DARKNESS & MOONLIGHT

A WORLDSMYTHS ANTHOLOGY

978-1-7778385-5-3

❀ Created with Vellum

This collection is dedicated to all the writers, backers, friends and family, and our lovely editor Stephanie, without whom this anthology wouldn't be possible!

TABLE OF CONTENTS

LETTER FROM THE EDITORS

We are so excited to present our second anthology, Darkness & Moonlight! Worldsmyths Publishing has grown a lot since we founded in February 2021, and we anticipate a bright future filled with many more anthologies.

This anthology is brought to you by the Admins of Worldsmyths, Ally Kelly and Freya Bell, and two of our moderators, Odessa Silver and C.P. Miller. The four of us pushed the members of our community to put their best writing forward, and are proud to present our own words within these pages as well.

Worldsmyths Publishing is an offshoot of Worldsmyths, a writing group dedicated to speculative fiction. We started in 2016 as a Facebook page, moved to a website forum, and in 2019, moved to a Discord server. We are a community that is low pressure and supportive, and aim to raise up the new writer and give them publishing opportunities where we can guide them through the process.

So let's talk about Darkness & Moonlight! We wanted to pick a more focused theme, and provided the community with a list of potential ones to vote on. Darkness & Moonlight came out on top! The blurb we gave was 'Stories that take place at night, deadly secrets, daring heists, secret trysts' and the community certainly took that and ran with it.

We would like to extend our most gracious thanks to our editor, Stephanie Cullen, who has been able to wrangle our stray commas and help bring these stories to their brightest shine. We would also like to thank the Worldsmyths community. Without their constant enthusiasm and interest we never would be able to do this. Our lovely ARC readers also deserve thanks, you take time out of your busy days to provide us with reviews, and we will always be grateful. Lastly we would like to thank the friends and families of all the writers who allow us time to pursue our passions. Writing is a lonely venture, and the support of those around us means everything!

We would also like to thank our cover artist Asterielly for our beautiful cover art! Visit her Facebook page here https://www.facebook.com/asterielly/ to see her work.

Worldsmyths Publishing is at the start of a great journey. Follow us on social media or join the Discord to see what our next publishing opportunities are, as there is always something in the works! Look out for Seasons Unceasing, our third anthology coming out in November 2022, and a Love themed anthology, Sugar and Spice, coming February 2023. The best place to keep up with anthology news is through our Discord server, at https://discord.gg/dCW3b6g.

Thank you again for reading, we sincerely hope you enjoy Darkness & Moonlight!

TRIGGER WARNING

This anthology contains some stories that contain the following:

Graphic violence;

Descriptions of blood and other injuries;

Sacrifice (human and/or animal);

Abuse (implicit and/or explicit);

Death of family, friends, or lovers;

Incapacitation;

Slavery (implicitly and/or explicit);

Exploitation;

Religious overtones;

and Sexism.

There might be other content some may find triggering. We apologize.

HIGH MOON JUSTICE
BY D.A. GATLIN

D.A. Gatlin is a new YA Fantasy writer living in Bakersfield, California with his wife, mom-in-law, two warrior princess daughters, Ellie and Matilda, and a freeloading white rabbit that burrowed in one day and never left. A middle school teacher by day, D.A. loves writing short stories and is currently working on a series of novels about triplets with superpowers who live in a medieval world. His debut novel Maiden to None will be available soon.

* * *

She was the youngest bounty Wyatt had ever seen advertised. Her raven pigtails and freckled cheeks were better suited for a "Missing Child" poster. Instead, she had earned a different type of billing: WANTED—CASSIE SANGE. Crime: Murder. Age: Eleven. Alive: $5000. Dead: $3000. Wyatt hadn't known they hanged people that young.

"Course they do, chickenshit," Dermit said as the two of them fastened their saddles for the long ride. "She's a murderer, ain't she? Young. Old. Don't matter much to Judge Stone. She'll swing. And you can bet we're gonna have all five thousand in our pockets before she does. I ain't settlin' for anything less."

"Damn. That's a lot of money," Wyatt said, examining the torn poster once more before rolling it into his rucksack. He knew he'd be lucky to see a thousand of those sheriff-sponsored dollars before Dermit had his take. "You seem sure we'll get it all."

"Sure as shit. Come on boy. You gonna stand there jawing, or are we gonna go get us the easiest money we ever got?"

Wyatt made no reply. He climbed on his horse and followed after his partner, not wanting to get on Dermit's ornery side again. He rubbed at his chin—the place where Dermit had struck him last time —and cringed at the clicks of unhealed bones within. Still, the pain was only second in his mind. He hoped everything went as smoothly as Dermit assumed because he didn't like the idea of having to kill a kid. No matter how guilty she was.

He and Dermit had been bounty partners for the better part of five years now. Before they'd met, Wyatt had been sleeping on the dusty streets of New Waco. Sometimes he could earn up to a whole two dollars a day shining boots near the post office. Most folks passed by his way anyway when going to Miss Selma's saloon, and the cowpokes that entered there were sometimes sent packing if they brought crusted horse apples onto Miss Selma's freshly swept floor. A shoeshine like Wyatt could really make a way for himself, meager as it was.

That was how things had been at first. Whenever he was thirsty, he'd just scoop himself a hat's worth of water from the horse trough. At night he'd have himself a can of beans or dried jerky for dinner. Wyatt would set himself up on the edge of town where the coyotes passed through and the stable hands sometimes played cards over barrels. He kept to himself mostly. A dull fire and a hot can were the only company he needed.

But then some days, no one needed a shine. That was when he learned to steal. He'd been the recipient of his fair share of black eyes and busted ribs during his earliest attempts at making quick grabs. His wounds would heal, and his hands would get a little faster. It was either that or starve, and having a buzzard circling overhead was *not* the last sight he wanted to see. No, someday he was going to make it all the way to one of the big cities, like New York or Boston. Maybe he'd catch himself a train and marry one of those fair lady types, like the kind he'd sometimes see in the catalogs over at the general store.

Dermit had found him purely by chance. Wyatt had just so happened to be coming out from the general store, untucking a recent steal from the folds of his shirt, when he bumped into a man who was rushing in to rob the place himself. The man had stopped to curse him —doing so rather loudly—and that's when Dermit showed up like a black tornado and blew a hole right into the side of the man's head.

All told the robber had a bounty of two-thousand dollars on his head. Dermit thanked Wyatt for his convenient assistance as he'd been tracking that particular bounty for days. Wyatt gratefully accepted the man's offer to share a campfire that evening. The bounty hunter was a surly old cuss, Wyatt had come to figure. Had to be, in a profession that killed people. Dermit was the sort that could make a grizzly stumble back some if he encountered one on the plains. His hair was short and ragged, looking to be self-cut from the long knife tucked on his hip. Both of his shrunken eyes were like two sapphire hurricanes; they were terrifying to stare directly into, but a thing of harsh beauty nonetheless.

They got to talking. And later that night Dermit got to drinking. It wasn't long before he reached into his wallet and gave Wyatt a one-hundred-dollar bill—leftovers from the bounty. Wyatt had never seen that much money before. Whatever this man's business was, he wanted more.

"Couldn't have done it without ya, kid," Dermit had told him, shortly before belching and passing out with his head near the fire. Wyatt had to drag the man to a safer bed of cold dirt.

That was pretty much how their partnership came to be. In some ways, Dermit reminded Wyatt of his own Pa. He always smelled of the cheapest whiskeys and he smoked Big Chief tobacco, which had been his Pa's favorite. Dermit taught Wyatt how to fire a gun, and how to bring a man in alive to face the rope. They made a good team, just so long as Dermit was in one of his *better* moods.

* * *

ACCORDING to the sheriff's poster, Miss Cassie Sange was last spotted out in the desert past Sidewinder Gulch and up near the Dakota pass. The sheriff had taken a posse to that territory the week prior, but they had returned without their bounty. What's more, they rode back with less men than they had ridden out with. They say a couple of men in the posse had tried their luck going deeper into the pass—a dry canyon filled with the old bones of poor souls who had died of thirst. The men hadn't returned, and that was when the sheriff updated Cassie's poster.

It was as good a lead as any to go off of. Dermit insisted they ride up the pass during the coolness of dusk with plenty of water packed between their two horses. As they rode, Wyatt gazed all about the narrowing canyon. He half-expected to be done in by a stray cougar or worse. There'd be no way of fending off a surprise attack on this skinny trail.

Dusk came quick and night settled fast. Dermit had already taken to sipping from his flask, but the cherry-nosed man wasn't about to rest when he felt they were on a hot trail so Wyatt had no choice but to freeze atop his horse as the night grew colder and darker. His dark bangs felt rigid over his wary, amber eyes. He watched as shadows crept across the land like packs of hungry wolves. Wyatt looked up to see the moon blotted out by heavy clouds. *The Devil plays at night*, his mother would say whenever he'd be outside too long. *Evil lurks on a starless night.*

Wyatt cleared his throat, ready to finally suggest that they should turn back. But Dermit shushed him then as the trail widened and the end of the canyon drew near. Wyatt could see for himself then the cabin in the distance. At first glance there was nothing extraordinary about it: just an old wooden shack with a tin roof and a broken pipe chimney. But as they drew closer, the ground became more uneven, and Wyatt saw that much of the land around the cabin had been freshly dug. The dirt was splotchy and red, and there rose a stench so foul that Wyatt had to cover his nose with his shirt.

Dermit stepped down from his horse, stumbling forward clumsily, then turned and motioned for Wyatt to accompany him. Wyatt dismounted and stepped cautiously towards the cabin behind his partner. He hadn't noticed before, but there were several half-gutted deer carcasses laying against the side of the shack. Wyatt shuddered at the sight of a rotting deer head staring back at him. Dermit pointed at the wood door.

"Cover me, *boy*," he said, sharply, drawing his gun from his holster.

Dermit lurched forward and then raised his foot to kick the cabin door open. He entered with his gun ahead of him, cocked and steady despite the holder's intoxication. Silence filled the canyon. Dermit had been swallowed up by the darkness of the shack. Wyatt stood there alone; his gun shook so nervously in his hand that he considered for one foolish second putting it back into his holster.

"D-Dermit?" he called out in a choked whisper.

A deafening scream shot out from the shack, echoing throughout the moonlit canyon. Wyatt hesitated, but forced himself closer to the cabin's door. There beyond the threshold he could see for himself the little girl at gunpoint who had just been given the fright of her life.

* * *

DERMIT HAD BEEN RIGHT. This was one of the easiest bounties they'd ever gone after. Cassie didn't have any weapons on her. She had begged and sobbed like the scared child she was until Dermit had enough of her wailing. He struck her with the back of his hand and then tied her hands and feet together using a cow-hitch knot. She could've been a calf awaiting a hot-iron brand with the way he handled her.

"She'll ride with you," Dermit ordered. He scooped the hogtied child up from the ground and handed her up to where Wyatt was sitting on his saddle. "Try not to drop her or screw this up, chickenshit. If she dies, you're gonna wish you had too."

"Shouldn't we rest up tonight?" Wyatt asked. "Seems loco to go riding back this late." He looked down at the girl now seated in front of him on the horse. "Shoot Dermit, she's likely to freeze before we get to town. I think we should make camp."

"What the hell you say to me boy?" Dermit snapped. He raised the butt of his gun and rammed it into Wyatt's ribs. "I says we're going back tonight. You give me any more lip and I'll bring her back myself. Ain't no one gonna kick up a fuss for a worried little prick like you."

Wyatt was hunched over, trying to catch his breath again. "Sorry Dermit . . . you right . . . we should ride."

Dermit always rode his horse faster when he was drunk. Wyatt could hardly keep up. It was too dark to see much of anything anyhow, and he was too focused on making sure Cassie didn't slip from the horse. His rib also bothered him some. He worried that Dermit might have broken it.

Cassie eventually turned around to face him. It was the first time Wyatt had really set eyes on her face, aside from the poster. She didn't seem like the dangerous criminal type. Her big black eyes sorta glimmered, even in the dead of night. Her freckled cheek was puffy from where Dermit had hit her, but she wasn't bleeding. Actually, she didn't even look bothered by any of this. Wyatt could almost swear she was enjoying the ride. Usually when they brought someone in to face the noose, there was a good share of begging or swear-filled threats. Sometimes Wyatt would even see tears when he looked into a helpless bounty's face. He didn't enjoy hangings, unlike Dermit, who always watched the dangling bodies with relaxed composure, as if he were on some sadistic Sunday picnic. When Wyatt met Cassie's eyes though, there weren't any tears. Instead, she gave Wyatt the biggest of grins.

"How's your rib?" she asked, with a twang in her voice. She sounded as woodsy as a plucked banjo. "Think it's broke?"

"Not sure. I'll be fine though."

"Don't sound fine. Say, why you let him hit you like that for? Don't seem right, ya ask me."

"Dermit didn't meant nothing by it. That's just the way he is. I shouldn't have mouthed off. That's all."

"That's funny. Cause last I checked, you had a gun too. If I were you—I'd shoot him dead and take the reward all for myself."

Wyatt reeled back some, startled by the rising glee in Cassie's voice. "I—no. Dermit's my partner. Always has been. I could never double cross him like that."

Cassie scoffed. "I seen plenty guys like him. You wanna know something? They're all the same. They only care about their own wallets.

You just watch. As soon as he don't need you anymore, why, he'll plug you himself."

Wyatt scowled. "I think you should hush now, Cassie. Start worrying about your own skin. They're gonna hang you, ya know?"

Cassie started to giggle. She could've just finished skipping rope for how carefree she was acting. "Aw hell, I ain't afraid to die. But your friend there is." She narrowed her black eyes. "Ya know you're nothing more than a wall for him to hide behind when the bullets start flying, right?"

"I said that's enough."

"Think about what I said some. Only reason he didn't send you in first to fetch me is cause he didn't think there was no need. I'm just a little girl to him."

"You *are* just a little girl."

"And you're just somebody to take the first bullet." She stared quietly at him, and for the first time appeared as if she genuinely cared about Wyatt and his situation. She pursed her lips together. "When I see a young fella like you...well, you still got the whole world to see. What you doing wasting your time with trash like him?"

There was some truth to what she was saying. Wyatt usually was the first one that had to approach a bounty. It had been that way ever since they started working with one another. It used to make him so scared he could piss himself, but Dermit had seen to beating that terrible habit out of him early on in their partnership. Even now his stomach was churning as Dermit's horse rode further and further ahead of them. If Wyatt didn't catch up soon, he was sure to be injured again. *Maybe permanently this time.*

Cassie looked to the sky. For a second, Wyatt could swear that her eyes shone yellow. "Clouds are thinning," she said, almost warning. "It's a full moon tonight, ya know? Say scary things happen under a full moon. What you think?"

"Shoot, I think that's something a kid would believe."

She leaned in closer to his body, raising her eyebrows as she spoke. "Be honest with me now. If I took care of your little *partner* problem, then you'd let me go. Wouldn't you?"

Wyatt laughed, appreciating her little joke. "Oh, Miss Cassie. I would love to see you try."

They were nearing the gulch again. The town was only a few miles ahead and the trail was growing brighter as the moon drifted out from behind the clouds. Then, without warning, Cassie threw herself backwards and fell from Wyatt's horse.

"Shit!" Wyatt exclaimed.

He turned and tried to see where she'd rolled off to, but he couldn't see anything amidst the kicked-up dust and poor light.

"Cassie! Cassie!"

He jumped down from his horse and began checking through every nearby bush he could. She wasn't there though. It was as if she had vanished. Wyatt intensified his search, until he heard a sound that made his heart leap from his chest. Dermit was riding back, and Wyatt could already tell he was angry with how hard he was kicking his horse.

"What the hell's keeping you, boy?" Dermit shouted when he was close. "My own grandma rides faster than...where is she?!" he barked savagely, realizing now that Cassie was gone.

Wyatt looked up to meet him. Dermit was seething with anger, and his gun was in his hand once more. He fell off his horse, but didn't let his drunkenness slow him. He shot up with that cussed speed of his and belted Wyatt across the face with his gun. Wyatt fell onto the flat of his back. He tried crawling backwards, desperate to get away. His hand brushed over something familiar laying in the dirt. He turned to see busted fragments of rope strewn across the trail. *Cassie's rope?*

"You dumb bastard! I shoulda known you'd screw this up somehow."

"I'm sorry Dermit," Wyatt wailed. His jaw made a painful click. Tears rushed to his eyes. "She just—she fell off. Honest."

"Just fell off my ass! Hell, I reckon this was your plan all along, weren't it? Soon as we come up with a real bounty you gotta find some way to keep it all for yourself. After everything I done—this is what I get, is that it, boy? Huh? Answer me you little prick!" Dermit aimed his gun at Wyatt's head. "After all I gave to you, boy, this is the respect you show me?" His face was redder than a stoked fire.

"Please Dermit!" Wyatt yelled, before whirling over in the dirt. His only chance of getting away was a mad sprint. He'd make for some brush or a rock—anything to keep from being shot in the back of the head.

A gut-wrenching scream rose suddenly from Dermit's direction. Wyatt paused his escape to look back, and his blood turned cold. His own stomach twisted in knots at the horrific sight. Cassie was upon the older man, only she didn't look herself anymore. She'd sprouted wings—huge monstrous wings, like the kind you'd see on a bat. She'd grown claws, as well, and two long fangs that protruded from her mouth. She used them to bite into Dermit's neck and then she tore the man's throat clean from his body. Dermit fell over, and Cassie let loose a screaming hiss. She dropped down and began to feed on the dying man, now shaking with violent convulsions as his body was ripped to shreds by the child.

Wyatt rushed to his feet and drew his weapon. He cocked his gun and aimed right towards Cassie's head, just like Dermit had taught him. Cassie paused her feasting, and looked up at Wyatt. Those big black eyes of hers were now completely yellow under the light of the full moon, yet, they still retained that same look from before. The one she'd given him on his horse when she told him he was better than all of this. And, admittedly, she still resembled an adorable little cuss— despite the bits of Dermit's cheek dangling from her fang.

Slowly, Wyatt lowered his gun. Cassie gave him a bloodstained grin, and continued on with her meal in peace. Wyatt didn't think twice when her hungry eyes left him. He bolted away, his boots pivoting and scraping at the dirt like a hunted raccoon. He saw his frightened horse galloping a ways down the trail, heading back towards town. Wyatt caught up and jerked at the horse's reigns, pulling himself up into the saddle. It took some doing, but he was finally able to calm the animal, though neither of them looked back to confirm their clean getaway.

Wyatt rode off in a direction that wasn't aiming for the town. After all, he was his own man now. That town had made him feel like a boy, the way Dermit always had. *Dermit.* Was he really gone? Somehow it was harder to believe that his grizzled partner could actually be killed than it was to believe in winged evils of the night, or whatever the hell Cassie was. He couldn't help smiling a little at the thought of her despite his cold sweat, his aching side, and the lightning pace he kept his horse riding at. She *had* taken care of his little partner problem. Now, the world was his to see, just like she had said. Maybe he'd take a train to California. Or perhaps he'd see what was due east. It didn't matter, so long as it was his decision. He called his own shots now, though he didn't expect to be doing much shooting anymore. Still, Cassie had taught him one other important lesson that night beneath the full moon. There were some monsters that deserved to die.

INTO THE BRAMBLES
BY FREYA BELL

Freya Bell is a Canadian writer residing in Alberta with her husband, cat, and dog. As one of the admins of Worldsmyths, Freya has helped shape this anthology alongside her co-editors, all driven by her love of speculative fiction. Find out more at www.freyabellcreates.com

* * *

I know I'm not supposed to go outside at night, Mama always said so, but he was waiting for me. My friend, the prince of shadows. Mama also told me that fairies weren't real.

She says a lot of things. I don't always believe her.

My bedroom door creaked as I opened it and I paused in the hallway, the sound of my breathing loud in my ears. Mama's bedroom door was closed, her snores leaking out under the door.

I smiled and continued down the hallway, careful to avoid the squeaky spots in the wooden floor. I knew where they all were now. It was nice, knowing things Mama didn't.

The kitchen door creaked when I opened it, and my breath stopped in my chest, but Mama didn't stir. I made my way outside and paused at the edge of the grass. Grandmama died last month. One day she was here, the next she was in the hospital, and then we had to go to her funeral where lots of people were crying. I got hugged by so many old people. At least the flowers there were pretty.

I missed Grandmama. She believed me when I told her about the prince of princes.

My prince! He must be waiting for me. I skipped down to the end of the garden and flung myself onto the grass. I slapped my hands over my mouth before I could laugh but a little giggle slipped out. The stars were bright and sparkling above me as I laid and looked up through the rose brambles at the end of the garden.

I closed my eyes and pretended to be asleep. It was hard not to peek to see if it was working but I had to be good. The prince said I had to play all their games, or else.

Tiny feet walked across my forehead, and I wiggled with anticipation. A second set of feet joined them, dancing across my face, stepping on my nose, my eyes, my lips. I wondered if they were leaving any tiny footprints. I should wash my face before bed.

The feet vanished and someone tapped me on the forehead. My eyes popped open and I sat up. Sitting cross legged beside me was a boy my age and size, with shaggy black hair and eyes bluer than paint. He wore strange black clothing that was part rags and patches and part old fashioned stuff like out of my book of fairy tales.

He smiled at me and my heart fluttered. I felt funny when he was around, but I liked it. The prince of shadows made me feel special.

The prince stood and offered me his hand. I took it, letting him pull me to my feet. Other fairies flew through the air around him, wings like bugs' but large and pretty. Some had butterfly wings, others moths, and some had sparkly wings like a dragonfly.

They flew so fast, I knew I'd never be able to catch one. I had tried once and the prince became so angry he didn't talk to me for a week, no matter how much I'd cried. I was allowed to chase the fairies but only when the prince said it was time to play.

But the prince was smiling now. He kept hold of my hand and led me around a clump of bushes where an old shed stood. My house wasn't visible and he relaxed as soon as we were out of sight of it.

"Are you going to tell me your name tonight?" I asked him.

The prince shook his head with a twinkle in his eye. "Only if you can fall in love with me!"

My cheeks turned red. "I'm too young to fall in love, Mama said so."

The prince tilted his head. "No one is too young for love. Or too old."

"Have you been in love before?"

The prince looked up at the moon with a distant, sad smile on his lips. "Oh no, it is not my fate."

"That's so sad," I said with a frown. "Why not?"

His answering laugh made tingles pop up on my skin. "Love is wonderful. But it is a human thing. But enough of this. Catch me, and maybe I'll tell you my name."

He spun around and leapt into the air, shrinking until he was the size of the other fairies, and darted past me. He tugged at my hair and I tried to grab him but he was too fast. Not that I wanted to catch him. I never wanted the games to end.

I chased the prince back and forth across the garden, laughing. He laughed too, like the ringing of a bell, and almost let me catch him once. But he flapped his wings and sped away at the last moment, and I nearly crashed into the bushes before I could stop.

I dropped to the ground, breathing hard. Chasing was one of his favourite games, probably because he always won. When we played hide and seek, I sometimes hid better than he did, and he didn't like that.

It was okay with me if he wanted to win. So long as we got to keep playing. I wanted to play with him forever.

When I turned around, the prince and the fairies were gone. I groaned and let my head fall back to the grass. Was it midnight already? The fairies had a bedtime too, though the prince never said what would happen if they were late. Did he have a mother who would growl if she caught him awake?

I sat up and walked back towards the house. Tomorrow was another night. I wondered what games we would play.

. . .

MAMA WAS MAD AT ME. I sat at the breakfast table, trying not to cry as she scrubbed at my nightgown. There were grass stains in it from tumbling around in the garden the night before.

"I told you, Mirabel. I told you not to go out into the garden at night and what do you do? You go outside anyway!"

I sniffled and stared down at my toast. "I know, I'm sorry."

Mama wrung my nightgown out over the sink and set it on the radiator to dry. "If you were sorry, you would stay inside. What would happen if you fell into the pond? You could drown!"

"I'm a good swimmer, I could get out," I said.

Mama shook her head. "Not good enough. There are weeds in that pond. I would know! I went swimming there once, when I was your age. Plants wrapped around my ankle and nearly pulled me under. I would have drowned if your Grandmama hadn't pulled me out. She was so upset . . . "

Mama looked so sad. I almost felt bad for going outside last night. Almost.

Mama sat beside me and took my hand. "I need you to promise me you won't sneak out again. I can't sleep at night thinking you're out there, playing by yourself. It isn't safe."

"But–"

"No buts! I'll have your promise or you won't be allowed back at school again."

"Mama! I need to go to school, my friends are there!"

"And they will still be there, but only if you promise me."

I poked my toast with a sad finger. It was cold. "I promise," I said, in the quietest voice I could.

Mama squeezed my hand and leaned in. "What did you say?"

Tears started to fall down my cheeks. What will I do without my prince? But to not go to school, and stay locked away inside helping Mama with chores all day . . .

"I promise, Mama. I'll stay inside."

Mama released my hand and patted my head.

"That's my good girl. Now eat up."

I ate my toast through my tears, and tried not to think about my fairy friends. They would be so mad. But I knew I had to wait until

Mama had forgotten before I could go back outside.

* * *

I LASTED AN ENTIRE WEEK. Pictures of the prince filled the margins of my notebooks and I got called into the principal's office twice for daydreaming. But at last Mama stopped asking me to stay inside when she tucked me in at night. I was ready.

The prince was ready too. He waited for me at the end of the garden by the shed, arms crossed. I gasped at the sight of him.

"You don't want me to pretend to be asleep first?" I asked.

He shook his head, lips tight. "Where have you been?"

"Inside. Mama made me promise not to come outside at nighttime. She's afraid I'll drown in the pond."

The prince glanced over his shoulder, where the pond lay beyond the garden shed. Tiny waves rippled across the surface, caught by the light of the full moon.

"This pond?" He crossed over to it and walked across its surface as casually as he strolled over the grass. His feet left little ripples in his wake and my eyes went wide.

"Can you teach me how to do that?" I asked.

The prince glanced over his shoulder, surprise flashing across his handsome face. He held out his hand to me and wiggled his fingers.

"I could try. Come with me."

I approached the edge of the pond. The water was all moonlight and shadow as the tiny waves flashed over its surface, and I gulped.

"Mama says to stay away from the pond."

The prince's eyes narrowed. "Your mother says a lot of things. She wasn't always so strict."

I placed my bare toes onto the surface of the pond but the water didn't hold my weight and my foot got wet. He wiggled his fingers again, impatiently, but he was too far away for me to reach. I took a step back and crossed my arms.

"I don't want to walk on water," I said.

The prince's eyes narrowed before a smile flashed onto his face. "Why not?" He spun in a circle and danced a few steps, droplets of water catching the moonlight as they flicked through the air. "It's fun!"

I eyed the water. "I don't want to get wet."

The prince stopped dancing. "You don't trust me. I thought we were friends."

My mouth fell open in dismay. "We are friends! I do trust you. I just . . ."

His lip trembled as though he was about to cry, and I reached for him. He was too far away to touch, though, so I took a step into the pond, and another, all while he watched with clear eyes. His lip no longer trembled once I stood knee deep in cold water, mud seeping between my toes.

The prince bowed and offered his hand once again. I took it, and he pulled me out of the water. He was stronger than he looked; I don't think I could have pulled him like that.

To my surprise, my feet landed on the surface of the water, smooth and cold as glass. His smile was full of wicked delight as his arm snaked around my waist, pulling me tight to him. He stepped backwards and lead me into a dance.

We spun in circles, skating over the surface of the pond like it were ice. There was no music, but I didn't need any with my prince holding me. The stars reflected off the pond until we were in a bowl of moonlight, illuminated like a stage. The little fairies spun in their own dances around us like darting fireflies.

I don't know how long we danced for, but it wasn't long enough. The prince loosened his grip on me and pulled back, a startled look on his pretty face.

"Someone is coming," he said tightly.

The little fairies vanished into the brambles, and the prince began to pull me towards them. I wiggled in his grip.

"I can't go into the brambles, I'm too big! The thorns will get me."

The prince gave me an exasperated look. "The thorns will do as I say. But if you truly wish to stay here . . ."

The prince shrank into his tiny form and darted away. For a moment after he let go of my hand, the water supported me. Then it turned to jelly and my feet sank. I had only the briefest glimpse of my prince's light vanishing into the rose brambles before the water closed over my head.

My arms flailed and I pulled myself towards the surface. My legs kicked, propelling me up towards the light of the moon. Before I could reach it, arms closed around me and pulled me up. My head broke the surface of the pond and I sputtered in surprise.

Mama gripped me tight, anger and concern at war on her face.

"Mirabel! My Mirabel, what are you doing?"

"I was dancing, Mama. Dancing with the prince of shadows."

"Dancing? Don't be ridiculous. I don't care what you think you were doing out here. You disobeyed me," said mama as she pulled me towards the edge of the pond. She pushed me onto the grass and then hopped out beside me. We sat for a moment, looking at the brambles on the other side of the pond.

"You scared me, Mirabel. Do you understand that?"

I looked away, down at the moonlit surface of the water. "I didn't mean to, mama."

"Well, you did. You scare me every time you leave the house at night. This talk of princes and fairies and dancing, it stops now."

Tears blurred my view of the pond and I refused to nod.

Mama sighed and stood.

"Come," she said as she offered me her hand. "Let's get your dried off and back to bed."

I took her hand. It was large and warm and familiar, but I wished I was still holding the prince's hand instead.

My bedroom had a lock now. Mama locked me in when she puts me to bed. For my own safety, she says. She even nailed my window shut, to make sure I couldn't get out! She didn't listen when I told her I was never in any danger! This was just her being selfish. So what if it scared her? I wasn't afraid!

The weeks passed slowly without my prince, and even my friends at school couldn't distract me. The only thing that interested me was Grandmama's boxes. Mama had cleaned up her room and piled all of

Grandmama's things into my closet. She said mine was the only room that had space for them.

That was fine with me. It meant I could look at him again.

My prince.

Grandmama had always been a good drawer and she had pictures saved that were very old, from when she was my age. And among the flowers and rainbows were drawings of fairies. Not silly fairies like in the movies. My fairies.

I recognized my prince immediately. I think Mama did too, the way she got mad when she found the pictures in my bed. The prince was old, he told me that himself. But I didn't know he was as old as Grandmama. I frowned, jealousy welling up in my chest. Had he danced with Mama and Grandmama too? The prince was mine! He had said so himself.

He belonged to me, and if I went with him into the brambles, I would belong to him, too. He would even tell me his name if I went to live with the fairies.

The longer I was locked up, the more tempting it seemed. To live with the fairies and to dance under the moonlight forever sounded so much better than homework and chores and Mama being mad at me.

And Mama was still very mad. I flopped back on the floor with a groan. I had done more chores in the last three weeks than I had in my entire life. I didn't know why she was punishing me.

Why couldn't she understand?

The wind made the tree outside my window rattle and shake and I stirred, warm under the covers of my bed. Sometimes it sounded like someone was knocking at my window but whenever I checked, there was no one there. It wouldn't be my prince; he never came up to the house.

I sat up as the knocking came again. That didn't sound like a tree.

Lights flickered beyond the curtain and I sprang to my feet with an excited gasp. I flung the curtain back, and there on my window sill were three tiny fairies. The green and gold of their dresses shimmering in the light given off by their fluttering wings.

They looked scared but determined. One waved to me and motioned for me to stand back. The three fairies lined up and peered at the nails that kept my window in place. One by one, the nails twisted, squealing in the wood before lifting up and clattering to the ground.

I wasted no time and heaved the window open. I didn't even pause to see if Mama heard. I didn't care. Crawling out of the window was scary but the chiming voices of the fairies encouraged me. Branches from the bush under my window scratched me when I landed on it but I barely felt them.

The fairies fled ahead of me as we raced around the side of the house towards the garden. My feet made slapping sounds on the cool flagstones, too late in the season to keep the heat of day. It was almost fall, after all.

And then I was in the grass. Wild laughter erupted from my chest, and if Mama heard, so be it. I was home.

I reached the end of the garden and pulled up short, aghast. It looked like a tornado had passed through the brambles, tearing them up at the roots and leaving them in messy piles.

My insides went cold. Mama. It had to be. She was destroying the fairies' home!

I raced towards the pond, fearing the worst, but it was still there, as were the brambles on the far side.

I fell to my knees. But where was my prince?

A hand landed on my shoulder, and I bit off a scream. I spun, ready to apologise to Mama for being out, but it wasn't her.

It was my prince.

His clothing was more ragged than ever, and dark circles bit into the skin under his eyes. But he was still the most handsome boy I had ever seen. I threw myself into his arms and he hugged me back just as tight.

"I'm so sorry, Mama locked me up! I couldn't get away!"

My prince squeezed me before standing back. "I know, I sent my fairies to spy. Your mother is a wicked woman, keeping you from me."

My heart clenched. "I love my mama, but . . ."

"Do you love me?" asked my prince.

I look up at him, blushing. "Love?"

"Yes, love. The greatest of human emotions. Do you feel it for me?"

I stepped out of his arms and looked down at my bare feet before nodding.

The prince tilted my head up with a gentle hand. "I'm glad to hear it. I've always wanted to know what love is, and I think you can teach me."

I shook my head, confused. "You don't know what love is?"

"No fairy does. Our hearts are too wild."

Shouting sounded from the house and I froze. Mama was awake, and she sounded angry.

The prince reached down and grabbed my hands. "Come with me. The summer is almost over and without it, my power will fade. If you want to love me, you must come with me. Now."

I glanced over my shoulder. Mama was running towards us, terror etched into her lined face. "Mirabel!" Her voice shook as she raced forward.

I looked back to my prince. There was nothing in his cold eyes, no hope, just that pretty smile. His words echoed through my head. *'Our hearts are too wild.'*

My eyes squeezed shut. Mama's shouts reached my ears, begging me to stop, to stay.

I took a deep breath and reached out my hand.

SELENE
BY ALEX K. MASSE

Alex Masse, AKA Fairything, is a 21-year-old writer, musician, and neurodivergent nonbinary lesbian residing in what is colonially known as Vancouver, BC. The arts are a longtime love of theirs, and their work has been seen everywhere from the Scholastic Writing Awards to Vancouver Pride, as well as in collaboration with Penelope Scott, She Does The City, and more. When not writing, they're often making music, and vice versa.

* * *

Selene looked up to the stars for help, but they'd been long ago smothered by buildings and billboards. They'd grant no wishes, heal no wounds, and were no help in getting her home. She forced her head back down—the movement left her dizzy and she was already struggling to walk. Though anyone would be struggling in her shoes.

She'd just had what was, to anyone with eyes, a career-ending injury. In front of about a thousand people, at that.

It'd been stupid, too—an orchestral cue had come early and she'd quite literally forgotten to look before leaping from her platform onstage.

Like an idiot.

"And this is why," she muttered under her breath, "the only rhythm you trust is your own."

A new rhythm persisted in her leg now, the pulsating agony a low drum in sync with her frantic, pounding heartbeat.

It was a miracle she'd bolted before the ambulance got there. A miracle she was walking at all.

She'd never be able to perform here again, not without another miracle. But luckily, while Selene was a dancer first, she was a witch a distant second. And if she wanted to keep dancing, she'd have to wear that hat again.

She murmured another simple mending spell—"*grand pas, grand pas*," one of the countless ballet terms she'd repurposed—to put off the worst of the pain, but it wouldn't last. After all, as she'd honed her body, her magic had rusted, one craft chosen and smothering the other. Anyone who knew would be able to see it—the need to speak any spell aloud, for example. A lifetime ago, she'd been able to calm calluses and banish blisters with a thought, a skill which had been invaluable for breaking in pointe shoes.

But now she needed something significantly more heavy-duty than her own amateurish work. She needed someone who could set a bone with a silent wave of a hand. Someone who'd kept with the practice. And for that, she had to get to the witchlands. It was the one spell she'd never grown rusty with, the one spell every witch knew. She just needed open space and clear exposure to moonlight.

Which meant she had to get to her apartment. After all, casting a spell in the middle of these crowds? Risky as all hell. Even if she didn't get jumped by panicked strangers, she'd be met with the tongue-lashing of a lifetime for a public magical display. She'd also be banned from leaving the witchlands for at least a few months. Worse, in this land she saw as a second home, her final public act for *weeks* would be falling from a twenty-three-foot platform and landing in the unknown. It'd be an embarrassment.

It was best to get home, where no one could see her and no one could stop her. She veered off into an alleyway, her favourite shortcut, and prayed she'd make it to her apartment.

Already, her spell was falling apart. She leaned on her cane—a simple theatre prop she'd snatched on her way out, the only thing she'd taken besides her coat—and cursed through clenched teeth. The winter air bit at her skin through her costume, insult atop very literal injury.

Almost there, Selene told herself. *Almost there. You can do it, Selene. Someone in the witchlands can help you. Just keep walking—*

"Selene?"

Selene froze, teetering against the cane. She wasn't sure she had the strength to turn around.

"Selene Choquette?"

The voice was low, almost androgynous. Breathy, too, like its owner had raced all the way from the theatre to meet her.

"Y'know, there's a a search party for you . . . "

Selene forced herself to face the stranger.

Immediately she had no doubt this woman had come from the ballet. She was dressed in her Sunday best—a frilly blouse and some dress pants, plus heels that made Selene's feet ache just to look at—and even in the dark there was no mistaking the glimmer of recognition in her eyes. Surprisingly, Selene felt the gears spinning in her own head— she'd seen this face before. Maybe in the front row?

"Folks are worried about you," the woman pressed. "And, y'know, not without reason. I mean, one of the other girls onstage needed a shock blanket, and all she did was *watch* it happen."

Selene held back a laugh—Marie, the prima of the company with an ego as wide as her tutu. Watching her shriek and fall to the ground was what had emboldened Selene to escape in the first place. "Sounds like she caused quite a commotion."

"I'm pretty sure the audience thought *she'd* been hurt," she said, "but I know what I saw, and I heard the other dancers whispering about you. So now I'm here."

"Oh," Selene murmured. "Well, there was no need to do that. I was actually on my way to take care of it by myself. I have my methods."

"You *have* what might be a career-ending injury," the woman deadpanned. "You should know that. I mean, you've been dancing since—"

"I've been dancing long enough," Selene interrupted with a sneer.

"Long enough to not need unsolicited medical advice. Who even *are* you?"

"A fan," replied the woman breezily.

Selene rose, tried and failed to puff her chest out. "If you can't even give me a name, I have *no* reason to trust you."

This at last cracked the facade. The stranger's face fell and she sputtered out, "My name's Stevie. At least let me help you get checked out, okay? I don't even know how you're walking—you must be in shock. You fell, what, twenty feet?"

Twenty-three, Selene thought but didn't say. "Can I at least drop off my things before I'm ushered into a hospital? I hate those places." She tried for the sympathy angle. "My apartment's only a five-minute walk from here, and I already have a cane."

"Where did you get that, anyway?"

"Prop room."

"Ah," Stevie said, nodding as if that made perfect sense. "I'm surprised it works."

"It doesn't," Selene muttered. "I feel like if I lean on it too much, it'll snap."

"Well, that won't do," Stevie remarked. She took a step forward, and then another, and it took all of Selene's instincts not to flinch back —she was vulnerable right now, after all. Whatever this woman did, she was at her mercy. . .

But Stevie simply slung Selene's arm over her shoulder.

"I'll call us a cab," she declared. "And once you drop off your stuff, we'll get you to the hospital. Okay?"

Selene held back a slew of curses—why did she have to be stopped by the one *nice* person in this godforsaken city? She had to get to the witchlands, and *fast*. Even the most skilled healers wouldn't be able to undo the damage if she put it off too long.

But she couldn't tell Stevie any of that.

So she just smiled and said, "Oh, you're my *hero*."

* * *

THE CAB RIDE WAS AWKWARD, but—much to Selene's annoyance—not silent. Stevie, undoubtedly not from around here, asked about several old buildings they passed and alleys they cut through. The questions varied from the typical, "Is this safe?" to the more inquisitive, "Whoa, how old is that?"

And Selene, ever the performer, humoured her, answering what the taxi driver couldn't. She peppered in anecdotes, rattled off what she'd read online, the whole nine yards. When Stevie told a bad pun in response, she even managed a laugh. All the while, though, she found herself studying the woman's face. She was so familiar—more so than any stranger in the dark of the audience had any right to be—and she couldn't for the life of her place it.

One clumsy exit and generous tip to the driver later, they ambled towards her apartment building together, a bizarre, three-legged beast that tripped over itself every few steps. Carefully, Selene untangled herself from Stevie's arms and hobbled towards the door. She thumbed in a code and made a beeline for the elevator.

"Wait here."

"Like hell." Stevie passed her with quick, long strides, calling an elevator down with a press of the button. "You're *not* playing hooky on the ambulance."

Yes, I am, Selene thought, *by any means necessary*.

"If it's a money thing, don't worry about it," Stevie went on. "I have connections."

She gave Selene a wink.

As they piled into the elevator, Selene asked, "How do I know you're not trying to corner me and kill me when I'm so vulnerable?"

She thumbed in her floor and leaned against the wall. The elevator rumbled to life around them.

"Oh, that's the problem?" Stevie stroked her chin. "Well, if I were going to kill you, I would've done it in a dark, damp alleyway." She looked to Selene, a mischievous glimmer in her eyes. "In fact, how do *I* know you're not trying to kill *me*? Like, how do I know you're not Bundying my ass here and now?"

"That I'm not *what*?"

"Bundying," Stevie pressed, suddenly indignant. "You've never heard of Ted Bundy?"

Selene snorted. "The serial killer?"

"Yeah. He used to feign a broken arm so women would pity him. He'd lure them into his car, then do his . . . y'know . . . " She mimed the stabbing of a knife. "Serial killing. Granted, you're already a famous ballerina—"

"Semi-famous," Selene muttered, a blush crawling up her cheeks. "I'm semi-famous."

The elevator came to a stop. The doors slid open, and Stevie eased her arm under Selene's shoulders yet again.

"You know you don't have to do this, right?" Selene asked as they ambled out into the hallway.

"No, I do."

"I don't remember you being my doctor."

Stevie gave her a stern look. "I'm not *your* doctor, but would you believe me if I told you I'm *a* doctor?"

Selene raised a brow. "You are?"

"I teach Sports Medicine at the local college and do talks at ballet companies."

Selene felt the blood drain from her face. "You're Stevie Ashton, aren't you?"

"I was wondering how long that'd take!" Stevie exclaimed, clapping her hands together. "I did a talk at your company, what, three years ago? And that's when I became a fan."

This was, undoubtedly, the worst-case scenario. "You have glowing reviews," Selene murmured. It was all coming back: Stevie Ashton, leading them through basic stretches like their lives depended on it. Stevie Ashton, complimenting her form as she'd left the studio. Stevie Ashton, talk of the changing room for weeks after, mostly for a viral video where she'd popped a guy's shoulder back into its socket backstage, then gently restrained him from racing back to his role. "So you know exactly what's wrong with me."

"Yes," Stevie replied, "which is why I'm making sure you get help."

"Why didn't you mention it earlier?"

"I like to be mysterious."

They reached the door to her apartment, and as Selene grabbed the doorknob, her mind raced. She needed, somehow, to escape.

"*Ouvert*," she whispered, and her apartment door slid open. Another simple spell, one she'd been using her whole life. She reveled in the soft *click* of the lock and hobbled inside.

Stevie whistled. "Did that thing just answer to your voice? Fancy."

"Sure. Wait here."

Selene went to close the door, but was interrupted when Stevie's foot flew out and blocked her.

"You aren't going to leave me sitting out here all night like a fool, are you?" she asked, cocking her head to the side.

Selene snorted. "What do you think I'm going to do? Sit in my room until you give up?"

"I was thinking along the lines of sneaking out."

"We're on the third floor," Selene pointed out.

"And you shouldn't even be *walking* right now," Stevie shot back, "so I'm not underestimating you."

Selene sighed, opening the door so Stevie could follow her inside. "I promise, Stevie. I'd die if I tried hopping out my window right now."

Selene thought she saw there was a flash of panic in Stevie's eyes.

"Okay, hey, we don't need to talk about dying."

"It was a joke." She watched the other woman curiously.

"Sure." But Stevie sounded unconvinced. Maybe it was Selene's imagination, but there was a skittishness to her gait as she entered the apartment.

The moonlight pouring in from her window dyed what little Selene could see silver—the book-covered coffee table, her old loveseat, and a modestly-sized television.

"Nice place," Stevie remarked.

Selene dropped her bag on the loveseat unceremoniously.

"I'm getting a drink before I go," she declared, hobbling into the kitchen. *Just stall, just stall, you'll get a moment to bolt.* "Do you want anything?"

"I *want* you to stop walking on that leg," Stevie muttered, but she'd already sat down. She gazed at the mess of the coffee table. "Lots of, ah, pagan works here."

"It's an interest of mine," Selene said with a shrug, shambling into her kitchen. "Tarot, astrology, the works." She poured herself a glass of wine—anything to fight the anxiety, and anything to bury the pain that'd begun to resurface. If she had to guess, the *grand pas* spell would last her another ten minutes before it became unbearable. "You sure you're not thirsty?"

"I'm sure." Stevie's face softened. "Y'know, if you want to just *talk* about what you're going through, I'm also open to that."

Selene suppressed a groan of frustration and pretended she hadn't heard that last part. *Time to bring out the big guns.*

"Tombé," she murmured into her glass. *Fall.*

It was a spell she'd woven years ago but never had the chance to use. She'd created the thing after a particularly bad incident with a ballerino stalker, and swore that she'd never have anyone in her home again unless she could effectively banish them at the drop of a hat. It also meant everything from here was automatic—no whispered chants, no hand gestures. Selene would look just as human as anyone else.

From here, it was a matter of endurance before the inevitable.

"A bit of liquid courage?" Stevie teased as she returned. "If it's what gets you to the hospital, I won't judge. I used to be the same."

"But now you work in medicine?" Selene eased herself into the loveseat, leaning against the other woman's shoulder.

"I get spared most of the gory details," Stevie replied, looking away almost sheepishly. "My specialty is in, y'know, physical rehabilitation. The aftermath. I swear, miss your daily stretches enough, and your body *riots*." She looked back to Selene then, a nervous smile on her face. "But hey, it's not the end of the world. People can come out on the other side—and you'd be surprised what they come back from."

Selene hummed in acknowledgement. "You seem more worried about my leg than I am."

"Maybe I am," Stevie admitted. "But, you know, that's because a lot of the time it's more than the leg. It's also the trauma, y'know—loss of control, loss of autonomy, maybe jeopardizing your future if you don't get help. I've seen people go down some . . . pretty dark paths."

Her face fell, and she looked down to her hands, wringing them together.

"Dark paths?" Selene echoed.

Stevie blinked, catching herself. "We're getting sidetracked. You said you'd let me look at your leg, right? And like I said, if you want to talk—"

The TV flickered to life before them. Praying it'd be enough, Selene watched her first trap spring into action.

Static overtook the screen, and an earsplitting whine pierced the air alongside its roar.

"Shit!" Stevie yelped, leaping from her seat. "Did one of us sit on the remote?"

She was barely audible over all the noise.

"Maybe." Selene didn't move. Her eyes fluttered shut. "Of course, it might be the ghosts."

"The g-ghosts?" Stevie echoed.

Selene chuckled. She'd spent *days* scheming up this backstory. "In 1982, a woman was murdered by her husband . . . in this very apartment. That's why the rent's so cheap."

"You're messing with me."

"Am not. Try turning off the TV."

Stevie pawed around for the remote. Selene opened one eye to catch a glimpseof it—the poor woman looked wildly out of her depth.

Any moment now, she'll bail.

But let's up the ante a bit, just in case.

"The TV isn't even the worst of it," Selene said. "Any minute now, the lights. . . "

She snapped her fingers and the lights dimmed, dropping to a flicker. Stevie cursed, still scrambling to find the remote. In the strobe, she looked almost animated, some strange form of pixilation.

"Well, all the more reason I shouldn't leave you here," she said, sweeping Selene's books to the floor. Her hands found the TV remote, and the room was plunged into silence as she pressed the power button. The lights followed, and soon they were left in blackness. Stevie was rendered nothing more than a silhouette in the moonlight, and Selene watched her drop the remote, scowling.

"I think I got a papercut when I manhandled your books," she muttered. "Sorry about that, by the way. Do you have any bandages?"

Checkmate, Selene thought.

"In the bathroom," she replied. "I'm sorry, too. I should've warned you. I didn't expect it to act up like that." A lie if she'd ever told one, but she didn't even care. The night was almost at its close.

"No, no, it's fine. I'm just glad you weren't alone when all that happened."

Muttering under her breath, Stevie disappeared into the bathroom.

Selene snapped her fingers one last time, and the door slammed shut, locking with a click. Stevie didn't react right away, and Selene took the stillness of the moment to assess herself. Sure enough, a steady, thrumming pain had picked up again in her leg and the rest of her body ached from dragging it around. The worst of it stayed submerged under the spell but she didn't have long.

On the—somewhat literal—bright side, the moon awaited her just outside her window. The ritual could begin.

Selene raised a hand. The moonlight danced on her palm.

The doorknob jiggled.

Shit. Be quick.

"Selene?" called Stevie. "I think your door's, uh, stuck."

Selene ignored her. The sooner this was over, the better. Her charms never lasted all that long, and by the time Stevie broke out, she'd be long gone.

"I'd really like to not be stuck here," Stevie pressed. "I mean, after tonight, I think—"

"I can help myself," Selene interrupted. She brought her palm to the floor and the moonlight followed, pooling like liquid. "Trust me. I've got this."

The doorknob jiggled again.

"Unless you have a doctorate hidden in your tights, no, I don't think you do."

Selene groaned, her face clenched. Fighting off the pain was one thing, but drowning out Stevie's voice on top of that? The edge of desperation in her voice didn't help.

"Just what do you think I'm trying over here?" Selene demanded. The portal grew, and soon her hand fit through it. Just a few more moments and she'd be able to squeeze out of here. "This is what has to happen."

There was a bang against the bathroom door. Selene cursed—Stevie was trying to ram it open.

"Please—" *BANG.* "Don't do—" *BANG.* "Anything drastic!" *BANG.*

The portal grew. The door rattled. Selene's leg burned.

"Please," Stevie said again, punctuated with a *BANG.* "I can't lose another like this." *BANG.* "You fucking *dancers*—" *BANG.*

Selene tried in vain to drown her out. Just a few more seconds, and she'd be gone.

"Please, accept the help." There was no bang this time, just Stevie slumping against the door, defeated. "I can't stand seeing you throw your life away."

"I'm not throwing my life away!" Selene shouted back to her. The portal crackled—in all the chaos, her grasp on the thing had wavered. "I'm getting proper help."

"By *avoiding* the hospital?" Stevie retorted.

"You wouldn't get it." she growled. She'd already said too much. While she doubted Stevie would conclude she was a witch seeking supernatural aid, one rule of living in the mortal world was to avoid drawing suspicion. Disappearing from her apartment in a flash of light? Suspicious.

The portal's glow dimmed. It bulged awkwardly, and a leg of Selene's coffee table dipped in. Cursing, she shoved it back.

"Then explain it to me! Please—" This time, she cut herself off with a sob. "Please, explain it."

And maybe it was the pain in Stevie's voice, or the pain in Selene's leg, but something impaired her judgment.

Selene flicked her hand out and the door unlocked. Stevie stumbled out, collapsing in a heap on the floor. She looked up at Selene with the eyes of a kicked puppy, and the witch knew she couldn't lie a second longer. If she got a few months of travel ban, that was fine—better than scarring this poor woman for life, at least.

"Don't tell anyone what I'm about to tell you, okay?" Selene asked.

Stevie nodded, already rapt.

"I'm a witch," Selene said. She strained to keep her voice even, keep breathing, keep the portal open. "Not a great one—just a basic spellcaster, really—but a witch nonetheless."

Stevie's head rose from the floor, her eyes shiny from crying. "*What?*" she rasped. "And here I thought you were gonna kill yourself. I've seen too many dancers get hurt, and last year a patient . . . " Her voice petered out as she took in the portal. "What's that?"

"It'll take me to the witchlands," Selene said. Her words had a slur to them—her leg was a useless, throbbing mass now, and the agony threatened to overtake her. "There I can find someone with the magic to heal me."

Stevie blinked away tears. "Okay, we *both* need to go to the hospital. Because you're crazy, and I must be, too, if I'm . . . "

"How can I prove myself to you?" Selene asked. She forced herself to sit up straighter despite her leg screaming at every movement. "Everything I've done tonight. . . has been magic. My apartment isn't haunted—it was *magic*. My door isn't voice-activated—it was *magic*. All of this—" She gestured to the apartment walls, to the portal before her, to herself. "All of this is *magic*. Minor stuff, but magic. Do you want me to light something on fire, too?"

"I mean, you're showing off already, sure," Stevie mumbled.

Selene groaned. She thrust a hand out, to the candles atop her bookshelf. "*Fondu.*" With a flick of her wrist, their flames flickered to life. In the dark, they dyed the corner of the room a warm gold. Another simple spell, one even children could do, but Stevie gawked at her like she'd split the room in two.

"Do you believe me now?" she asked.

"Okay, fine, I do. You're a witch, and you're going to a magical world to have another witch look at your problems. Is there anything I can do to help you with that?"

Selene pinched the bridge of her nose, felt the blush burning her cheeks. Even now, with everything under control, this woman insisted on being here, coddling her. . .

"No, I've got this. Just don't tell anyone what you saw tonight, alright? I'll never be allowed to come back if it gets out."

"Let me guess—a witchy code of secrecy?"

A smile played on Selene's lips. "Something like that." She thought the whole system was archaic, really, but seeing Stevie's eyes light up made her bite her tongue. Humans found whimsy in whatever you threw at them.

"And what's in it for me?" Stevie teased.

"You get to leave this room alive." She'd meant to tease right back, but the words came out colder than she'd hoped.

Stevie considered this, looking Selene up and down. Appraising her, almost. "Was that a threat?"

"Not really," Selene replied. She'd heard of it as a legal defence in the witchlands—*price of protection*, they called it. Selene didn't have the nerve for such an act, but there were few things tougher than a witch's bluff. "But are you sure you want to find out?"

"Tough talk from someone with a mangled leg."

The reminder seemed to empower her pain and Selene winced as it fought through her spell. "What, is there something you want?"

"Just one request," Stevie said, stooping down to Selene's level. Her eyes, Selene noticed, were a shade she'd never seen before: bright, almost glowing green. Of course, that may have been the portal's light and her delirium.

"What *is* it?" Selene pressed. "If you let me go, I'll give you whatever it is you desire. Money, a shoutout, industry connections..."

Stevie held her index finger to her lips, and Selene cut herself off. With her other hand, she took Selene's own.

"One ticket to your next show, please," she murmured. "If you really can dance after this, I want to see it. I've spent most of my life in theatres, but I've never seen someone move how you do. It's like your body's reduced to the barest elements—the air moves to your will, your body's fluid as water, there's a fire in your soul—"

"And the earth rushed right up to meet me when I fell off that podium," Selene finished flatly. Still, she couldn't help the blush that crept up her skin. It was nothing she hadn't heard before, yet coming from this strange, stubborn woman . . .

"But when you get back up there, I want to see it. Even now, barely able to walk, you have this way of just. . . " She gestured vaguely to Selene's crumpled mess of a body. "You carry yourself like a dancer, whether or not you're dancing. I want to see that again."

Despite it all, Selene smiled. "You have a way with words, you know." She couldn't see it, herself—she felt like a beached mermaid: legs useless and stabbing, covered in pearls that have lost their sheen, sweat bringing salt to her skin. "And you have a deal—though if I do perform again anytime soon, it'll probably be in the Witchlands."

"Smuggle me in, then."

And Selene couldn't help but chuckle at that. They shook on it. Stevie had a warm, strong grip. And then she did something peculiar: she planted a kiss on the back of Selene's hand. Selene knew the gesture was little more than that—a gesture, the kind not uncommon around touchy performing artists. Still, it made her heart skip a beat.

"You've charmed me, Miss Choquette," Stevie murmured, looking up to Selene with a grin.

"We witches have that tendency," Selene replied with a shrug, trying and failing to keep her cool.

The portal crackled, its edges fraying. It'd evened out, its turbulence calmed, but soon it would wane away, not unlike the moon it drew power from.

"I should go," Selene said. She pressed an arm against the coffee table, hissing through her teeth as she rose to her feet. In an instant, Stevie was at her side, offering a shoulder to lean on. Selene fell against it with a sigh of relief.

"You know," she said, "if you want, you could come with me." She felt foolish even suggesting it—and selfish, so selfish, after what she'd put the poor woman through.

But she didn't want to walk in there alone. Not when she could barely walk. Not when there was someone who cared so much and would help her along.

"I could?" Stevie's eyes lit up.

Selene gave her a stern look. "Only if you want. Don't be impulsive about this kind of thing, okay? It's dangerous, and I don't know how long you'd be there, and I—"

"I'll take whatever witchy vow of secrecy they throw at me," Stevie declared. "If they hand me some kind of magical truth serum, I'll chug it. If they make me sign contracts with blood, well. . ." She held up her bandaged finger. "I've got easy access already."

"You wouldn't be able to pronounce half the words in our vows," Selene said, smiling despite herself. "We don't sign our contracts in blood, either—we left that practice behind *decades* ago."

"*Just* decades?"

Selene shrugged. "Crazy, right?" She took a tentative step to the portal. Stevie followed so faithfully, it felt like a *pas de deux*. "See, it stopped in the late 19th century, but was never officially criminalized, so there was this rogue sect. . . I'm rambling, aren't I?"

"Keep rambling," Stevie said. "It'll keep you alert, and I just learned magic is a thing, so all of this is cool as hell to me." She laughed, the high and uneasy sound of someone whose life had been irrevocably changed.

But they took another step forward, and Selene hoped she'd changed this woman's life for the better.

"Very well." Selene cleared her throat. "There was this rogue sect of magical scholars, known as the Children of the Lone Angel, and they were *very* insistent on honesty. So, every single one of their contracts was bound. . . with *blood*."

Stevie's eyes went wide, a thousand questions undoubtedly on her tongue. But she only asked one: "Did it work?"

And it was Selene's turn to laugh, not at Stevie but at her unabashed wonder. "I mean, so the legend says. But one day, someone actually brought them to *court* over the whole thing. . . "

As Selene prattled on, the two of them stepped forward. Stevie looked to the unknown, before them, and Selene looked to the unknown right beside her—this strange, selfless woman she'd let in. She had a feeling she wouldn't regret it.

The moonlight portal took them in, and took them home.

DAUGHTER OF DARKNESS & SON OF THE SUN

BY KIERAN LAMOUREUX

Kieran Lamoureux hunts for fairy rings while hiking and wouldn't be surprised if cats were shape-shifting dragons hiding in plain sight. Her stories reflect her fascination with mythology and fairytales and the archetypes in humanity's narratives that resonate across cultures and throughout history. She daydreams of devious plot twists and ways to reduce weeds in her rather wild garden, and someday, she'll succeed in transforming her house into Bag End.

* * *

She watched him with envy, the son of the Sun, the golden child with his gleaming hair and bronzed skin and radiant smile as he followed his father across the sky. She watched him from her place in the shadows, watched the weight of his legacy slow his steps with every sunrise and sunset, watched him stare longingly at the shade and the gloom and the dark places where the Sun could not reach.

She wished she could speak to him, wished she could feel and see the world as he did, in all its glorious warmth and color. Had she a form that could endure his light, she'd have found the courage. Or so she told herself.

But what had she to offer—she, a daughter of Darkness, of nightmares and deepest fears and darkest truths whispered in the dead of night? She had no place in his hours of stark sunlight and sharp shadows and saturated colors so bright her eyes burned. And she had been warned: light destroyed darkness.

But she couldn't stay away, drawn to his radiance like winged creatures to flame.

So she sat on his windowsill under the cover of night, wrapped in her great black wings, and she wove him dreams. She showed him the beauty of the shades of shadow, the pale luminance of the few plants that survived in the depths where she lived, the symphony of sounds in the quiet and solitude. And she sang.

She sang to him of the stars and the planets and the shimmering lights she saw on clear nights when she crept to the edge of the cliffs along the wild sea. Of her desire to be free from the cold and dark she'd known her entire existence, to see the world as he did, to feel the warmth of the Sun's dying light.

And one night, the son of the Sun awoke.

She tensed as he stirred, ruffling her feathers, readying herself to flee. If he caught her—

A word, no more than a whisper. "Wait."

* * *

HE SAT UP, staring. He'd never seen one like her. Cloaked in shadows and starlight, her very essence seemed to shift, her form wavering as she spread her wings wide. And what wings—glossy feathers deeper than night, their tips swirled with the colors of the cosmos, as if each had been dipped in a different part of the galaxy.

His father had warned him of the daughters of Darkness, each one lovelier than the last but deceitful as Darkness Himself. Women who would steal his light, bind him to shadow. . . . But this woman, who sang to him of such beauty and wonder—surely she couldn't be one of them?

"Are you . . . ?" He slid slowly from his covers, struggling to discern her expression in the shadows. "Are you the one from my dreams?"

She watched him warily, then nodded.

"Stay. Please?"

Her wings rustled, then relaxed. He took a step. She tensed.

He sat back on his bed, not wanting to startle her. "Will you sing again?"

"Of what?"

Her voice—ah, to hear her voice. In all his centuries, he'd never heard a sound so sweet, its edges soft and sultry, sending shivers down his spine. He'd thought it merely his dreams, seeking to torment him, but to hear her speak as she sat before him—

"Of anything," he said, hearing the desperation in his voice. He, who had never wanted for anything. "Please."

* * *

SHE COULDN'T RESIST his pleading eyes, the deep, clear blue of a summer sky. So she sang, night after night, as he crept closer to her perch, until one night she peeked out from behind her feathers to find his fingers a mere breath from hers.

She snatched her hand back and spread her wings. Hadn't she been warned? "If he touches you," her father had said, "his light will burn your very soul."

The son of the Sun smiled. And she shivered, his smile piercing her shadows with the light of a thousand suns, warmth and promise and pain and desire.

In the silver glow of the slip of a moon, his eyes shone like pale blue stars. "I will not harm you," he murmured.

She shook her head, arranging her wings to shelter herself from his radiance. "But my father said . . . "

"What did he say?" he asked gently. When she stayed silent, he cleared his throat. "My father said you would steal my light."

She shook her head. "I have no such intent." She paused. "Mine said your light would destroy me."

"And if they are wrong?" The son of the Sun held out his hand.

She hesitated, then touched her fingers to his. Warmth and feeling flooded her form, fulfillment of the promise in his smile, pain and desire and the weight of her betrayal, and yet—she hadn't disintegrated. He hadn't destroyed her. She curled her fingers around his and slid off the sill.

Her heart—oh, to feel it—she could feel the rhythmic thrum as he slid his arm around her waist and tilted her chin.

"May I?"

She nodded.

He leaned down and brushed his lips over hers, and she had never felt so warm.

* * *

AND SO THEY met by moonlight, learning each other's hopes and fears and dreams. Learning the secrets of skin against skin, the pleasure of light piercing shadow and of darkness swallowing light. He learned what made her shiver and sigh and how to tire her so she could sleep in his arms until dawn.

It wasn't long before the son of the Sun began to live for the night, for those hours when her dark caresses drove away all thought of his father's legacy. The world might revolve around the Sun, but the son's world revolved around her.

As spring gave way to summer, as the days grew longer and the nights grew shorter, the daughter of Darkness began to watch the shadows with fear in her eyes, her form weightless in his embrace, lighter than the brush of her feathered wings.

"He knows," she whispered. "I know it. He will take me from you."

The son of the Sun held her tighter, the same fear darkening his own heart. But he refused to lose her.

"We will find a way," he said, smoothing her sleek hair to brush his lips over her brow. "Our fathers' lies have no hold over us."

"How?" she asked, her voice the barest whisper of silk against skin, her eyes shimmering with tears. "How, when they refuse to see . . . "

He didn't know. But now that he'd found her, he knew he had no life without her. So he caught her tears with his thumb and kissed her until she sighed, her body eager against his.

* * *

HER FEAR CAME to light as dawn crept over the horizon. Darkness Himself rose from the depths, his ancient face etched with fury as he strode across the room, fashioning shadowed shackles with a sweep of his great arm.

But they bound not his daughter, with her flurry of wings; they latched instead onto the son of the Sun, dragging him down into darkness. Fearful for her lover, she followed, throwing herself before her father's throne, pleading until her voice failed.

It did no good.

Darkness stared at her, his eyes unreadable. "You were warned. He would have destroyed you. He is now mine to do with as I wish, and for your treachery, you have lost your place and the protection of the shadows."

She shook her head. "You were wrong."

Her father's eyes narrowed.

"You were wrong," she repeated. "It is not his light that harms me. It is you."

Darkness rose from his throne, his shadowed form soaring high above her. "Would you so readily betray your own?"

She lifted her chin. "I am the oldest of your children. Would you cast me aside so easily?"

Her father's eyes smoldered. And a fragile hope fluttered in her heart.

"A bargain," she said. "If I survive the Sun's light, and my love survives the shadows, you will grant us pardon."

Darkness loomed. "One night," he said at length. "When shadows reign over the light of the Sun."

The solstice. She would need to endure one year for one night. She nodded, and with no chance for farewell nor to warn her lover of the trial to come, her father cast her out.

So she wandered the world, her soul battered and broken, longing for her son of the Sun, for the comfort of his warmth and the light of his smile.

Bereft over the loss of his son and too weak to fight, the dying

Sun's light waned further, subduing the beauty she'd longed to look upon at her lover's side.

Days turned into weeks, weeks into months, and her heart grew heavy with cold. And though her shadowed form paled and her wings weakened until they could no longer lift her from the ground, she refused to fade.

AS THE DAYS shortened and the nights lengthened, the daughter of Darkness began to watch the Sun set with stirrings of hope. Hope that her lover had withstood the shadows, that his light had endured.

One evening, when the snow settled in great drifts and the wind whistled through the pines, she flew to the place where they'd met, to the windowsill where she'd watched him sleep as she'd sung to him in dreams. And as the Sun sank toward the horizon, as the stars began to shimmer in the sky, she waited with growing hope in her heart.

The crescent moon rose higher, and a glow gathered in the distance. Bound in shadow, his light glimmering weakly, the son of the Sun rose, his shackles held triumphantly by Darkness Himself. The Sun, a mere sliver where earth met sky, shivered, for he feared Darkness had won.

But when the son of the Sun saw the daughter of Darkness, a smile spread over his face, a bright burst of light piercing his chains. Her heart pounded in her chest, each painful thud thawing the chill of his absence. With a long-stifled cry, she spread her wings and leapt from the sill, riding the currents to reach him.

And as the daughter of Darkness approached the son of the Sun, her sable wings spread to cover the starlit sky, and his light shone all the brighter.

And Darkness was swallowed in the last brilliant flare of the dying Sun.

WITHIN THESE TWISTED VINES
BY ALEX HARVEY

Alex is a queer writer and mountain of incomprehensible goo living in the Pacific Northwest. When they aren't being paid to fix other people's financial mistakes, they're researching whatever interests them, reading from their arsenal of books, or playing video games. They can be reached at authoralexharvey@gmail.com or by howling into the woods when you're alone at night.

* * *

Isabella was missing. That's what the officer kept telling me from across the living room. I was listening—almost. But every time I tuned in to what he was saying, his words were lost again to a thick, unrelenting static.

Isabella was missing. It didn't make any sense. I'd just talked to her yesterday, hadn't I? We'd been Snapchatting back and forth for hours because she couldn't sleep. If I focused, I could recall the last image she'd sent: a blurred forest yawning behind her. Though it'd been a selfie, the vastness of the space she'd been in had made her smiling form seem minuscule in comparison.

And that, according to the police, was the last anyone had heard of her.

"I don't understand." I fiddled with the popsocket on the back of my phone. In, out, in, out. The clicking soothed me; anything to keep from listening to Mrs. Herrera's lamenting wails in the kitchen or the badge on this man's chest.

"We aren't here to harass you, Macy." He leaned back as he spoke, legs spread. For him, this was undoubtedly just another day. Another life lost, another case to make. "You're the last person we know of who spoke with Miss Herrera. Anything you can give us would help."

In, out. In, out. The popsocket continued to click as I pondered his words. All I had were our Snaps—except the photo. I hadn't saved it, which now struck me as odd. I always saved Isabella's photos. This one had fallen through the cracks, as though it'd never existed.

"Miss Floros?"

I met his stare, so direct it must have been the reason he shrank in response. My mouth moved on its own. "All I have is our Snapchat conversations." And in them, vague clues. Some party, but she hadn't said who with or where. This wasn't uncommon for Isabella.

"We've already reviewed those." He sighed, pen tapping against his notepad. Before this impromptu interview, he and some other officer had loomed over me as I played each Story over and over again. "Can you think of anything else? What kind of party she went to? Anyone who might have attended?"

I'd taken to scanning the Stories of our mutual friends while I'd waited to be interviewed. With each short clip, I had prayed beyond hope there would be some sort of clue. Alas, nothing. None of them had gone with her, nor did they know anything more than I had.

"No." My attention shifted to the pendant at my throat, cool to the touch. *Let her be safe, please.* Then, "She can be frustratingly private, when she wants to be."

He wrote this down, mouth set in a thin line. "Do you think she was going to be with anyone in particular?"

"No." My screen flashed. A text from my aunt, likely telling me there weren't any updates. Not that I was expecting them. I turned my phone back over. Isabella had only been missing for less than a day, after all. Under normal circumstances, missing persons cases weren't opened immediately. It was the frenzied insistence of Isabella's mother that had the police involved at all. I'd seen this scene too many times the last couple of years.

"Do you think," I said, testing each word as I said it, "this is related to all the other missing women?"

He sighed again and sagged into the couch cushions, writing pad landing with a slap. His foot beat out an uneven staccato. "We currently don't think so. The other missing persons have no relation to each other. To have it all come together now?" He sucked on his teeth and shook his head. If he had something further to say, he didn't say it. Minutes dragged on like hours before, finally, he rose.

"This is my card," he said before scribbling a series of letters and numbers. "If anything new comes to you, or if she tries to contact you, give me a call." Then he handed me a sliver of cream cardstock, thin and wrinkled as it molded to my palm. I held it as the officer wrapped up his questioning, and as he made a final attempt to console Isabella's hysterical mother. And then, the moment his shadow vanished from the glass on the front door, I crinkled it up and tossed it to some forgotten corner of the couch.

* * *

THE TIMELINE of Isabella's and my ever-changing relationship had grown murky, but the night we met was one of its stronger points. Some friend of a friend of some drug dealer had hosted a party at his house while his parents were away. Jasmine, my best friend at the time, had invited me and I hadn't wanted to leave her to the dangers of a hoard of drunk teenagers.

And then I met Isabella.

I was in a corner of the basement, positioned so the music wasn't as intense. Though the noise made concentration difficult, I stared at the book in my lap and willed the words to stop swimming. Jasmine had long since abandoned me.

"You know, a party isn't the best place to be reading," said Isabella, though I didn't know it at the time. I didn't look up, content to pretend the party didn't exist and that I wasn't really there. Soon enough, this stranger would get bored and leave me for more active company.

But she didn't. Sighing, she sat down next to me, reeking of weed and strong alcohol and mint. The sound of her gum chewing gnawed at my nerves.

"Mind if I sit here?" she asked between obnoxious smacks.

I flipped to the next page. "Would it matter if I did?"

"Probably not." Then, clearer, "Whatcha reading?"

I lifted the book so she could see, still focused on the words.

"Hymns? You don't seem the church-going type."

Frowning, I flipped forward again. "I'm not."

"Could have fooled me."

"They're Orphic Hymns," I said. "Like from Orpheus." Now I looked up, in time to see her thick brows crinkle. Long black hair, curly and lighter at the ends, framed her narrow face. Her eyes looked dark enough to suck me inside of them. A smattering of freckles, like stars in the sky, curved over the bridge of her nose, which wrinkled as she regarded me.

"So . . . " She scooted closer, until I could feel the heat radiating from her. "Are these about Jesus or . . . ?"

"No. They're Greco-Roman—about the Olympians. Hades and Zeus and Demeter and." I paused, chewing on my lip. "Right now I'm reading about Dionysus," I said at last.

"I think I've heard of that last one," she said, dark eyes twinkling.

Of course you would know the god of wine and madness. Then, as quick as the thought came, I reprimanded myself for it. He wouldn't encourage such judgmental thinking. Instead, folding the corner to the page, I shut the book and met her curious stare. "Oh?"

"Yeah. I think they mentioned him in *The Secret History* or something. Some mad god. Name's familiar. But, still, you don't strike me as the party-girl type."

My cheeks grew warm with embarrassment. "I'm not."

"But you're reading about the *king* of partying . . . at a party."

"He's not—" I caught myself as my voice raised. Several drunken teens turned our way between music beats before deigning to ignore us once more. "He's . . . much more than that," I finished, when they'd all looked away again.

She held her hands up in surrender. "You don't gotta defend him to me." Then she took another look around the basement. "You come alone?"

"N-No, um." As I stumbled, I scanned the room for Jasmine. She was probably upstairs. "I came with a friend."

"Some friend, leaving you to nerd out by yourself. You drink?"

My heart lurched. "Not often."

"Smoke?"

"Only marijuana."

"Oh, good. Me too." When she turned back to me, it was with a fox-like grin and a lighter in one hand. "Wanna come outside with me?"

I looked her over once again. Though looks could be misleading, she didn't seem the sort to leave me abandoned somewhere—like Jasmine had, I recalled bitterly. As I hesitated, Isabella held up a crushed bag of weed and gave it a shake. "Huh?" she said, the way one might to a dog they're trying to entice.

"I guess for a bit," I said at last.

Until that moment, I had been completely sober. But touching her made me the drunkest I'd ever felt, like I'd stumble and the world would fall away from me. She was the most perfect, intoxicating disaster.

Later, hiding in the woods behind the house, we were watching the stars side by side when she said, "So. Dionysus."

"Yes?"

"You read about him for fun?" With a chuckle, she continued, "Or am I about to find myself sacrificed in some blood orgy?"

"It's not like that," I said, for not the first time. The weed, though skunky and weak, had been enough to dull my discomfort some. "Like any god, He has multiple forms. These hymns focus on some such variations."

I heard her shift beside me. When I dared a glance, she was on her side, staring at me through her lashes and leaning on one palm. "What's he like, then, to you?"

My stomach stirred. "Well," I said, regarding the stars through the branches. "He's . . . have you ever had a family friend? Or like . . . a really cool aunt or something?"

Her smile grew crooked. "Sure."

"He's a lot like that. Very paternal, but not in a fatherly way. Like . . . " I wrung my hands together. "If I'm sad, I can play His music or burn His candles and he's right there, yaknow? Not in a 'I can talk to God' kind of way, but." The fog in my brain thinned. "Now that I'm trying to explain it, I guess I sound crazy."

"You don't."

I turned my head. "Really?"

She bit her lip before replying. "Yeah. Like. A lot of my family is pretty Catholic. They talk about Jesus and Mary and all them the same way."

I nodded. "Makes sense."

She leaned closer. Mint and weed and booze-laden breath drifted on the breeze. "Is your dude better about gay people, at least?

I blinked. "He kind of has to be."

"Good." With this, she flopped back down, sending a scattering of leaves swirling around us. They drifted down like snowflakes and settled on our clothes. "Your god or deity or . . . whatever you call him, he sounds alright to me," she said.

I didn't get a chance to respond. The flashing of lights sent us both bolting upright. Red and blue. Police cars. We took one look at each other and broke into a run, scattering like leaves on the wind.

I didn't learn her name until days later, when we met by chance between classes. Like stars, we fell hard and fast, tumbling headfirst into an ever-changing relationship. And yet, a few years later, Isabella's sudden disappearance was a black hole I couldn't escape from.

* * *

TWO WEEKS WENT by with no sign or sound of Isabella. I joined every search party that opened, scanned every inch of our small, haunted town as thoroughly as I could, prayed until my knee ache was unbearable. All of it to no avail.

At the end of these two weeks, the gravity of the situation was settling hard on top of me. Each day ended the same: I'd come home from work or search parties or candlelight vigils and throw myself into bed, dreading the day to follow.

This day, three weeks to the date of her disappearance, was more of the same. The door clicked shut behind me, echoing around the empty house. Mom was still at work. Though it was still early afternoon, exhaustion and sadness had wormed their way under my skin and continued to gnaw at me. My drive to do anything but sleep had long-since abandoned me. And so, after a beat to observe my surroundings, I hauled my way up the stairs and prepared for the end of another soulless day.

My bedroom door creaked as it opened, throwing a sudden breeze that sent the curtains fluttering. The scent of pine needles and lavender hung thick in the air. It coated my senses like perfume. I hadn't remembered leaving my windows open, but many of the smaller details of my life had been consumed by a thick fog. It was possible I'd just forgotten.

But then, sitting on my bed as if she'd never disappeared, was Isabella.

Her features seemed sharper, somehow, like her selfies had sanded down the edges. When had I last seen her in person? It had been a few weeks, at least.

The door shut behind me, loud enough to startle. She didn't stir.

"Macy."

My fists curled as sudden anger consumed me. Here I'd been, hunting past the point of exhaustion, and she'd just . . . ghosted. No calls, no texts, no sign that she was okay. What gave her the right to suddenly come back?

With a sigh, I looked away. "What are you doing here?"

"Aren't you happy to see me?"

Startled, I maintained a wide berth as I headed for the window. What an odd question for her to ask; of course I was. But, "Everyone's been looking for you."

"So they have." She declared it like a weather forecast, predatory gaze locked on me. "I should feel bad people are worried, I think."

The shutters struggled as I fought to close them, but my renewed strength won out. Never before had she sounded so cavalier. "You say that like you aren't."

I looked away—just for a second, to give the window my attention —and she was on me at once. Palms of ice cupped my cheek. She carried the scent of the forest on her breath.

"Just you," she said. "Only you."

I swallowed hard, breath battering my ribs. Dozens of emotions fluttered inside my chest. Anger. Heartbreak. Love. I repressed the urge to look at her lips, to kiss her, to *want* to kiss her, more than anything in the world. This couldn't be real.

"I came to say goodbye, Mace." A slight hesitation, sadness crinkling the corners of her eyes. Then, "I won't be coming back this time."

"What do you mean?" I reached for her, but she broke contact in the space of a blink. "Where are you going?"

For the first time, her assuredness slumped out of her. Her eyes glistened as she stared at me. "I can't tell you."

"I thought—"

Whatever I was chasing was lost on the softness of her lips. She kissed me the way she used to, soft and slow, a fire coaxed to life. As we came apart, I swore I felt her tears on my cheek.

Then they—and she—were gone.

* * *

I didn't report her appearance. I couldn't. Every time I thought to, I froze with feelings I couldn't place. Was it fear? The feral gleam in her eyes? For all I knew, she'd been a hallucination, a manifestation of my guilt and sorrow.

Likewise, I couldn't sleep. Understandable, given the circumstances. Instead, I sat on the cluttered window nook, tracing oily lines into the glass. The moon stared back at me from its perch in the sky. The soft light painted my skin with shades of grey.

And I was drunk. So very, stupidly drunk.

I hadn't meant to drink this much, but the moment I'd wrapped my lips around the first bottle, it'd all become a blur.

There was an army of them now. Glass clinked whenever I moved. A stray Mike's Hard rolled and came to an uneasy stop by my foot. As I watched it, brain numb, a strawberry-flavored belch escaped. I lurched to pick up the bottle .

Before I could grab hold, a dark shape at the foot of my bed caught my eye. On wobbling limbs, I dragged myself towards it. It was a hard-cover book, larger than the ones on my shelf. As my vision swam, I slid it closer. Slivers of moonlight illuminated the cover. I felt each word on my tongue as I read it. My high school yearbook.

I hadn't been the best student in high school. Most of it had been left to a weed-addled stupor. I wasn't a good fit for any social niche. Extra curriculars were a waste of time. My strategy for survival had become, "Keep your head down and survive." Isabella, on the other hand, had been a total social butterfly. Her face was everywhere in this yearbook. Sports, debate, jazz band. Somehow, she had done it all, forcing me into the frame with her wherever she could.

With every flip of the page, my heart shattered a bit more.

"This can't be it." My voice came out slurred and hollow. I wiped excess spittle away. "She's not dead. I . . . I just . . . she can't be. I would feel it if she were."

The moon remained as impassive as ever.

"Wherever she is, she's alive." A soft, slurred sigh drifted from me. "You'll make sure she's safe, won't you?"

When people speak of the Gods appearing, they often speak of physical manifestations, of seeing Them in person or hearing Their voice. Dionysus rarely worked that way. He spoke in soft scents and gut feelings, in cryptic dreams I struggled to remember. Now, the soft scent of lavender wreathed me, a reminder of His presence.

"Dionysus." His name came out a croak. I pushed myself up on unsteady legs. The world spun and showed no signs of stopping. "Is it wrong I want to find her?"

Outside, the wind picked up. Branches scratched at the windows.

"I just . . ."

The room swirled. Before I could stop myself, I dropped to a cruel rendition of a bow, knees sore with the impact. A weight planted against my spine and held me firm.

"I need to find her. I'm not going to be able to get over this." The floorboards muffled my words, but I carried on anyway.

"Dionysus Soterius, help me find her. Help me find Isabella."

In these moments I spent prostrating myself, He came once again in the soft tugging of my heartstrings. If I strained hard enough, I could hear His thoughts within my own: "I am here."

* * *

THAT NIGHT, I dreamed of shadowed forests and yowling cats. I chased them through the woods until I was certain my legs would fall off. I screamed Isabella's name until my throat was hoarse. Still, I couldn't catch up.

The next night, the visions returned. One moment, in an edible-fueled stupor, I watched the ceiling swirl overhead. The next, I was chasing Isabella through the forest.

We found momentary peace in a clearing. Figures in disfigured animal masks leered down at us from the trees. As each mouth opened, Isabella's voice poured out like smoke.

"Find me," they intoned. "Find us."

My gaze darted along the clearing. There was something familiar in the scene, but I couldn't place what. "Where?" I asked. "How?"

"Find me. Find us."

The figures dropped from the trees in unison, shambling towards us on all fours. A stiff breeze rustled the trees and tugged at my clothes. When I looked back to Isabella, she wore the stiff, bloody head of a bobcat over her own. She reared back with a roar, ichor dripping from the decapitated neck. As I stumbled back in shock, the ground rumbled and fell apart. I plummeted into the blackness beneath.

When I opened my eyes, the kitchen door flapped in the wind like a paper bird in a tornado. Outside, the rain fell in sheets, bouncing off the concrete as it landed. Lightning streaked the sky with thick fingers of white. Seconds later, thunder boomed.

This wasn't part of the dream. I knew the moment I could read the time on the oven. Two in the morning. Another flash of lightning whited out the room. I swore, for a split second, that a figure loomed in the doorway. Then they were gone. The low rumble of thunder overtook me once again. The edge of the forest glowered at me beyond the backyard.

How did I get here?

The hairs on my arms pricked up. Uneasy, I rushed to close the door. The wind howled, fighting back. The hinges squealed like an animal injured.

Then, as I was ready to give up, the door slammed closed. I flew back, landing on my ass with a groan.

It was a sign. It had to be. It was what I had asked for, after all.

Quiet as I could and still woozy from the alcohol, I rushed back to my room to change. In a pair of too-loose sweatpants and a dye-streaked crop-top, I pulled my boot laces tight. Whatever I was going to find about Isabella, it would be in those woods.

* * *

THE FOREST'S edge goaded me, each branch a crooked finger. My guts lurched, as if something had plunged into my stomach and was trying to pull me forward. Chin tipped, I marched on. Perhaps this would all be a dream. Still, I owed it to Isabella to exhaust every option.

The deeper into the forest I was, the more awake I became. The truth prickled my skin. This was real, for better or worse. The lurching in my gut worsened.

Something fluttered in the canopy overhead, sending leaves and twigs to the earth like rain. With a shriek, I planted myself against the nearest tree. Then, a soft hoot.

Just an owl. Embarrassment kept my cheeks warm. *Nothing more.* I clung to the shadows with a pounding heart, waiting for the shape to recede.

Look.

The thought wasn't my own, lurking in the depths of my mind like a shark below surf. My gaze returned to the twisted overhang, where I thought I had seen the owl make its haunting departure. There wasn't anything I could pick out of the darkness, but then—

My chest tightened as it dawned on me. Two reflective eyes gazed down at me from within the branches. Every muscle tensed, preparing me to run. Sweat beaded my palms.

During spring break our senior year, Isabella and her parents and I had gone camping at Mount Rainier, split into two plots. On the final morning of our trip, I'd left our tent and found myself face to face with a bear. It had rummaged through the trail mix I'd forgotten to pack up, uncaring of my presence just feet from it. Isabella had joined me with a hurried whisper. "Back away. Slowly. No sudden movements, no loud sounds."

I thought of her advice as I regarded the eyes in the tree. One after another, each eye fluttered shut and then opened once more. The branches creaked as the creature shifted its weight. Then it pounced, landing with a cloud of dust a couple of feet away. A bobcat, I thought, based on the straight back and small paws.

Isabella's voice filled my head. "Back away. Slowly. No sudden movements." Before I could stop myself, I was mouthing along, her voice cradled within my own. I shrank into the undergrowth, placing each step with the care one might in building a castle out of playing cards. The bobcat glared at me and growled.

Maybe this is what happened to her. Without looking, I ghosted a hand along the trees, searching for a branch thick and long enough to be a useful weapon. *Maybe a bobcat ate her.* Even as the thought emerged, I dismissed it as foolish. She was alive. She had to be . . . right?

With a yawn that cracked its mighty maw in two, the large cat turned and strode deeper into the forest, vanishing with a final wave of its stubbed tail.

* * *

BEFORE LONG, the long ferns gave way to a small clearing. Tree stumps formed a ring at the edges, new sprouts unfurling in nature's proudest display of defiance. Scraps of paper, tattered and sunbleached, mixed with the foliage. Something hard rattled underfoot. A bottle rolled from where it had tripped me and stopped with a clatter. A scant ray of moonlight splashed across the label. Hard lemonade.

Isabella and I had been partial to such alcohol in our teens, since it was fruity and weak and cheap enough to acquire. In the months after graduation, we'd taken to drinking cases of it here, trading stories as we did. Mine were of the folk tales a relative from Greece had told me, while hers were about the boys she'd taken to bed.

Our stories had made each other uncomfortable in different ways.

I picked up the bottle. Traces of someone's lip prints clung to the rim. Despite the darkness, splashes of moonlight revealed the red smudges.

All at once, it clicked. This was our old hangout spot. Dozens of half-formed footprints littered the clearing, the remains of countless search parties. I myself had scoured this part of the woods time and time again, numb to its significance.

There was a final test, just to be sure. The day after we graduated, drunk on love and Mike's and higher than we had any right to be, we'd carved our names into the ring of stumps. I crouched beside a stump whose new sprouts threaded together like a chair back and felt along its top. *There.* So faint, I almost didn't believe it, two large letters. M + I.

The bottle slipped from my hand and clattered, leaving a red smudge on my thumb. The forest blurred around me. Woozy, I sat down and waited for my mind to settle.

* * *

BEFORE LONG, a woman's shrill laughter pierced the quiet, too far-off to place. Birds took flight overhead. Tendrils of smoke wove together before me, thick with the scent of fire.

Then, as my heart lurched, another shout. *Isabella?*

My legs moved of their own accord now, carrying me deeper into the dark. I exploded from the bushes like an animal crazed, breaths ragged and knees sore where I had collapsed. The damp earth clung to my palms. Pin-pricks along my skin urged me to not look up.

"A newcomer." The voice was one and yet many. "Dionysus Maenoles has brought us another."

The remains of my dinner churned. Like most devotees, I was

aware of His cult throughout the centuries. The maenads, a cluster of women embroiled in Bacchic frenzy. I was also aware of their favored sport. Sparagmos. Ritualistic dismemberment. They had invoked His epithet in speaking to me: Maenoles, the Mad One, a sharp contrast to the epithet I used. Soterius, Savior from Madness.

"I can smell her terror from here," said a different voice, farther away. Glasses clinked. The scent of pine needles and lavender drifted to me like fog. Then, with such gentleness I could have imagined it, a hand on my cheek.

"I knew you would find me."

Isabella. Her hand remained against my skin, soft despite the callouses. I kept my eyes glued closed, so convinced she was a hallucination, my deepest desires made cruel reality. A minute passed, then another. We remained bathed in the silence.

Then, "Macy, would you look at me?"

The moment I did, the tears rushed out. She was here. Real. Isabella, my best friend. I threw my arms around her with a sob and relished in her warmth.

"You're alive," I said into her neck. "You're actually fucking alive."

"Who is this?"

The voice sliced through me. Slowly, I released the fistfulls I'd gathered of Isabella's hole-riddled sweater and peeled myself away. Her tears soaked my shoulder.

"Forgive me, Serena." She rose, brows furrowed, her body a wall between me and the rest of the clearing. "This is—"

"Macy. My name is Macy."

From between Isabella's legs, I watched the throng of women sweep closer. A whole cluster of them, old and young and each of them as wild as the last. They smiled at me with rows of too-sharp teeth. At the lead, an older black woman with several clinking bracelets approached me on hands and knees.

"Be not afraid," she said. The feral smile didn't drop as she reached for my necklace. "All of His children find safety here."

"She *is* a devotee, is she not?" asked another.

The woman sat back on her haunches. "She is."

In the silence that followed, I studied her. Her bracelets gleamed in the moonlight, countless bands of gold and silver and crusted with crystals. Her face was wrinkled and leathery, her eyes two ethereal garnets. Her hair rolled into thick twists, tied back and laced with ivy. The longer I stared at her, the more her presence gnawed at me. I knew her, somehow.

"You're Serena Briggs," I said at last. "You disappeared a couple of months ago."

Her canines glistened. "So I did."

"And this is where you went."

"So it is."

Isabella took my hands in hers. "Most of the recent disappearances have ended up here. We all went missing, in some fashion or another . . . all so we could be here with Him."

My nose crinkled. "You never expressed an interest in Him."

Serena set a cold, weathered hand on my calf. "If one feels His call, that is enough." Then, long tongue swiping across her teeth, she leaned in close. "Have *you?*"

I supposed I had, in a way. After all, it was my pleading to Him that had brought me to this very spot. With a firm nod, I said, "I have."

When she spoke next, it was within my mind, her thoughts bleeding into my own like ink through water. *Then we welcome you.*

* * *

THE BOBCAT WRITHED UNDERNEATH ME. I felt each twitch of its powerful muscles in my thighs as I pinned it down. In a circle around us, the maenads chanted in high-pitched shrieks. They called it the final devotion, a slow stripping of our inhibitions.

The creature bucked, sending chunks of dirt and clay flying. I gripped its scruff to keep myself steady. Isabella dropped to her knees before us, keening and tearing at the earth. The spear she'd clutched rolled away from her.

Over the time I'd spent in this forest—difficult to quantify, between the chaos and the drugs—several women had undergone this initiation. I'd stood where they all stood now. Watching. Waiting.

Eager to release another mad woman back into the clutches of our Father.

Another buck. My fingers twitched and, in a flash, our roles had reversed. The bobcat was on me at once, teeth gnashing. Isabella scrabbled forward, spear back in her hand.

With eyes as wide as saucers, she lunged.

This was the last memory I had as a human: a year after we graduated high school, Isabella and I were dating. It was a firecracker kind of relationship—bright and flashy and gone too soon. On a brutal summer's day, we'd watched the stars above us dance. Isabella had held my hand hard enough to hurt. "No matter where you go, I want to be there with you."

I remembered the way the world had swirled, like I'd been put on a playground swing and spun again and again and again. Holding her tight, I said, "I want to be there with you, too," just as a shooting star flashed overhead.

Blood, thick and metallic. Back in the present, the bobcat paused, as stunned as I by the spear sticking out of the back of its throat. Its eyes glinted in the moonlight, flashing my reflection back at me. We stared at each other for an eternity. Then, with a watery growl, it collapsed.

For a while, there was only the whistle of the forest. The warmth from the bobcat fled in waves. When it was nothing more than a frigid corpse Isabella helped me haul it away.

Its skin split like paper. I peered through its now-loose jaws, pelt an uncomfortable weight on my shoulders. The maenads began to chant again. One by one, the stars blinked to life above us. As a star fell from its perch in a white streak, I collapsed on the ground and lost myself at last.

* * *

A SHARP, cold wind ruffled my fur. The moon was a claw in the sky above. Beside me, a bobcat slightly smaller than I drew close, nose wet and warm as she nuzzled me. I rasped my tongue over her fur. In the distance, the shrieks of human women echoed into the night.

WHEN THE RAVEN ATE THE MOONS
BY NICOLE L. SOPER GORDEN

Nicole L. Soper Gorden is a speculative fiction author with a not-so-secret identity as a biology professor at a small liberal arts college. She has been reading and writing fantasy and science fiction stories her whole life, and has a special soft spot for fantastical writing with nature or biology themes. When not writing or teaching, Nicole enjoys growing heirloom vegetables, baking award-winning cookies, and plotting new ways to make people appreciate how wacky plants are. She lives in the Appalachian Mountains with her elderly puggle, affectionate black cat, playful goats, colorful chickens, rescued box turtle, bearded husband, and dinosaur-obsessed toddler.

* * *

Five days after the raven spirit ate the third moon, Minji was hired to steal eggs.

Apparently, the eggs were important to her noble employer. The money he offered was impressive, probably because they were hidden deep in the catacombs of the moon temple. Stealing ordinary eggs from a holy place. Well, Minji wasn't in it for pride. She'd once stolen a woman's undergarments back from an estranged lover.

But still. Eggs.

Koraki preserve me from the whims of rich nobles, Minji prayed silently as she collected the empty mugs from the table of one such noble. He responded with a leer, tossing her a silver coin. It was way too much to tip a barmaid, but Minji wasn't about to explain that to the drunk man. Instead, she threw him a wink and tucked the coin in her apron pocket, waiting until she had turned away to let the sour expression colonize her face.

The nobleman was only at the Crow's Nest to gamble with people of lesser means—easy to outbluff everyone at pikes when no one could outbid you. It probably gave him a feeling of control when everything else was chaos. The catastrophe of the three lost moons had left the city in a state of anxious bedlam. A month ago, the sky-wide raven spirit had risen from the shadows of the world to devour the biggest white moon, Ao. A handful of days later, it appeared again to gulp down the craggy brown moon, Xo. And just five days ago, the raven spirit swallowed the smallest moon, red Ne.

All three moons gone, and it was like darkness had descended metaphorically as well as literally. People mostly stayed indoors at night, terrified of the moonless sky. Tempers were short and fears were large. Murders and fights had risen starkly, as had suicides. More people than ever came to Minji's unofficial soup kitchen for food. Even the city's stray dogs were in a frenzy, and people had stopped using horses past sunset because they spooked too easily. It seemed like everyone was going a little mad.

At least the chaos and darkness would make Minji's job tonight easier.

She pushed the door to the kitchens open with one hip, carrying her platter of mugs to the basins for skinny Paidi to wash. He grumbled at the unending dirty dishes, and again as Minji ruffled his mop of hair in passing. When Kathe had first taken Minji in, a starving child of eight, that was how she had started—washing dishes for the tavern. At the time, she had needed a crate to reach the basins, and had been too scrawny and weak to lift anything heavier than the tin plates. A lot had changed since then.

"Kathe!" she called, sticking her head into the stairwell to the beer cellar.

"Down here!" came the reply.

The staircase was short but dark, the only light coming from Kathe's single lantern at the far end of the cellar. Kathe had to be the only person in the city who didn't mind the dark these days. Minji shook her head, running a finger over the silver pendant she wore to activate it. The pendant had been blessed by Koraki, the trickster god and patron of thieves, to enhance her night vision. Useful trinket. It kept her from tripping on the uneven earthen stairs now, and was doubly useful when she played the thief.

Kathe was shifting inventory, moving casks of ale and cider closer to the front of the cellar to make room for tomorrow's delivery. Assuming it came. Shipments of everything from new hats and beer to food and medicine had been erratic since the moons were eaten. They hadn't been able to serve fresh fish at the tavern for over two weeks now.

Kathe was a stout, well-muscled woman, with graying auburn hair pulled back in a frizzy bun. At the moment, she had her sleeves pushed up as she rolled a barrel of ale on its rim. Minji swore, rushing over to help the tavernkeeper.

"Kathe, you can't be moving these by yourself! They're over 300 pounds!"

"Nonsense. I've been moving these barrels my whole life. No reason to stop now."

"You're in your sixties now!" Minji pointed out. "You threw out your back just last week."

"Hush your mouth," Kathe grunted as they settled the barrel in place. She paused, using her apron to wipe sweat from her brow. "I'll have you know, young lady, I am capable of much more than you can imagine."

"But what would the tavern do if you hurt yourself?" Minji demanded.

Kathe looked Minji up and down, one eyebrow raised. "Oh, we'd manage. I know what I'm doing."

Minji sighed, not willing to push the argument tonight, not when she had other things to do. "I need to go out," she said.

"What, now? Are you moon-crazed, child?"

She had anticipated this. The city wasn't designed for moonless nights, with narrow cobbled roads and no streetlamps to light the way. With three moons, there had never been a time when at least one of them hadn't been shining in the night sky—until now.

"I'll stick to the streets where the city guards tend the barrel fires. There's an overturned cart of potatoes down by the docks," she added. "Bruised potatoes for the taking."

She had chosen this lie carefully. Kathe knew her well enough to believe it.

Sure enough, Kathe's face softened. "Food for that soup kitchen of yours?"

"We have more people every day. If I can supplement with free potatoes, we can feed even more tomorrow night."

Kathe shook her head, clearly bemused. She had always been tolerant of Minji's desire to feed others; Kathe had adopted Minji when she was half-starved, so she understood. Now, she let Minji use the Crow's Nest's kitchens to prepare the free meals.

"Take a lantern," Kathe said.

"Worrywart. Fine, I'll take a lantern."

Kathe studied her for another moment, gray eyes inscrutable. "Do your best, but don't do anything that will get you hurt, young lady."

Minji laughed. "Don't worry. I'm not about to risk life and limb for a few bruised potatoes."

"Hm." Kathe's smile sparkled with humor, despite the dark cellar. She waved a hand, shooing Minji away. "I'll see you later."

In her bedroom above the tavern, Minji made a quick swap of her tavern dress for the dark navy thief clothes she wore when on a job. Hiding her lantern in her closet to avoid Kathe's suspicion, she slipped out her window and across the city's dark wood-shingled rooftops.

The salt-laced breeze brushed her skin as she ran. Below, most of the streets were dark as pitch—especially in the shadows of the taller two-story buildings. Anyone out this late carried large lanterns or massive glowing moon opals, as if afraid the darkness might nip at their toes if allowed to get too close. Arguments broke out at half the intersections, people's tempers sharpened by worry and hunger and pain—but fear most of all. The empty night sky seemed to press down on a city ready to explode.

With the help of her Koraki pendant, Minji saw the tall stone spire of the moon temple ahead and paused. Night was usually when the moon temple was busiest, but the turmoil over the missing moons left the temple half-dead during the post-midnight hours. Many moon devotees had left, disillusioned with their god for being eaten by something as lowly as a raven spirit. Sure, animal spirits had changed the world before, like the ancient badger spirit that had dug the land into Asvos Lake and the neighboring Chalikia Mountain. But those had all been small changes compared to the current chaos, and if the moons had really been *eaten* by the raven spirit, it was likely they would never come back. How could the moon priests reconcile that with their belief in a powerful moon god?

The priests who remained tried to rally spirits among the city people by maintaining regular midnight masses and lighting the interior of the temple with every moon opal in their stores. But even they became listless and tired after mass was over, locking away the opals to prevent thefts and retiring early.

That left her an opening.

Minji watched from her roof perch as the last of the cool blue light of moon opals disappeared from the temple windows. She stared up at the distant pinpricks of stars, burning so intensely but without any light for the land below, and counted another half hour before moving. Silent as a breeze, she slipped down the gutter pipe into the alleyway below.

To her surprise, Minji found a man there, thirty feet in front of her and sneaking in the direction of the moon temple. He was dressed all in black, blending well with the night, but he lacked the silence of a true footpad. In fact, as she watched, the man caught the soft toe of his shoe on a rock and spent a solid thirty seconds jumping on one foot and swearing.

She crossed her arms. The swearing had given him away. She knew this man.

Suppressing a groan, she shed her thief persona with a few practiced motions: unwrap her face and hair; tie the head wrap as a sash around her waist instead; unknot the ties to let the fabric panels fall loose like skirts. The overall effect was that she looked like a woman in a navy-blue dress instead of a thief. She removed the bag from her back as well, slinging it over a shoulder like a woman's purse.

"Hap," she called, putting a friendly note in her voice.

The middle-aged man squealed and leaped three feet in the air. Whirling, he spottedher and put a hand to his chest. "Minji," he gasped. "Koraki preserve me, girl. What are you doing out at this hour?"

Minji kept herself from grabbing her pendant at the trickster god's name. Hap was no thief—but he was a gambler, and Koraki claimed gamblers as their own, too. And pickpockets, pirates, footpads, actors, and even some politicians. Anyone who relied on their cleverness or luck to get by was within Koraki's purview. As the shapeshifter god's unofficial doctrine said, tricksters were made, not born.

"I'm restless, with the moons gone," Minji said. "Having trouble sleeping lately. Needed a walk and some night air." It wasn't a big lie. It was true for many in the city—that sleep had become difficult with the three moons gone from the sky. Personally, Minji slept better in the dark, but she wasn't about to admit that. "And what about you, Hap? What are you doing heading for the moon temple after the evening service is done?"

Hap went suddenly silent, face blank in the same way he used when keeping his cards close to his vest. Minji had seen that exact face often enough at the Crow's Nest when Hap was in the middle of a game of chance. She found herself mentally tracing the distance to the moon temple, feeling a sneaky sort of suspicion rise in her. Kathe often said the only true coincidences in life involved the weather, and there was no weather to speak of tonight.

"Hap?" she tried in her best admonishing-daughter voice. "You're not trying to cover your recent debts by any unsavory means, are you?"

"Shh!" he said, waving her down and looking around. "You'll be heard."

"You are, aren't you?" Minji whispered back. She crossed her arms, giving him a stern look. "What are you after, Hap?" He didn't answer, still looking around the corner of the building towards the temple beyond. Minji bit her lip, deciding to push one step further. She took his shoulder, whispering close to his ear. "I heard a rumor about the moon temple moving some valuable eggs to the sea temple by the docks last night." It was another believable lie; the sea god Dakrya and the moon god Fengaria were supposedly married, after all, and the two faiths were tightly intertwined. With the moons gone, the tides were sporadic and the catches of fishermen unpredictable. It was part of why so many folks in the city were hungry these days. Sharing holy artifacts between the temples to help increase the fish catches wasn't unheard of. "You're not after those eggs, are you?"

He looked at her in surprise. "The Dakrya temple?"

"Hap, tell me that's not why you're here."

"Hm," he said, sounding distracted. Minji caught him looking towards the bay where the docks and the sea temple were, neither of them visible in the moonless night. "Of course not," he said, patting her hand on his shoulder. "I should head home. I'll see you at the Crow's Nest tomorrow, aye?"

"Of course," she said. "Have a good night, Hap." She gave his shoulder a squeeze.

She liked Hap well enough, and knew he had debts from cavalier bets against another noble like the one that had been in the tavern tonight. But she remembered too well the pain of hunger from her own childhood to let Hap take her prize for the sake of his gambling.

She watched as Hap ambled in the direction of his house for a block or two, then paused and looked around, turning to head towards the bay instead. So he *was* after the eggs. Minji frowned, wondering if Hap had been hired by the same noble as she, or if there were multiple people after these eggs. Either way, she would need to be more careful.

She tied her navy-blue garb back in place, taking on her boyish thief persona again. She refastened the bag against her back then circled back to the moon temple.

Every good thief knew to never use the door if another entrance presented itself. And if Minji was one thing, it was a good thief. The temple had a series of windows along one stone wall, shaped as a moon waxing to fullness and then waning again. They were small and too high off the ground for anyone to reach from there. But Minji was also small, and very good at climbing. The rooftops were her second home and the pillars of the temple were easy to scale.

She almost dislodged a pigeon nest from the gutter as she reached the roof. It held three small white eggs, each no longer than her thumb. For the eggs to be left alone at this hour, the mother pigeon was probably in someone's stew. On a whim, she snatched the eggs and packed them carefully in her bag.

Ten minutes later, she hung upside down by a rope from the roof and looked through the round full-moon window. With one hand, she pressed her Koraki pendant to her chest, letting it enhance her night vision enough to see into the dark moon temple. There was no movement in the space beyond, the room dense with shadows. Minji slipped through the circular window to dangle by her fingertips. When no alarm was raised, she dropped silently to the floor below.

The moon-shaped windows lined the south side of the temple hall. Minji found herself on the raised dais at the front of the large open nave, near a lectern holding the illuminated lunar text and several stylized three-moon calendars. The only light in the cavernous nave came from under the door of the oratory, where a moon priest would be on duty to pray all night. Across the nave and next to the oratory was a twenty-five-foot-tall marble statue of the moon god, Fengaria. Ostentatious, if you asked Minji.

The smell of saltcedar and sage lay heavy in the air, the incense burners still warm to the touch as she slipped down the hallway to her right. Her employer had said she would find the eggs in the catacombs below. Of course they would be in the catacombs. Nothing like raiding the sacred resting place of moon saints to add some blasphemous spice to her normal diet of thieving.

She sighed, slipping silent as a shadow behind the curtain that hid the narrow stone stairs. She drew on her Koraki pendant again. She had been worried it would be too dark in the catacombs for it to work; after all, it could only enhance the light that was already there, not create light outright. She had brought a tiny candle with her, just in case. But now, as she quietly descended the stone stairs, she found that there was already enough illumination coming from below.

She frowned. Why was there light? Did they store the moon opals in the catacombs? But no, the light was tinted red, not blue. Was someone else already there?

The antechamber at the bottom of the stairs had arched hallways leading from it in three directions: south for the brightest moon, big white Ao; west for the brown-shadowed moon, Xo; and north for the smallest, the red moon, Ne. The strange light shone from the Ne arch to her right.

Minji padded softly down the north hall, matching her footsteps to the set of prints already in the dust to conceal her passing. The hall was lined with small square ossuaries, their engraved silver labels limned with the pale green-blue glow of bioluminescent bacteria. Ahead, the flickering glow grew brighter, clearly coming from a flame.

Nearly holding her breath, Minji crept to the end of the hall and peeked into the crypt beyond. It was recessed, giving her an excellent view from her higher vantage point. Three big tombs rested in the center of the floor, each chest height. Decorative carvings of moon saints and silver-gilt calendar murals lined the walls, with columns painted a shiny dark red curving towards the domed ceiling like rib bones.

In the space below, at the head of the center tomb, a figure with a torch knelt on the floor. They wore all black, similar to Minji's own navy-blue clothes. Thief garb. She frowned, narrowing her eyes at her competition. For a second, the figure straightened, holding an ordinary-looking chicken egg up to the torchlight. He frowned at it, clearly skeptical, before bending back to his task. The fool had either removed or never worn the head wrappings that hid a thief's identity, and that glimpse of his sharp-nosed face was enough for Minji to recognize him: Rask, a well-known actor who moonlighted as a pickpocket during lean times.

A silent breath hissed between her teeth. Clearly Rask had graduated from pickpocketing to thieving. Rask may be wiry, but he had a ferocious strength born of practice tumbles and acting stunts. Minji wasn't a fighter. Her small, lithe form was great for climbing to roofs and slipping through windows, but it didn't lend itself well to physical altercations. But she was here for those eggs, for the reward money for her soup kitchen, and she would give up her Koraki pendant before she let Rask walk out of the temple in her place.

She pursed her lips thoughtfully, adjusting her bag. Time to make her own luck, as Kathe would say.

She backtracked to the antechamber at the bottom of the stairs to prepare. Moments later, she heard scuffing footsteps on the stone floor and saw Rask's flickering light coming closer. Judging her timing by his footfalls, she stepped from the Xo hallway just as Rask entered the antechamber.

Rask let out a noise of alarm, pulling a knife from his boot. Minji froze, blinking at him as if surprised. She looked between Rask and the three glowing eggs she held, pigeon eggs she had coated in bioluminescent bacteria scraped from the catacomb walls, giving them an eerie blue-green glow. A beat passed—just enough time for him to see the eggs in her hands and notice their unearthly glow. Then she made a show of trying to hide them.

"Hey now," Rask said, shifting the straw-packed box he was carrying to his other arm. "What's all this?"

Minji took her bag from her back, stuffing her glowing eggs inside. "Nothing," she said, keeping her voice low. "Just a job."

She felt Rask study her thief garb again. It was unlikely he recognized her boyish thief persona as Minji the tavern maid, despite having come by her soup kitchen more than once. But he clearly recognized the importance of the outfit: a thief, and one devoted to Koraki. He licked his lips, eyes caught fully on the bag she clutched to her chest, gears clearly turning.

"I should . . . be going," Minji said, edging towards the stairs.

"Stop," Rask said. Minji felt the thrill of knowing she had him, that feeling like setting a hook in a deep-sea marlin. He still held his knife, and two steps brought him close enough to Minji to press her back against the wall.

"What? You're not . . . a moon priest, are you?"

Rask straightened his spine, the consummate actor accepting the role Minji offered him. "And if I am?"

Minji held the bag tighter, eyes going shifty. "Where is Koraki's luck when I need it?" she muttered, and watched Rask's smile grow wider.

"I saw the eggs," Rask said, voice stern. He set down his box, keeping the knife on Minji. "I was sent by the high priest to bring them to the altar tonight. I see it's good that I was." He used his free hand to grab one of the straps of Minji's bag. She gripped it tighter to her chest, making her eyes big.

"I . . . I was just . . . " She licked her lips.

Just then, a noise in the temple above drew both of their attention. Nothing loud—no crashes or shouts. Just the sound of steps on stone, ones not being hidden by the person walking. For a second, Minji's heart stopped. Was one of the priests in the temple? Doing rounds, maybe? If she was discovered here by a real moon priest, things would go much worse than being caught by Rask with his flimsy knife.

Rask pressed his knife closer to her throat. "Let go," he hissed, pulling the bag from her hands with a sharp tug.

That close, she could see the dark circles under his eyes, the gauntness of too many days without a solid meal. He was frantic, probably scared and hurting like so many others since the moons' disappearance. Few went to the theater these days, after all. For a second, she regretted needing to take this win from him. But he knew he could get a meal at the Crow's Nest if things got bad enough, and there were more bellies than just Rask's at stake here. So she made one last snatch for the bag, trying to sell the content's importance while letting Rask hold her at bay with his knife.

"Stay out of my way, boy," he hissed. Then he shoved her to the ground and took off running up the stairs.

She rolled with the shove, coming back to her feet. But she let Rask go. It was a shame to lose such a good bag, but her ploy had served its purpose. Rask had left the real eggs behind in favor of running with her fakes instead. She brushed herself off, shaking her head. Rask hadn't even been a good actor in the end, letting his ruse drop for the sake of expediency. Amateur. Or maybe just desperate.

She knelt for the box Rask had left on the floor, brushing through the straw packing it. For a second, she doubted herself, seeing nothing but ordinary chicken eggs of various sizes and colors. She could buy similar eggs in the market any day of the week. She reached for the big white egg, and the metallic chill that bit bone-deep at the touch made her *sure* she had the right eggs. They felt *important.*

Koraki preserve her, what *were* these things?

Not that it mattered. She wasn't here to understand the eggs. Just to steal them.

She suppressed a shiver, repacking the eggs in Rask's innocuous wooden box. She padded up the steps, silent in the dark, listening for more footsteps above. Even with the help of her Koraki pendant's night vision and her wariness from run-ins with two competing thieves, she almost bumped into the man in dark robes waiting on the other side of the curtain that covered the stairwell.

She froze, hoping somehow he hadn't seen her. Fruitless. He reached up to stroke his beard, and she realized belatedly that his robes weren't the silver robes of a moon priest, but the black robes of a city senator. She also saw familiar features: shoulder-length brown hair, neat-pointed beard, wide nose, sharp eyes. She recognized him— anyone would. Senator Savidi, one of the most influential men in the city. He had finagled his way to being speaker of the senate faster than any before him, and now spent his days working out clever tax plans that made the people think they weren't being taxed after all.

"Good evening," Savidi said. He had a practiced paternal voice, reassuring and resonant.

Minji said nothing, considering her options. She could run back the way she had come, into the catacombs, but as far as she knew there was no other exit from the basement. Savidi was blocking the hall that led to the nearest door out of the moon temple. She could run the other direction and try to climb back out the window she came in, but that would be slow with only one hand to climb—she had to keep the box of eggs safe, after all.

Savidi held up his hands, giving a warm smile. "I see you are unnerved by my presence. You needn't be. Your employer sent me."

Minji went rigid. "My employer has never sent someone to meet me before," she said bluntly.

"Ah, but there are complications. Others have been sent to steal the eggs, too." Savidi said it so matter-of-factly, as if stealing from a temple was a commonplace errand. Minji blinked at him, feeling struck stupid. "Have you seen any others yet?"

Minji narrowed her eyes. "I've seen you."

"But I'm here to help. Give me the eggs. As an upstanding, recognizable public figure, I can bring them to your employer without encountering suspicion in the streets," Savidi continued. "You can still collect your pay during your meeting tomorrow night."

He knew about the eggs, about her employer, even about the meeting scheduled for tomorrow night. The only way he could know all of that was if Savidi had indeed spoken with her employer. Should she trust him? He would definitely be less likely to encounter trouble on the streets than she would. But she hesitated. It felt . . . wrong to give up the prize she had worked so hard to steal. Did she just want the glory for herself, or was there something more suspicious going on? All of her instincts thrummed on high alert.

She squinted at Savidi, his warm smile welcoming. Her free hand clutched unconsciously at her Koraki pendant. Then she realized what was bothering her: if Savidi was trying to avoid suspicion, why had he come into the moon temple? No one was supposed to be in here after hours except the priests. If anyone saw him enter or leave, any innocence he might have otherwise claimed would be questioned. He should have waited outside. But if he wasn't here to ferry the eggs to her employer, why was he here?

Hap. Rask. Now Savidi. She pinched her lips shut against a curse. He was here to steal the eggs, too. Koraki preserve her, what were these eggs worth if this many people were after them?

"You have the wrong person," she said. "The thief ran out of here not two minutes ago with the eggs in a bag."

Savidi frowned, cocking his head to one side, clearly trying to read her. "I saw the man. You seem much more competent than he."

Minji wanted to snort. Instead, she did her best at looking abashed and a little angry. "I had the eggs. He pulled a knife on me and took them."

A partial truth—always the best kind of lie.

Savidi studied her for a minute, and then threw his head back to laugh. "You're clever, thief. But I saw the eggs he carried glowed. Did you fool that other rogue into thinking they were the real thing?"

Drat. "How did you know?"

He chuckled again, darker this time. "I did my homework. Do you know what those eggs are, boy? Do you know what I could do with them? Besides, I read people for a living. I can read you, for example. You're thinking about making a run for it." He moved himself more solidly in front of the exit. He likely wasn't a very spry man, considering his advanced age, but he was significantly larger than Minji. She had no illusions that she could get past him. "I don't recommend it," the senator said, giving a much less friendly smile this time.

Minji assessed her options again: straight at Savidi, back into the catacombs, or towards the windows she had climbed in. Or, she supposed, out across the open nave. Savidi growled, clearly sensing she was going to make a move. He took a step, trying to grab her arm, and she dived to her left through the nave and towards the oratory. Savidi gave a noise of annoyance, picking up his senate robes to chase after her.

"Stop," he hissed. "You won't get out of here that way."

Minji had no plans to get out of the temple this way. Instead, she reached the door to the oratory, turned to watch as Savidi raced towards her, and knocked on the oratory door.

Savidi grabbed Minji's sleeve as she tried to slip past. For a heart-stopping second, she heard eggs knock against one another in the box she held. Savidi heard it too, hand springing open with a curse. Minji ducked his arm and hoisted herself up the nearby marble statue of the moon good Fengaria, crouching in the crook of a giant arm. The senator stared up at where she had disappeared into the shadows. She saw him squinting, clearly unable to see where she was.

Then the oratory door opened, and the high priest looked out. The chapel interior glowed with the warm light of a fireplace and many candles, a cozy contrast to the rest of the temple at this dark time of night. Minji couldn't help but notice how tired the high priest looked, with deep bags under her eyes and hair limp and dull. No doubt the missing moons had dealt her a lot of sleepless nights and panicking parishioners. She blinked into the dark, seeing Senator

Savidi just outside her door, illuminated by the light leaking from her oratory.

Minji was fully aware that this was a bit of a gamble. Savidi could just as easily say he saw someone creeping around in the temple and ask the high priest for help finding her. But she had watched gamblers in the Crow's Nest since she was only waist-high on Kathe, and she was betting on Savidi's desire to keep things quiet so he could come after her himself. And that meant acting like he belonged here for reasons other than stealing eggs from the moon temple catacombs.

"Honored senator," the high priest said, eyes widening. "You should not be in the temple at this hour."

Savidi cleared his throat, sparing one final look in Minji's general direction. She could almost hear him pondering the decision—should he rat her out or try to deflect the high priest without drawing suspicion? Finally, he turned his big, warm smile on the high priest.

"My dear high priest," he said, voice thick with warmth and concern. "I'm sorry to go against tradition, but I'm worried about the people of the city in these dark nights, with our moons gone. I'm sure you're aware of the . . . problems." A mild word for chaos, murder, suicide, stealing, arson, and more—and that wasn't even touching on the change in food supplies or trade routes or medical staffing short-ages. "The people need hope—the hope of Fengaria—before our city devolves into civil war. I wanted to speak with you privately about how we might approach this challenge together, the city senate and the moon temple."

"Oh. Oh! Yes, of course," the high priest said. "You're very thought-ful, senator."

Savidi gave a gracious nod. "When can we speak more? I don't want to interrupt your evening prayers further—"

"Nonsense," the high priest said before Savidi could finish. "This is the city's highest priority. Please, come in and we can speak more."

She opened the door to her oratory wider, beckoning him forward. For a moment, he hesitated, eyes flicking in Minji's direction. But if he said anything about Minji now, it would look suspicious. He had guessed the high priest would want him to come back later, and he had been wrong. Now he needed to either admit to wanting to chase a mysterious figure in the temple or go along with the high priest. He was cornered. With a smile that was maybe just a little too much gritted teeth, he followed the high priest into the oratory, pausing on the threshold just long enough to glare into the darkness after Minji before closing the door.

Served him right. Koraki gave him a silver tongue. He might as well use it to do his job instead of harassing Minji. Maybe he'd even accomplish something useful for the people of the city instead of lining his own pockets for once.

As soon as the door to the high priest's oratory clicked shut, Minji climbed back down from her perch. She paused at the statue's feet. For a moment, she was overcome by a feeling of immensity from the stone form of Fengaria—not because it was four times as tall as a man, but because it felt large with power and importance. The shape of a god. The moon god.

She let out a breath. Here, in the presence of Fengaria's statue, holding her stolen eggs, the loss of the moons hit her anew. How would the world change with the absence of three celestial bodies beyond this period of transitional turmoil? Would there really be civil war, as Savidi had suggested? Or would it be worse even that? With the loss of Fengaria's source of power, the entire pantheon might shift. The sea god was so closely tied to Fengaria, he might fall, too. What god would fill that power vacuum? The world might descend into true chaos, unlike any seen since the Mid-Barbarian Wars. Chaos may be the provenance of Koraki, her patron god, but it was never a good thing for normal people like Minji.

She rested a hand against the statue's foot, sending a silent apology to Fengaria. The marble was smooth under her fingers, and a moment later it went so cold her bones ached, like she had slid iced silver under her skin. She gasped, snatching her hand back. But it didn't hurt, not really. It felt like . . . an acknowledgement, maybe. Or amusement?

She took a step back, eyeing the statue. Maybe she was imagining it, but it seemed like the entire marble statue was glowing faintly silver in the darkness. A part of her was tempted to leave the box of eggs right there, at the statue's feet. They belonged here, didn't they?

She shook her head. Growing up homeless had given her a practical streak she couldn't deny. The affairs of gods were above her, but she could at least use the money from these eggs to provide for those like her. She had things to do, and that didn't involve waiting around for Savidi to make another appearance.

Silent on her padded shoes, she crossed the temple nave back to the altar. A sash pulled from under a book of moon prayers served to secure the box and its contents to her lower back. Then she vaulted up the stone wall, using a metal torch stand to propel herself high enough to grab the edge of the round window she had come in, wriggling through in an instant. Her rope to the roof still dangled in the darkness outside.

It was late enough now that the whole city was silent, almost no one walking the streets with or without giant lanterns for light. This was Minji's favorite time of night—when there was peace in the city, a stillness that no other time of day could produce. She reeled in her rope and crouched on the stone roof of the moon temple. Breathed in the chill salty air. Reveled in feeling blissfully insignificant under the moonless sky. She may not be able to solve the world's problems, but with her payment she could make a difference to some. It was all she could do.

After a moment, she pulled the box around, setting it on the roof in front of her so she could rustle through the straw and make sure the eggs were still in good shape. She pulled them free, holding them in her hands as she checked their shells for cracks: the brown-shelled egg with darker speckles, the small coppery-red egg, and the palm-sized egg so white it almost glowed in the darkness. For a moment, she worried about what her employer would do with these eggs that were not eggs.

"I would have placed money on you being the one to win, if I had anyone to gamble with," a voice said behind her, startling her so much she almost fumbled the eggs.

She laid them back on top of the straw, spinning to face the figure on the temple roof. After so many others trying to steal the eggs tonight, it shouldn't surprise her to find yet one more person in her way. Only this person was different—someone she had seen many times over the last decade, always in the shadows. Tall and straight, long white hair, deep gray eyes, and a cloak of silk so fine only the richest nobles could afford it. Her employer, almost as if her thoughts of him had summoned him here.

"Not the biggest or strongest, but cleverest by far," he said with a chuckle. He adjusted his cloak's hood so that his face was hidden in shadows.

"We're not supposed to meet until tomorrow night," she said.

"Ah, yes. That is what I said."

Minji narrowed her eyes, drawing on her Koraki pendant to try to see her employer's face in the shadows of the cloak's hood, to judge whether those words were meant to be joking or dismissive. But the darkness there was too impenetrable, even for the trickster god's magic sight. Something about this whole situation didn't sit right with her.

"You hired those others to steal the same eggs as me, didn't you?" she asked. "Why?"

"Oh dear. And after I just complimented your cleverness, too. Didn't I just say that it was a competition? And you won, dear Minji!"

She jolted, taking a step backwards. She had never given her name —never used her real name when working as a thief.

"Who are you?" she asked.

"Tell me—have you figured out what the eggs are yet?"

She looked down reflexively at the box she held. She had, of course. It was obvious, when she had seen the three eggs: large white, medium brown, small red. She remembered the cold she had felt when touching them, and again when touching the statue of Fengaria. She remembered the mass of them—not weight, but the feeling that they were so much larger than they appeared.

"Ao, Xo, and Ne. The eggs are the three moons," she whispered. She looked at her employer, who was still hidden in the darkness of his cloak's hood except for a wide, toothy smile. "Are you the raven spirit?" she asked. "Or are you hunting the raven spirit?"

"Ooh, good guesses! Both of them!"

"That's not an answer."

His laugh split the air. "No, it's not."

"You also haven't asked for the eggs yet."

He spread his hands. "That's because I never wanted the eggs."

Minji looked down at the eggs—Koraki preserve her, at the *moons*. "Then you are the raven spirit, not a spirit hunter."

"I both am and am not the raven spirit." His teeth glowed white in his grin, but no matter how hard she drew on her Koraki pendant, she couldn't see anything more of his face. And suddenly she knew.

She let out a breath like she had been punched in the gut. "You're Koraki," she said.

"My clever thief." The figure removed their hood. For a moment, they wore the pretty male features of Minji's employer, then the hungry beaked face of a raven, and then the face of the god she expected: long black hair, pale complexion, androgenous features, eyes like chips of silver.

The pieces all fit. Koraki was, among other things, a shapeshifter. They could turn into a raven if they chose—even one as big as the sky. And who but a trickster would steal the very moons from the sky, and hide them in the moon temple, of all places? They had hired several people to try to steal the eggs—thieves, pickpockets, gamblers, actors, politicians. All people under Koraki's trickster purview. They had been hired to steal eggs Koraki themself had stolen first, in a game of quick wits and clever thievery. It was all a game. *It was all a game.*

But games with a trickster were never trivial.

"So I've won your challenge," she said carefully. "What's the prize?"

"The moons, of course."

The box of eggs in her hands suddenly felt like they weighed more than the world. These three small, fragile things were the reason the entire world had gone mad. She licked her lips, feeling small. "What am I supposed to do with them?"

Koraki shrugged. "That's entirely up to you, isn't it? You could sell them on the black market. You could give them to the moon temple priests. You could keep them as family heirlooms. You could crack them open and cook them into the most celestial omelet that's ever existed."

The possibilities stunned her. She held the moons in her hands, and knew she could leverage them for more riches than she could even imagine. She could take care of Kathe in her old age. She could keep everyone in the city fed forever. But at what cost? Anyone who would want to buy the world's moons would likely have no kind use in mind for them. Could she justify that, even for the idea of the greater good? Could it even be the greater good, in such circumstances? She could keep them herself, protect them and care for them, but she didn't want the moons. They shouldn't belong to her. They shouldn't belong to anyone. And their absence was wrong. The bad kind of chaos.

"Put them back," she said, holding the box towards Koraki.

They made no move to take the box. "You would rather give up the moons and gain nothing than collect your well-earned riches?"

"Tricks and cleverness are all well and good. But when it comes down to it, the world is more than just me. And the world needs these moons more than I do. So put them back."

Koraki grinned widely, their dark hair suddenly floating around their head like a halo of dark writhing mist. "I knew you were the right choice," they said, voice suddenly somehow familiar. They glided closer until Minji was looking right in their silver eyes. "But I can't put them back."

"Why not? You're a god."

"Yes. But even gods get old, dear." There was another shift in Koraki's appearance, hair going gray and auburn, eyes dulling from silver to gray, arms thickening with stout muscle. Minji let out a noise, stepping back.

"Kathe?" she whispered.

It was too much to believe, seeing the tavernkeeper here. It had to be a trick, another game of Koraki's. But she knew the lore: Koraki could take any face except one that already belonged to another. That meant Kathe was Koraki. And Kathe was her mysterious employer, who had hired her to steal so many things. *Kathe*, the stubborn, elderly, tough-as-nails tavernkeeper who'd had the soft heart to adopt scrawny, starving Minji as a child.

"Why?" she asked, her voice gone rough.

"Oh, Minji." Kathe reached a hand to smooth Minji's hair, like she had a million times before, but Minji pulled back reflexively. "Don't be foolish, young lady. I'm the same Kathe I've ever been. And I've been Kathe longer than I've been Koraki. But you get a sense for when your time is waning as a god. My power is trickling away. I wanted to be proactive about my successor."

"Successor." The word stopped her heart like a fist of black night sky.

"Of course, dear girl. Who could take the mantle of Koraki but the one I've raised as my own? The thief who steals to give to others? Who would put the world's moons back rather than take them for personal profit?"

"I can't," Minji breathed. And she didn't mean that she couldn't put the moons back. She meant the bigger thing—yes, bigger than moving moons in and out of the sky. She meant the offer. "I *can't* be Koraki."

"But you can. Tricksters are made, not born. And you've made yourself quite the trickster."

Minji's brain whirred. Be Koraki, the trickster god? Her? She was just an orphan with a gift for stealing. That, and a driving need to help others. And she suddenly realized that was the true test. It wasn't until she demanded Koraki put the moons back that they'd known she was the right choice. They wanted not only someone clever, but someone compassionate as well. It suddenly hit her how terrible a place the world could be if the trickster god, the god of chaos and cleverness, was also cold and vicious. The world could be torn apart—like it was at this very moment, in the absence of moons.

But a compassionate trickster? That was maybe something she could do. Something she already was.

"What about you?" she asked Kathe, chest already aching.

"My time is done, dear Minji." She smiled sadly, reaching again to smooth Minji's hair. This time, she let her. "I have other places to be."

"What do I do?"

Kathe reached into her apron pocket and pulled out the key to the Crow's Nest. "Do what you've always done. Just do it *more*."

Minji reached a tentative hand for the key. The instant her fingers touched the metal, Kathe fell into an explosion of black feathers, an inky swirl in the already dark night sky. The feathers circled Minji, tightening until they pressed deep under her skin with a familiar warmth. She felt the immense power of it, filling her up until she gasped. She blinked open eyes that were newly silver.

She flexed her hands into fists and felt the power there, ready to do her bidding. With a grin, she tossed the eggs into the sky, and they stuck to the black like they belonged there. Because they *did* belong there. Three moons again shone down on the world.

Mere moments later, she heard the first cry of gratitude mixed with confusion and wonder. No one seemed able to tell where the moons had come from, or how they had gotten back in the sky.

On the rooftop where Kathe had stood moments before now sat an ordinary-looking raven, feathers dark enough to blend in with the night. But Minji could see perfectly despite the dark now, better than she had ever been able to with her pendant. As she watched, the raven cocked its head at her, let out a low caw, and took flight into the night.

"I'll see you later," Minji whispered after the bird. Koraki preserve her, but she would miss the stubborn old woman.

She clutched the tavern key, still warm with Kathe's body heat. The mingled light of three moons etched the nighttime city in relief around her. There was much to do—tricks and cleverness and compassion alike. But first, she had a tavern to see to. Those barrels of ale wouldn't move themselves.

THRONED

BY JULIA SKINNER

Julia Skinner is a modern-day Hobbit who loves writing fantasy stories about broken people in broken worlds. She is a sinner saved by Jesus, and fiercely believes that life is a precious, beautiful thing. Residing in South Texas, she spends her days juggling college, happy-ranting about Brandon Sanderson's books, and discovering new noises she can annoy her siblings with. You can follow along with her writing journey on Instagram @litaflameblog.

* * *

Once again, Diah was breaking into her own castle. She shifted uncomfortably, back pressed against the palace wall while neatly mani-cured bushes brushed her bent knees. The space was great for hiding under the cover of darkness, but it was ridiculously cramped. After this was over, she was going to have to have some words with the gardener.

Boots clicked on the other side of the bushes and Diah peered through the thin space between the shrubbery. A guard in an ashen orange suit marched down the stone path. In the distance, she could make out the pale figure of another straight-backed figure. There would be others as well, scattered across the courtyard and hidden by the night.

Bother.

She leaned back against the wall, and counted off on her fingers how many times this particular guard had passed. It was somewhere around seven times, if she remembered correctly. Which meant—as long as the stupid enchantress hadn't bothered to change their schedule—they had just one more round to do before they changed guards. She patted the small pouch hooked to her belt and squeezed her eyes closed. Exhaustion laced her chest like a string, pulling tighter and tighter with every ticking second. Life had been nonstop after she'd been crowned Queen of the most cursed kingdom in the four desert plains, at age seventeen. Apparently, when people heard that such a young queen sat on the throne, their first thought was, *'Hey! Let's go take it from her!'*

And *apparently* they didn't expect her to make it out alive, let alone *reclaim* the throne each time.

Jokes on them.

The guard strode past again.

Diah tensed, and leaned forward to peek. Another guard approached to take his place. As their low voices murmured across the space, she rolled onto her knees, nearly faceplanting into the bristling bushes. She gave them a glare then shoved herself under.

Branches snagged her hair and clothes as she crawled out. *Those guards better be too distracted to hear this,* she gritted her teeth. Once she broke free, she scrambled to her feet, and crept across the yard. The guards didn't even turn. Which was good for her, but also made them terrible guardsmen. She'd have to reevaluate her hiring methods later.

She made it to the side of the castle as the first guard left for his break. The new one started down the path, heading away from where she was huddled. A grin crept across her face. *See, Calihn?* It *was* a good idea not to hang any lanterns in the courtyard! Her former advisor had opposed almost every single decision she tried to make—*nasty old man.* And then he'd tried to get her people to rise up against her and put *him* on the throne. Now *that* had been a close call.

Edging cautiously along the shadowed side of the castle, Diah kept her hand on the stone to steady herself. It felt like forever before she reached a spot where she could spy the single, familiar bedroom window which overlooked the garden. When she was little, she'd broken the window's latch and no one had ever bothered to fix it. Well, until *Calihn* became Advisor. *He'd* wanted to go through and repair everything in the castle—obviously she'd won that argument.

Running her hands along the cold stone, she finally found the deep grooves she'd cut precisely for this reason. There were other seemingly random changes she had made to the palace over her four years of queenship to help her sneak back in should a circumstance like *this* ever occur. Which . . . seemed to happen a lot.

Stupid usurpers.

She huffed, hooking her fingers into the grooves, and slowly pulled herself up the wall toward the window. In this particular situation, an enchantress—of all people—had just waltzed into the throne room one day, and cast a spell on all her guards. She'd only barely escaped, and it had forced her to go to Katrine for help.

Katrine. Her *cousin.*

Who had been the *first* person to try—and fail—to take the throne from her, but who had promised to never try something like that again.

Who was annoyingly perky *all the time*, and had a weird laugh.

Who Diah could barely stand the *sight* of.

Ugh.

After hauling herself onto the sill, she pushed the glass open, quietly dropping into her childhood bedroom. A thin line of light peeked out from beneath the door directly in front of the winow. She hurried toward the pale shape of her old desk. Crouching, she felt beneath it for the tiny bag of explosives she'd stashed there.

Pulling the bag free, she dumped the crystals on the floor, took a match from her pocket and lit it. The flame cast a flickering orange glow across the carpeted floor, causing shadows to curl up around her like ghosts. She nudged the crystals on the ground with her foot. This particular type took just the right amount of time to ignite and, when they did, they'd only create a *little* explosion. Nothing like the time she blew up her entire throne to get an extremely frustrating usurper off of it—*Finnigan the Unmoving*, he'd called himself. *Bleh.*

Flicking the burning match on top of the crystals, she eased the door open and peeked into the dim hallway. A guard paced the corridor ahead. *Korgen,* if she remembered correctly. Diah let out a low whistle. He spun around, and she kicked a plank on the wall. It clicked inward and a single, tiny dart shot out and hit him square in the shoulder. A heartbeat later, Korgen thudded to the floor.

"Sorry," Diah said to his unconscious body. After all, it wasn't *his* fault he'd been spelled into believing the ugly enchantress was queen. She turned and jogged down the hall, passing a huge painting of her bright orange throne—the one she'd turned to ashes. It had been . . . an unfortunate sacrifice. Diah fingered the pouch on her belt as she turned the corner, heading for the corridor that led to the stairs.

She could see the stairway just ahead when the explosion went off, sending vibrations reverberating through the walls and floor. A heartbeat later, a second explosion boomed from the other side of the castle——compliments of Katrine. Alarmed shouts erupted from across the castle.

Right on time! She dashed toward the flight of stairs leading down to the main floor. Obviously, guards would go up a set of stairs on the opposite side, since they would lead to the room faster, leaving a clear shot for her to get to the throne room, and—

Footsteps echoed from the stairs. Three soldiers burst from the stairway, armor rattling with urgency. Diah backpedaled. So . . . maybe not *all* the guards took the other stairs.

"Hey!" the soldier in the front barked. The black pistol on his side contrasted sharply with his starched orange suit, giving him a threatening air. "Don't move!"

"Captain Ghen!" Diah raised her hands innocently. "How's your wife?"

He reached for his pistol. "Silence, *traitor*! We're under orders to—"

The floor dropped away from beneath the guards, and they plummeted downward with panicked yells.

Smoothing her hair back to compose herself, Diah inched forward to peek into the gaping hole. The three men lay moaning on the floor of the kitchen. Diah waved at a bewildered servant, then jumped over the hole, landing on the top step of the stairs.

Katrine stood at the bottom, wearing an entirely too bubbly expression for this late at night. *Oh bother*. Diah rolled her eyes at her cousin before starting down toward her.

"Did you know you had a lever that activated a *trap door?*" Katrine said.

"No," Diah said flatly, "I had absolutely no clue that I had a trap door installed in my own castle." She reached the bottom of the steps, and pushed past Katrine to continue down the hallway, which banked narrowly to the right.

"Well it's awesome," Katrine said, following, "I *love* this place!"

A little too much. Diah sniffed. They slunk down the hall in silence, quickening their pace as they turned the corner into the broad passageway that led straight to the throne room. As they approached Diah eyed the closed throne room door with disgust. The gold trim lining the arch of the door had been ripped off last year by some raiders, leaving it a dirty white. *One would* think *that the dumb enchantress could cast some kind of spell to make this place look better.*

"Here's the plan," she whispered. "You go in there and get the attention of the guards, have them chase you out, then I'll go in and take care of the Enchantress."

Katrine bobbed her head. "Sure, sure, and you're positive you can handle her?"

"Of course," Diah said, tapping the small pouch at her side, then pressed herself against the wall on the side of the doorway.

Katrine shrugged, and ducked into the throne room. There was a crash, and shouting, and then she came pelting out, heading back down the corridor in a panicked sprint. The guards in the throne room rushed blindly after her.

Diah smirked, then shoved the door open and stepped into the throne room. A tall woman in a black dress occupied the bland-colored chair that had replaced Diah's beautiful tangerine throne. On the woman's right, squashed flowers and broken glass littered the floor.

"Wow, what did Kat do?" Diah said. "Throw a vase at you?"

The enchantress looked up. "*You!*"

"Me!" Diah shouted, grinning victoriously.

The enchantress narrowed her eyes. "You should have never returned, *child*."

"Well, you see," Diah said, hand on the pouch on her belt, "I just wanted to thank you for an educational few days. Turns out, the throne I blew up a while back was *enchanted* to stop people like you from waltzing in and doing what you did."

The enchantress scowled. "Meaning?"

"Meaning, I'll be needing my ugly throne back." Diah jerked the bag from her waist, and tossed the bright orange ashes—the sole remains of her original throne—onto the imposter.

For a horror-stricken moment, the enchantress didn't move. Then, with an awful jerk, she collapsed, unconscious. As Diah tied the bag onto her belt, Katrine slipped through the doors, grinning her usual stupid smile. "The guards just collapsed! What'd you do?"

"Took care of the enchantress." *Hopefully, they'll wake up free of her spell.* Diah stepped over the woman's body, and sat on her throne. It wasn't the most comfortable or beautiful chair, but at least it was *hers* again. "And that's that!" she leaned back. "Another perfect plan well executed, and all before the sun came up!"

Katrine, who was *still* hovering about for some reason, bobbed her head. "I love perfect plans!"

Diah eyed her. "I suppose you'll be leaving, then?"

"Ah," Katrine paused, "well . . . "

Here we go again. Diah sighed, and straightened on her throne. She had enough experience to know what was coming next.

"I . . . " Katrine cocked a smile at Diah. "I want to thank you for getting rid of that pesky enchantress for me, and let you know that we'll always be family, and all that . . . but I'll need you to get off *my* throne now."

Diah rolled her eyes. "Yeah, no."

"How about yes?" Katrine slipped her hand from behind her back, revealing a pistol. She pointed it at Diah. "Off the throne, Diah. *Now*."

Diah glared. *Well when she puts it like that . . .*

"Fine." she spat. As she stood, she flicked her finger under the bottom of the chair's armrest, tapping the button hidden there. She stepped aside, waving dramatically to the throne. "There you go, *congratulations*."

Katrine eyed her for a moment, then grinned. Striding forward, she plopped down on the throne. "See? I knew you'd be reasonable!"

Diah nodded. Of course. She was always perfectly reasonable.

Something clicked inside the arm of the throne. A small cavity on the back of the throne snapped open, and a tiny dart shot out, burying into Katrine's back. Her eyes widened in realization a split second before she slumped forward.

Sighing, Diah dragged her snoring cousin off the throne and sat down once again. Hopefully soon her guards would wake up, these two usurpers would be sent off to the dungeon, and she'd be Queen once again.

Until the *next* time she was forced to break into her own castle, of course. But she'd deal with that when it came. For now, Diah tipped her head against the back of the throne. *Yup*, she thought, satisfied, *another perfect plan flawlessly executed.*

BENEATH TSUKUYOMI
BY ODESSA SILVER

Odessa has been stuck in her imagination since a child creating strange ideas and weaving them into stories. Often fusing fantasy and science with darker themes, her stories tend to dig into all aspects of human nature. Worldsmyths moderator, logo creator, and strange Brit who doesn't actually like tea.

***

"The moon is beautiful, isn't it?" he asked, his lithe body sprawled in the silvery moonlight.

I wasn't looking at the moon though. Only him.

"Yes, it is. I can hardly tear my eyes away."

He turned to me then, a chuckle gracing his lips, black strands of hair falling across his face as he pulled himself up. His movements were slow, teasing, skin uncovered and covered again. He was enjoying this. As was I.

I found myself wandering closer, passing the open door, bare feet padding on the tatami mat, heart racing, lips parting.

"Don't look at me like that," Ryoichi said, smile widening.

"So should I take my Lord's words as a love confession to Tsukuyomi? I'm sure he is enjoying the view of your body from the skies."

I knelt down in front of him and he reached up, pulling my kimono open; his eyes wandered up and down my deliciously-bruising body, red marks deepening after his rough touch. "And now he is enjoying yours too."

"Then should I shut the door?"

"Hotaka." Ryoichi grabbed my chin and pulled me to his lips. Breaking the kiss, he breathed, "You, I love you."

"Only poets try to say it in fancy ways." I stopped to smile and kiss him again. "And you are no poet my Lord."

"Please, we are alone. I am more than your lord like this."

I licked my lips. "I love you too . . . Ryoichi."

The air around him changed, subtle to most, but not to me. A magical warmth exuded from his skin; I ran the backs of my fingertips up his bared arm, absorbing the traces. He couldn't feel it, he didn't even know it was there, exiting his body in streams as it had all evening.

Blood rushed to my cheeks. Earlier. The hot water of the onsen surrounding us, steam rising up and up, our bared bodies relaxed and calm. I'd opened my eyes then. Not in the way most did when seeing the world around them. No, I saw vivid colours and magic. Purple bubbles floated in the soft wind, and Ryoichi sat amongst them all, growing magic that he couldn't see. It clung to his blemished skin, to its creator, begging to stay longer.

Now that we had grown closer, each touch of mine sent it wild, responding to the budding feelings deep in his heart. I needed him to feel more. The magic would only last for so long, and I wanted every drop. I'd spent years looking for someone like him.

Smiling, I inched closer, fingers rolling down the defined muscles of his chest. Most vassals didn't dare touch their lord so, but I wasn't like them. The warmth of the onsen soared as I straddled his lap, Ryoichi stared but said nothing.

"You've wanted this and I am here to please."

"Hotaka."

I'd wanted it too. Somewhere, I'd fallen for him.

Ryoichi wrapped his arms around my chest, hands resting on my lower back. I smiled as the magic reached me, storing deep inside my own body, a blooming mental ecstasy.

Leaning to his ear, I brushed away his wet black hair and whispered, "It can be our secret. We're here alone. We don't even have to be lord and vassal . . . just two men who want each other. There is nothing wrong with that."

Pressing the softest kiss to his neck, I faced him. Black eyes watched me hungrily, torn between duty and desire. I'd seen this look so many times before, and each time he'd picked duty. I would not let him pick it again.

"Perhaps . . . " I glanced away shyly, feebly attempting to slide back off his lap.

"No," he growled and held me tighter. "Don't move. I can't admire you from far away. Here," his hands moved, gliding along my soaked skin above and below water, "I can see everything. Almost everything."

I whimpered before my Lord, his touch arousing all my senses. He'd touched me a thousand times, but not like this. All around him the magic grew, purple deepening to blue, then to black. I needed it, but I needed him more. Ryoichi didn't hesitate then, lips finding skin, fervent, needy, wanting.

My Lord led us from the water. We made it as far as the inn's futon before our bodies collided. Fingers rolled through hair, gripping, pulling, as limbs tangled. I straddled his bare hips, looking down at my Lord flustered and lustful. As our ecstasy grew, so did the magic. I breathed in his scent, breathed in his magic. It would all be mine. He would be mine.

The night had grown late; Tsukuyomi had continued on in the skies. Only once exhaustion had taken us and the tatami mats beneath us were slick with sweat did we notice the passing of time.

I sat before him now, my own body gorged on his magic, yet still hungry. The magic gained would keep me going for many months, but I wasn't here for just a few extra months of life. I needed more.

"Would you care for some sake my Lor—Ryoichi?" I caught the

look in his eyes and corrected myself quick enough. My fingers still brushed his skin, making my way to his shoulders. "Or I could call for a meal to be made."

Ryoichi nodded. "Only a few cups tonight, I need a clear mind for the morning. We need to return to the real world." He took my cheek in his palm, a sly smile forming. "I am not done with you yet, Hotaka. I'll find a way for you to be by my side without issue. If that is what you want."

I placed my hand over his as my heart lurched. "You would do that for me?"

He snorted. "Do you think this is the first time a vassal and lord have fallen for each other? You've proven your loyalty, your love."

My eyes fell to my lap. I couldn't look at him. This had to end. "Then we should toast."

Leaving my lover, I hurried to the low table we'd pushed aside and poured two cups of sake. Ryoichi followed, kneeling next to me, our legs brushing together. I pressed a cup into his hand and lifted my own.

"Kampai, my Lord."

"Kampai."

"Your hands must be tired, let me." I lifted my cup to his lips, tipping it until the clear sake flowed freely. Once empty, I stopped to refill. "I hope the sake pleases you."

"Slow down." He chuckled and wrapped an arm around my waist. "Tsukuyomi is blessing us with a long night."

Taking a deep breath, I held it before letting it go gently. "You're right. This night could last forever if we wished it."

Slower this time, I continued to press the cup to his lips. Like me, Ryoichi couldn't handle much sake before the room began to spin and words fell freely. Too many times in the years spent in his service had we ended up drunk out of our minds. I'd enjoyed my time, and my sake, but now I needed a clear head. No mistakes could be made.

But why did it have to be tonight?

Four years I had planned this moment, weighing up every action and interaction. Scenarios played over and over until just one way remained. First, I was to get him drunk until he passed out. It was always hard to wake him from those sleeps. Next I would say farewell to him and . . .

The next cup lifted to his lips with another pang in my chest, the sake flowing free once again.

I had to do this.

I had no choice.

If I waited, the magic would dwindle back to nothing, and I'd spent too long here eking it out, making his magic stronger. His kind were becoming too few now, and I couldn't live without magic.

Ryoichi's cheeks flushed in the moonlight, whether from my touch or the alcohol's, I wasn't sure. I'd grown to love this face, his crooked nose and lopsided smile, the way his lips would quirk when he was trying to be stern but he couldn't help but laugh. I'd known from the start how this would end; it was the sole reason I was here. I just never expected *this*.

Sake cup discarded, my thumb rolled across Ryoichi's bottom lip, wiping away droplets of alcohol. I licked them away, tasting the sweet tang.

"Ah I see, you would rather drink from me."

I smiled and kissed him, breath lingering on his skin.

"Sake tastes better like this."

"More," he whispered, voice needy and wanting, hands reaching for me. "I want to drink from you."

Ryoichi leant close, fingers pulling away my silken kimono, baring me fully to the moon once again.

"The moon—" Words caught in my throat. My chest hurt. "—Is very beautiful."

He smirked against my neck, arms winding around my waist. "Yes, you are my poet, Hotaka."

"L-Let me get you some more sake."

I climbed to my feet and shuffled over to the door; I'd ordered two bottles to make sure. They sat neatly on a tray lined up perfectly.

"Hotakaaa," Ryoichi called, crawling across the damp tatami mats, swaying with drunkenness. "You are too far from me."

"Just a moment, my Lord."

Behind the tray lay a sheath filled with a blade I'd used many times before. This time, however, regret filled both of us, overspilling from my body.

I have to.

"Hotakaaa, what did I tell you," Ryoichi called once more, his breath now upon my skin, his voice luring me away. "Don't call me that here."

But if I do . . .

Turning my head to him, I kissed him, once, twice, lingering on his taste. "Ryoichi."

One hand grasped at regret, the other dug fingernails in his shoulder. I forced a smile as the blade sunk into his chest. He cried out, confusion bubbling over his sweet-tasting lips, and horror clouded his black eyes.

I hadn't planned to kill him quite like this, watching his life fade, stealing my lover away. But I couldn't miss the opportunity. If I had waited any more, I . . .

My hands shook.

I didn't want to watch.

Magic filled the room, swirling in a black miasma. I could feel my body soaking it in as my Lord grew heavy in my arms, blood running down his bruised skin. Bruises I'd made.

"Forgive me," I choked out, my tongue thick and dry.

I lay him down, his sightless eyes far away now, my own filling with tears. I couldn't cry though. My job was done. Mission complete.

I should be happy.

The moonlight bathed Ryoichi in its light once more, soft but cold. Tsukuyomi still watched us brightly.

"Forgive me," I whispered to him, begging the deity for any kind of mercy.

The room was empty now, magic depleted, soul departed. I was alone. I knew I should have left by now, but my body was heavy and tears still fell.

I wrapped my bruised body in clean clothes, bruises he'd made, the kimono that smelt of him discarded. Returning to Ryoichi, I kissed his lips one last time while removing the blade. Wiping the blood on his black kimono, I returned it to the sheath filled with regret.

I didn't look back as I exited the room. Clouds now covered the moon, bathing everything in darkness. I ran on and on, feet taking me further and further from where I wanted to be but . . . I had the magic now. I wouldn't need to kill again any time soon.

I wish the moon wasn't so beautiful.

THE GROVE
BY ERIN SLEGAITIS-SMITH

Erin Slegaitis-Smith is a fantasy author from Upstate New York in the Adirondack mountains. When she's not teaching, drinking far too much tea, or writing, she enjoys attending Ren Faires and playing D&D.

* * *

What I am saying is important to me; otherwise, there'd be no point saying it. One day very soon, I'll be gone, and it will be too late. So listen, or hand me off to someone who will—I need someone to hear my story—someone to know what I could never tell the people I loved, the people who knew me . . . anyone, really. This is my last chance. Will you stay?

I traced the line of moonlight on the ceiling. The wooden bones of the roof stretched broad shadows across the room. The night air was stuffy and, for some reason, I was restless. I tried to lie very still to not disturb my brother. He got grumpy when someone woke him so rubbing the coarse blanket between my fingers and counting the knots in the stitching was my way to tire myself. It wasn't working. My mind was still alert. I tilted my head back to look out the window at the moon, which was too bright.

To my surprise, Michael was standing at our window, looking out into the night. He cocked his head and slowly lowered his shoulders, slumping as if falling asleep while standing. His pale skin and dark hair made him a phantom in the moonlight. I flipped to my belly and pulled myself closer to the head of the bed.

"Michael," I whispered. "What are you doing?"

He didn't respond. So, I crawled out of bed, my bare feet hitting the cool rough floorboards, and tiptoed up to him to minimize the risk of waking our parents. I pushed the sleeves up on my nightshirt. It was Papa's, and at only eleven it was like a dress on me that I hoped to grow into one day. Looking into Michael's eyes, they were distant and glossy.

"Michael." I pushed on his shoulder.

"Stop that." He brushed my hand away without breaking his gaze from whatever he was staring at out the window.

"What are you doing?"

"Be quiet, Henry. I'm listening."

"To what?"

"I said be quiet."

I strained to hear whatever Michael was listening to, but the only sounds were the village cattle lowing at the sky and a disorderly racket from the pub two roads over. Maybe a bird or two.

"What are you listening to?" I asked again.

"The music."

"From the pub?"

"No."

"From where?"

"The hills," he said. I tried to trace his line of sight. My eyes shifted along an invisible line that landed my gaze on the hills beyond our town. Lights danced on the hilltops, and a sense of foreboding eked its way into my bones. In these hills lay a grove we had been warned about since we were small children. Light on the hills was a sign of misfortune.

"I don't hear any music."

"That's because you talk too much." Michael started pulling himself into the window frame.

"What are you doing?" I grabbed his arm.

"I'm going to the music."

"No, Michael, there is no music."

"Get off." He shook loose and began lowering himself down the front of the house. I gaped for a moment. It wasn't like Michael hadn't snuck out before this way, it happened far too often, but this wasn't his usual rebellious nighttime outing. Something wasn't right.

I rushed to pull on some slacks and stuff my feet into my boots. Stopping Michael from leaving hadn't worked. All that was left was to get him back before our parents noticed we were gone. Tomorrow there would be trouble for both of us if he was caught sneaking out again. Going through the house would wake my parents, as Michael's early attempts to sneak out proved, so I lowered myself out after him.

Michael was bigger than me at sixteen and I struggled to reach many of the handholds and footholds he had used. Michael had already made it a good way down the street when my boots hit the ground. While rushing to catch up, I tucked my nightshirt into my slacks.

"Michael, you can't go to the hills." I protested.

"I don't want you, Henry," Michael said.

"I don't care if you want me or not. We're going home." I grabbed his arm and pulled back on him, but he kept pushing forward and pulling me with him.

How did he get so strong? All he did all day was help Papa with the mending nets. It wasn't easy work, but it wouldn't make him this strong. I had wrestled with him often enough to know. But then something glinted in his hand and I looked to see an ornate coin clutched in his fingertips. "Where did you get that?"

"I've had it."

"No, you haven't."

"Yes, I have."

"The only way you would get a thing like that is by stealing it."

My brother turned on me, ripping me off the ground by my shirt collar.

"No one calls me a thief!" I had taken and given my fair share of black eyes with my brother, but now I was terrified by him. His brow furrowed in anger but there was an absence in his eyes I couldn't explain. It was as if he really were asleep.

"Then where do you get it?" I asked, pushing him away.

"It was a gift."

"A gift?" I re-tucked my shirt.

"From someone who said I deserved it, and more like it." He continued walking towards the hillside. I grabbed his sleeve again at the edge of the hills, where the road disappeared into the grass.

"Wait." As his foot hit the grass, a buzz rushed through me. It ran from my hand on his sleeve through every inch of me. Then everything changed.

Strange creatures I had never seen before overran the hills, milling about in grass that turned a greyish blue under the moonlight. They were a variety of shapes and sizes and looked as though someone had taken a bucket of different toy parts and glued them together at random. They were slithering things, bouncing things, striding things that milled about on their bellies or limbs that dug into the soft sod of the hillside. As their chilling eyes turned on us, their otherworldly gaze chased the air right out of me. If the creatures had mouths, they stretched into sinister smiles over the creatures' alien faces upon noticing us.

One of the creatures that looked like an old hacked-off stump slithered toward us on roots like snakes. Its large golden eyes fixed on us. It came to our toes and reached its twig-like arm up towards Michael. Its knotted finger touched the coin in his hand, and Michael smiled at it as if he knew what was going on. On the other hand, I couldn't suck in enough air; everything was too real and too wrong. It didn't make any sense, like old stories spinning to life off my mother's tongue. Maybe I was the one dreaming.

I heard a crackling noise behind me and, out of nothing, a boy close to my brother's age came sauntering over. He was dressed in rich clothing and flipped a twisted dagger-shaped scale in his hand. Whatever creature that scale belonged to was larger than anything I would ever want to meet.

He had the same eerie calm smile as Michael. Gold accented his brown skin around the eyes, so he wasn't just pretending to be wealthy. The creatures gathered up around his ankles, and he greeted him like an old friend. Then, turning, he spotted my brother and me.

"Good evening." He walked up to us. "I'm Dietrich. Have we met before?"

"No, I think I'd remember," Michael spoke informally to someone from such a high station. "I'm Michael."

"And who's this?" Dietrich looked at me. His eyes were glassy.

"What?" Michael looked back at me. "Henry, when did you get here?"

"I've been with you the whole time," I choked out.

"No, you haven't."

I couldn't believe it. How could Michael not remember me being with him? We were arguing only a minute ago. The stump-like thing sniffed at me and sneezed before retreating to its like beasts, and they glanced among each other with shifty eyes.

"Michael, we should leave," I urged, but Michael was too fascinated with meeting Dietrich to listen.

"Been here before?" Michael asked.

"No, but I should have. I mean, look at this place. It's amazing, and this," Deitrich scooped up a small ball-shaped creature.

Another crackling sound rippled behind us as, this time, a girl stepped through.

"Well, hello." Dietrich sidled up to her. "Name's Dietrich." She cast her eyes down and pulled her hands up to her chest.

I had seen that kind of reaction among many serving class girls who were used to such "hellos" meaning trouble. The bruises clinging to her dark collarbones were evidence of this. Their bluish-purple hue matched the small flower she clutched in her slim fingers.

"Come on." Dietrich put his arm around her. "What's your name?"

"Alai," she whispered.

"Now that's a fine name." Dietrich patted her shoulder and scooped her like a wheat fold over to Michael and me. "This is Michael, and—and—I'm sorry, who are you again?"

"Henry."

"Right," Dietrich said. "This is Michael's brother Henry."

One of the stump-like creatures scuttled back to me. It looked up at me with its yellow blinking eyes. Then, it pulled something like a fig off one of its few branches and presented the fruit to me.

"Go away," I tried to shoo it but the creature kept pushing the fruit towards me.

"What's wrong?" Dietrich asked. "It is just trying to give you something."

"If you eat spirit food, the spirit steals your humanity. Then no creature can recognize you as human, even your own family," I said.

"That superstitious garbage," Michael mocked. "You don't really think we're in a spirit realm? Grow up already."

"How do you explain all of this?" I pushed the stump thing away with my foot.

"I don't know, but it's not supernatural. Those stories are for scaring little kids into staying indoors and not taking questionable gifts from strangers. There's no such thing as spirits," Michael scoffed.

The stump thing threw its fig at me and wormed away on its roots with what I guess you could call an angry expression.

"You hurt its feelings," Dietrich said.

"I'm sorry—maybe, we should just go before we upset them further." I gestured back towards the town.

"You go if you want to," Michael said.

"Let's go exploring!" Dietrich grinned. "What do you say, Alai?"

She simply raised a timid knuckle to her lips.

"You don't talk much, do you?"

"I agree with you," Michael said. "Let's explore."

"It's settled." Dietrich grabbed Alai's hand and pulled her forward. "Let's go."

"Wait!" I called after them. The three of them ignored me and walked further up the hill. I followed.

We crested the hilltop and looked down into a shallow valley. We gasped, seeing more odd creatures the size of grown men. They looked like empty husks of paper hives spiraling up into the air. Yet, aside from their ashy paper skin and being empty inside, they seemed disturbingly human, with arms and legs like ours and faces like people.

There were hundreds of them trudging in circles through the wide basin.

"Woah," Dietrich abandoned Alai's hand, which she appeared grateful for, and rushed over to one of the husks. It seemed to ignore him even as he peeled off a layer of its gray skin. "This is so strange. It's like they're made out of paper!" Michael joined in with Deitrich's prodding.

"You don't have to stay," I said to Alai. "We can go back."

"No, I want to stay," she said in a hushed voice.

Dietrich turned back to us. "Look at these things, Alai—hey," Dietrich turned to me. "Who are you?"

"Henry?" I said, puzzled.

"Are you not sure what your name is?" he laughed.

"You already met me, not two minutes ago."

"Did I? My memory is usually pretty good. I'm positive that it was just Alai, Michael, and me," Dietrich mused. I was moving from wary to perturbed. How could he have simply forgotten I was there? "Let's keep exploring."

We moved our way through the husks. Some of the other kinds of strange creatures were following us. One looked like the meanest dog you've ever seen with taloned bird feet instead of paws. One had a long body with purplish-blue fur. It slithered as much as it walked. Another looked like it had goat feet, a fat man's belly, and a bird head with short, floppy ears. And those stump things were always following en masse on our heels.

We came upon a small grove. A bluish light danced inside it, bouncing off small pools of water and glass plates that seemed to float in the air. We all marveled at it for a moment.

As we entered, the surfaces picked up our reflections. Alai touched one, and it rippled like water beneath her finger. Suddenly, an image appeared on it of another place. It was daytime in the picture, and people moved about in strange clothes through a peculiar town.

The others were enraptured by it. I thought it was fascinating too, but I couldn't shake my nerves off long enough to enjoy it like they were. The air of this place was heavy somehow, putting me ill at ease.

"You do not smell of the tokens like the others," a voice hissed. I turned around to see another strange creature. Its gray skin was wrinkled. Its body was like a lizard with a back bent sharply to the sky, its form partially concealed in a kind of cloak. "Most curious. Perhaps—perhaps you hold the answer."

"What are you?" I stepped back. The creature tilted its head to the side. Tracing its line of sight to the others, I put myself in its path even as I realized there was no sure thing to do to protect them if the creature turned out to be dangerous.

"What am I? What are you? Your kind could not enter this realm without a token. So I wonder if you are some other kind." There was an odd glint to the creature's eyes—something like hope.

"What are tokens?" I asked.

"Things of this realm; small flowers, long jagged scales. Things to trap and ensnare. To make this pretty place a prison," the creature said.

"What about some coins?" This creature might have answers about what this place was and how to get Michael to leave. As long as it was talking and the others occupied nearby, it couldn't hurt to ask.

"Yes, coins." Its head bobbed. "Or something like that."

"My brother has one," I gasped.

"And you touched him as you entered this place?" It tilted its long head.

"I did." I nodded, looking back briefly to ensure the others hadn't wandered off on me. They were captured by a new scene of fast-moving things that glimmered like they were made of steel.

"I see." The creature stroked its hooked jaw with its long fingers. Its wrinkled lips hooked up in something like a smile. "Yes, a rare opportunity. A chance—at last, a chance. I will tell you, human, that I am called Keeper. This grove is where the tales of this land and more intersect. I have seen and told many wisdoms over so many centuries. So heed me. Leave this place, now. It is the only way."

"I want to, but the others won't listen to me. What do you mean the only way?"

I looked back at them again to see the scene had shifted to rolling hills of trees with pink budding flowers. The petals drifted through a breeze like silken rain.

"They will not come with you. Those tokens resemble in the physical what is captured in their hearts. This place is like a dream to them. Nothing is real. Nothing is true. That is why these fables can enrapture them." Keeper gestured towards the standing pools. "You, little one, see this place as it is. If you leave now, you will still be able to return without the beguiling of a token. You may grow and become stronger. Then when it is right, you can return. You can break what has made my home into a wretched curse. Go, please."

"But, my brother—"

"No!" Keeper barked. It scuttled towards me and grabbed my wrists in its boney fingers. "You do not listen! You must go, or there is no hope for any of us. There is a creature here that has caught their scent, the Taegorak. None of your realm can survive it while beguiled. None of this realm can defeat it. This creature is what baited them here, to destroy them. Only you can stop this wretched cycle. Leave now. Train, grow, and come back to defeat this monster before it destroys all that is good between our worlds."

"But why is this creature so dangerous? Why does it want to hurt us? How am I supposed to defeat it when you say no one else can?"

I look back to see the others now looking at a scene that made it seem like there were flying through the air. The view swooped over mountains, and when they dipped close to a lake, the water exploded around them before they climbed back into the sky. Keeper shook my wrists.

"The Taegorak hungers, as all creatures do. It hungers not for flesh but souls, their humanity itself." Keeper took a ragged breath.

It was like the old stories of goblins and spirit creatures had come to life. Monsters that wanted not just your life but whatever it was that made you human. With a choking sound, Keeper continued.

"All you see here is a result of it. None of us have the power to stop it. The more humanity the Taegorak consumes, the stronger it becomes, but humanity is also the key to defeating it, and now, at last, we have a chance."

"I can't do anything about any monster. I'm not a hero from a fable. No magic will make me powerful enough to defend this place from a creature you can't defeat yourself. There is nothing I could learn or do to change whatever is happening here. I can't even get my brother to listen to me."

I yanked my wrists free and stared the creature down with false bravery.

Desperation choked Keeper's voice. "Of course, you are not ready. You are too young, that is true; you do not have the skills. That's why you must go now. Go and prepare and become strong enough to save this realm and your own. Don't underestimate who you may become, the value of your humanity, or what your being here means. Realize it or not, child, you have opened a door that I thought would forever be closed—hope."

"This can't be," I shook my head.

"Stop reasoning. This is beyond your reasoning!" Keeper tugged me down so it could grab my face and look me in the eye. I gasped and pulled back, but Keeper's hands held me with a strength it hadn't used before. "What you have known is only part of what can be."

Keeper released me, and I staggered back, sucking in a sharp breath as it wrung its hands.

"All the more reason to get them out of here," I said. "Even if I believe you, there is no way I can fight that thing by myself, not with all the time in the world, and not if I somehow could learn how to defeat a monster. They can help me. Michael would be a better help than me, and Deitrich would have the influence to get us access to information and training. Alai knows how to work hard and would help too. If you need humans to save you, we'd be far better off with all of us."

"They will not come. These others are dreaming. If you stay with them, you will only accomplish the loss of your own life, the wasting of this opportunity!" Keeper's lips trembled. "Never has a chance like this come, and it may never come again. You cannot save them, but you may save whoever would come after by leaving now."

"So be it," I squared my shoulders with the sternest expression I could muster. "I won't leave my brother behind just because some creature tells me to."

"Impertinent child," Keeper hissed. "So be it.' Then so be it! Keeper warned you. A chance, Keeper is a fool. Humans are too dense to hear, always." The creature howled a mournful cry. "Any trouble you find was bought with your own coin."

Keeper scuttled back into the thicket, muttering angrily to itself. As the rustling leaves settled, I almost thought I heard it whimpering.

I turned to the others to see they were laughing at a menagerie of animals dressed in clothing like people and working in a village as people would. I grabbed my brother's shoulder.

"Michael."

"Henry! When did you get here?"

"That's starting to get old," I sighed.

"What is?" Michael raised a brow.

"We need to go home," I said.

"Why? Haven't you looked at all of this? The grove is amazing." Michael turned to look at the new scene unfolding before Deitrich and Alai. It was underwater, surrounded by colorful corals and fish. They gasped in awe.

"Yeah, so very amazing. Let's go," I pulled Michael back to face me.

"What's your rush?" he asked.

"Don't you think there was a reason behind all the stories? It's dangerous here." I didn't know if I fully believed what Keeper had told me, but my twisting stomach tightened into a firm knot. It could have been fear or my exhaustion from staying up so late, but I couldn't shake that feeling of wrongness.

"You're such a baby," Michael tsked.

"I am not," I huffed. "Let's go."

"Henry, you are starting to annoy me." Michael turned a more fiery gaze toward me. Finally, he looked more awake.

"I wouldn't be if you listened to me!"

"Why do you have to bother me all the time?" Michael huffed.

"If you won't listen to me, Keeper will tell you."

"Who?"

"This lizardy creature." I looked back into the hollows of the grove. "Keeper!" It didn't come. "Keeper, help me!" I looked back to see Michael had gone back to watching the images. "Michael!" I shouted.

"Henry? When did you get here? Why are you yelling?"

"You can't be serious." I grabbed his arm and started pulling him out of the grove. "We're going home."

"What's going on?" Dietrich asked. The yelling must have broken him and Alai out of their trance. Michael wrenched his arm from my grip.

"It's just my little brother," Michael said.

"Oh, nice to meet you. What's your name?" Dietrich offered his hand with a smile.

"Henry, I told you that three hundred times. Every time you all look away from me, you forget about me. There are all sorts of strange things here. A creepy lizard said that there was some kind of monster out there that wants to eat us. We need to go back home!"

They all laughed at me.

"Come on, Henry," Michael said. "We've seen dozens of creatures here. None of them talk, and none of them tried to hurt us."

"So you want to wait until they do?"

"Maybe we should listen to him," Alai murmured.

"She speaks!" Dietrich gave a jovial slap on her back as his form of approval. "All right, we can go."

"What? Why?" Michael asked.

"If Alai is nervous, and so is Hennidy—"

"Henry," I corrected.

"Henry," Dietrich continued. "Then we should go. To respect them."

Alai smiled shyly at him.

"But there's so much more out there," Michael said.

"Yeah, we can come back another time and explore more."

"What if there isn't another time?"

"No, we should just go," I said, aiming to keep them on track.

"Well," Dietrich mused. "What if we explore one more thing? Like the top of that hill?" Dietrich pointed to a gentle hill not far away. "Would you be okay with that, Alai?"

She shrugged. "I guess so. But I wouldn't want to stay longer."

"Excellent. What about you, Benny?" Dietrich asked.

"Henry," I grumbled. "The sooner we leave, the better. Just to the top of the hill."

"Then a compromise has been decided," Dietrich declared.

"Let's explore," Michael urged, and so we left the grove and made our way further into the hills.

We reached the top of another dark knoll. The grass was a deep gray under the starlight, but we all gasped at the shimmering purple flowers forming wavering rivers down into the bowl of the next valley. Michael, Dietrich, and Alai laughed together and rushed into the basin. Deitrich threw himself down to roll to the bottom in fits of laughter. I followed cautiously, warily eyeing the empty space and subtle rolls of the earth among the flowers. It couldn't be that safe, that perfect, could it? Certainly not with the monster Keeper had warned me of looming somewhere.

The others began picking handfuls of flowers and breathing in their deep herb-like aroma. I leaned down and plucked one of the blooms. There was something familiar about this unassuming flower.

"Michael." I saw Michael handing flower after flower to Alai as she giggled. Deitrich was more cheery than ever, sitting among the blooms and braiding the dark stems of his plucked flowers into a crown. I crept closer and tugged Michael's arm. "Michael."

"Henry, when did you get here?" Michael asked.

"It's time to go home. We said we'd go to the top of the hill. This isn't the top of the hill anymore," I said.

"You go home. I'm having fun."

"This place is lovely, but we shouldn't be here."

"Maybe you shouldn't be here," Alai practically whispered. She took a deep breath of her bouquet. My eyes landed on the one flower tucked in Alai's hair, and I realized why the flower was familiar.

"Where did you get that flower?" I asked.

"From Michael," Alai said.

"No, the one in your hair."

"Oh." She raised her hand to caress the petals. "I'm not sure. I've always had it, I think."

"You couldn't have. It would have died, and the bloom is still fresh," I said. Alai tilted her head, considering it.

"Come on, kid," Dietrich stood. "Can't you just let us have some fun?" He placed his crown on Alai's head. She smiled, a blush rising in her brown cheeks.

"I'm not trying to stop you from having fun. I'm trying to make sense of what's happening. If my brother's gold piece came from something here, and Alai's flower probably came from this field, where did your token come from? Is it a scale from some creature or a dagger, or what? What does it belong to? None of you find this strange?"

"No. Quit worrying so much," Dietrich waved me off.

"He's right, Henry," Michael said. "If you're scared, go home."

"I can't go without you."

"Maybe he's scared to go by himself," Alai said.

"Grow up. You're not a baby anymore," Michael scoffed, plopping down and sending up a puff of purple petals.

"It can't hurt to take your brother home." Alai offered one of her flowers to Michael, and he considered her for a moment.

"No, he can take himself."

"Fine, I'll go with him." Alai took my hand. "Let's go. Don't worry, Michael and Deitrich will be fine." She started pulling me away.

"But—" I began to protest.

"Shh." She winked at me. "Boys are like this a lot. He'll change his mind."

"Wait," Michael stood. "I'll take him."

"What are you all worried about?" Dietrich huffed. "There's nothing wrong with this place. Let the baby go back by himself. He shouldn't ruin our fun. Everything is perfectly safe!" Dietrich threw down his token, the pointed end of the scale sinking into the earth. He stomped on top of one of the small knolls. "We're in a field of flowers. What do you expect to happen? Goblins to randomly appear and kidnap you?"

"No, I—"

I gasped as the ground began to rumble. Dietrich staggered off of the knoll as it slowly began to rise. We gaped as scaly arms and legs appeared from under the sod. A long neck unfurled, revealing a triangular lizard head and toothy maw. Each long, glittering, twisted scale reverberated with a deep rumble in the creature's chest.

"The Taegorak," I gasped. "Run!"

Finally, everyone listened, charging back up the hill as the creature shifted from an earthen hill to a jaggedly-edged, cow-barn-sized monster. We managed to scramble to the top of the hill before the Taegorak gave chase. It strode after us on claws as long as a man was tall, tearing deep gouges into the soft dirt behind us.

It craned its long neck forward, snapping up Dietrich in its massive jaws. We shrieked but kept running. The sounds—the crunching and wet shredding that followed—only speed us forward, sending ice water into our veins. We had neared Keeper's grove by the time the hulking form reappeared.

"Keep running," Michael huffed while running beside me. "I'll distract it."

"No," I cried. "You can't!"

"Alai, take Henry. Get to safety." Before I could protest, Alai yanked me forward.

"Come after me, you ugly demon!" Michael yelled.

He charged westward, away from us. Tears pricked my eyes. The pounding of my feet on the sod echoed the vibrations of the booming steps of the Taegorak.

Finally, we reached the Keeper's grove. The bright light from the mirrors that had attracted the others was shuddering and dim. My legs and lungs burned with each step. Between the Taegorak's size and speed, I knew we had no way to outrun it. Then Michael screamed—so sharp, and then, so quiet. It was a dagger in my ears, in my chest.

After a moment of our thudding feet and pounding hearts, we passed the grove, and the thundering of the creature returned. We just had to pass through the valley of husk creatures and climb one more hill to get back to where we had crossed into the foot of the grove. We barreled down into the valley. We forced our way through the husks, their papery skin crackling as we pushed them aside. As we started climbing that last hill, a crunching like charred corn husks fresh from the fire sounded on our heels.

Suddenly, Alai's hand was ripped from mine, and she shrieked. Skidding to a halt and looking back, my breath caught seeing the Taegorak throwing her high into the air before catching her brutally in its jaws.

I turned back towards the direction of the village and continued to run. Finally, reaching the stump creatures again. Almost home. The path's edge where Michael and I had crossed into this horrible place came into view. Too far and so close. The stump creatures began pelting me with their fruit, so that I had to dodge them and whatever else would slow or trip me. The thundering footsteps returned.

Slipping on one of the watery fruits, I thudded to the ground. With the Taegorak closing in, the sound of it snuffling as it ran echoed around me, and the smell of its moist stinking breath engulfed me. Pulling myself to my knees and gasping from exhaustion, my eyes meet those of one of the stump creatures. It was so like the creatures from the old stories. The things from the first stories I had ever heard might be the last thing to see me while I was still alive.

It clicked. The Keeper's words about how the creature hungered for our humanity, and the old stories my parents told of the spirit creatures in the hills. Snatching up the fruit, I took a bite, choking it down. The Taegorak skidded to a stop over me, right as the lump of bitter-sweet fruit scraped down my throat. The creature lowered its massive head spreading its jaws wide, its hot breath smelling of putrid metallic gore rolling over its long tongue.

I put my hands up as if that would protect me and gasped, seeing my skin turning gray and breaking apart like over-dried paper. Then, with a jolt, shadows burst from every crack in my skin, forming the odd creatures we had seen dotting the grove.

The Taegorak snapped its jaws shut, and I pinched my eyes closed, but no pain came. The ground reverberated with the creature's snarl and the crunching scrape of dirt under its talons. Its feet shook the ground as it adjusted its footing. I opened my eyes, suddenly face to face with one of its massive eyes, and scooted back with a whimper. Its oblong pupil tightened into a pin line of black in a sea of gold. It rolled its neck, curling back and opening its jaw with a gritty growl. The Taegorak's massive nostrils flared as it took in several huffs of air. It leaned its head back down, its sucking breath shredding free the loose curls of my papery skin. The Taegorak snorted at me, shaking its massive head, and lumbered away.

Slowly, I stood on shaky legs I couldn't quite feel anymore. Then, running my fingers over the papery shell that should have been my skin, the realization hit that I had become one of the husk creatures. It didn't matter; I was still alive. There had to be some way to fix this if this crinkling form could just get me home.

My body wobbled on unfeeling legs towards the village. My breaths no longer rasped in the empty cavity of my chest. The aching was gone. *All* feeling was gone.

I reached the place where the grass met the edge of the village road, still hoping this was some horrible nightmare. Yes, of course, that is what it was. I would wake up any moment now and Michael would make fun of me for having such a dream spun from children's stories.

I stepped forward and then tumbled to my numb knees, my paper skin crunching as they hit the ground. I shook my head and checked if there was damage to this frail form, but there was no easy way to tell with how this body coiled in papery shreds. My form struggled to stand, to find my feet. I tried again to take that last desperately needed step towards home, only to slide to the ground again.

I reached toward the road, and my hand met something solid I couldn't feel. A barrier kept me from going forward. I tried to speak, to scream, but whatever makes a person capable of doing so, I didn't have anymore. No sound came from me except the rustling of my limbs as I frantically probed the air, trying to find a way to slip through this invisible barrier. I wanted to cry, but no tears could come.

The Keeper. Keeper had to know how to help me. He knew what would happen to the others. He had to know how to fix this. I wobbled back towards the grove. It just had to work. I pushed past the creatures that were now odd kin to me and climbed back to the groupings of trees where Keep's grove was.

Reaching the grove with its floating mirrors reflecting the pine needles, leaves, and the night sky, it was so much darker. A few still held images of otherworldly things, but it was as if the grove was falling asleep with what pictures were there slowly fading into reflections of the here. I needed to get the Keeper's attention, but how without a voice? I grabbed the edge of a mirror and thrust it down. It shattered spectacularly loud. I looked into the shadows where Keeper had come from, but not even a breeze stirred in the grove. It didn't come. It never came.

I returned to the barrier many more times in the coming days and years but never could get through. Eventually, I realized it was because the same act that saved my life had trapped me here. As the legends said, my humanity was traded for my life, so there was no way to return to the human world.

I'm almost out of time now. My memories are the last piece of me that remains, and they are slipping away more and more. I can never go back to tell my family what happened—never explain to my parents why they woke up that next morning with no sons. You are my last chance. If you ever find yourself in Gethway, find a fletcher named Wendel. See if he and his wife Addie are well. If you can, help them have a measure of peace.

And if you are in another realm and can't go, please remember for me. Keep this story so that some part of us who died in the grove can survive. And, if you ever think to tempt the truth of your old children's stories for yourself, be wary. They might just turn out to be true.

ONE'S TRUE SELF
BY RYAN GALE

Ryan is a born and bred Central Floridian who likes neither Disney nor the beach. His hobbies include thinking about writing while staring at a blank page, owning more books than his bedroom could possibly store, and helping to care for 4 cats that he's fairly certain are plotting against him. Hoping to actually finish more stories in the future.

* * *

Everyone who knew him knew two things about Prel Verco: he was always up to no good, and he *always* came out ahead. There was no explanation for how such a dirty, rotten, yet physically-unimposing man could have such great luck, while so many of the people who crossed his path didn't. Of course, if you asked him, luck had nothing to do with it—just ruthlessness, ingenuity, and an irrepressible will to survive. There wasn't a dirty trick he wouldn't stoop to using, a trusted colleague he wouldn't sacrifice, or an opening—no matter how brief—that he wouldn't exploit. His enemies had all too often underestimated to their detriment just how tenacious he could be when it came to survival, and thus the list of those willing to challenge him grew shorter and shorter.

Naturally, no one dared to ask him about it, though, and all manner of myths and rumors had sprung up regarding him. Even now, in semi-retirement, the tales grew taller and taller. Not that that particularly bothered him. After all, he found it far easier to live his life how he pleased when people simply stayed out of his way.

Such was the case tonight as he strode down the streets of Tremela, a city he was loathe to visit on most occasions. Tonight, though, his presence was required.

As he walked, the few people that were out in the streets cleared his path like he had the spitting plague, eyeing him uncomfortably, though this wasn't necessarily due to his own notoriety. The people of this city had a superstitious streak a mile long; anyone who went out after nightfall did so fully hooded to hide their faces, and on moonless nights they didn't go out at all, staying at home in their brightly-lit dwellings as if the darkness itself was out to get them. All this superstition had to do with some witches or sorcerers or whatever a long time ago; Prel didn't know exactly, nor did he care enough to find out. All he knew was that the original reason had morphed over the centuries into a general superstition about showing your face in moonlight, taking the form of a common local proverb: moonlight reveals one's true self. Whatever the story was, the people of Tremela took it immensely seriously.

Not Prel Verco, though, far from it. He walked the streets with his face visible and uncovered for all to see, taking great pleasure in flouting that practice, for apart from not being a superstitious man, he had nothing to hide. He was exactly who everyone said he was—a scoundrel, a thief, a greedy, rotten person through and through, and he was proud of it. He didn't look like much at first, but with his attitude, he might as well have been ten feet tall. Since he had largely gotten out of the crime business, some might say he had mellowed somewhat, but he nonetheless wore his true self on his sleeve with vigor and dared anyone to do anything about it.

In the course of his . . . misadventures, Prel had accumulated a fair few treasures, valuables from all across the known world that had found their way into his personal collection in one way or another. The crown jewel of that collection, though, was the Ardel Parure: a set of jewelry made for some long dead noble comprising a crown, ring, neck-lace, brooch, and bracelet. What made these items so special were the jewels used in their construction: placed under light, the gleam that emanated from the gems was intoxicating in its beauty. Their vibrancy peaked when under moonlight. Prel had been obsessed with collecting the full set since he first laid his eyes upon the necklace as a boy and would do anything to do so. After many years of hard searching and 'acquiring', he had nearly succeeded. There was just one piece left to find . . . which was how he had ended up in this deranged town.

The lean man sauntered his way down the street in the soft moon-light, in search of one specific alleyway. Through the usual methods of secret letters, he'd arranged to meet a seller who claimed to possess the final piece of the Ardel Parure that his collection lacked—the neck-lace. Who this person was, he couldn't actually say; he didn't have a name or a face, barely any information at all to go off. All he did know was that their wares did not come cheap.

In a way, this anonymity worried him less than it would most crimi-nals—any serious player in the stolen goods market would make their identity known so the client would know they were professionals and could be trusted to have the goods in question. More than likely, whoever was going through all this trouble was just some amateur who was looking to make some quick coin and wasn't looking for trouble, which meant easy pickings for an experienced crook like him if it came down to it (and with him, it very often did). Most other criminals would be likewise concerned that such a shadowy figure might be a rival out to do them in, but at this point in his career pretty much everyone who wanted Prel dead was dead themselves, most by his own hand.

That said, he didn't typically deal with complete unknowns—most proved to be unreliable at best–but the temptation to finally complete the set that had bedeviled him so was simply too great to pass up. He hadn't spent nearly his entire adult life—45 long, grueling years full of close calls, narrow escapes, and clever trickery—searching for the pieces to let the one that had gotten away elude him again over silly over-cautiousness. After all, he wasn't throwing caution completely to the wind.

Finding the right alley at last, he paused, eyes searching every nook and cranny for potential danger. The only door was shut and there weren't any windows for easy access, so he edged his way past on the opposite side, on the off chance there was someone waiting for him behind it. Otherwise the alleyway was clear of hiding places for traps or lurking foes, and he breathed easier, straightening himself back up.

At the end of the alley stood his elusive associate, leaning against the wall in the shadow of an overhang, and so he approached cautiously. They wore the same large hood and face scarf as all the others, obscuring their face near completely, but didn't shy away as he approached despite his bare face, as if they expected him. In one hand they carried a scroll, the agreed upon identifier. Only a pair of violet eyes peered out at him, looking him up and down with curious interest before looking away.

'A peculiar shade, violet . . . ' Prel thought to himself. 'Don't see that too often.'

"Nice night out, don't you think?" The stranger didn't make eye contact, instead eying the opposite wall. Their voice was unfamiliar, a thin male voice that could have been mistaken for the wind.

"Let's cut the small talk. You and I both know what we're here for. Show me the necklace."

"Oh, I don't have it with me," the stranger said lightly. "That would be very foolish of me."

"Then how do I know you have it at all?" Prel's hand crept down to the dagger he kept on his belt. His patience was wearing thin.

The stranger just laughed. "Do you really think I'd be dumb enough to go to all this trouble, make such a specific claim, risk upsetting someone of your reputation, and not have the item in question? I don't take you for a fool, sir. Please don't take me for one."

Prel grumbled angrily to himself at this, but said nothing. The man's self-assured behavior unsettled him; he didn't like people acting like his equal. It gave them dangerous ideas. But he had a valid point and Prel was inclined to believe him.

"Alright," he responded hesitantly. "Where is it then?"

"At my home, outside the walls. Once I have my pay, I'll take you there."

Prel shook his head. "No deal, I ain't going anywhere with you." It was the oldest trick in the book, one only an amateur would use. Smarter men had tried cleverer ploys on him in the past; that that he'd killed them all may have made him confident, but not stupid.

"And I know better than to let you near it before I get my payment. It isn't as if you haven't resorted to cut-and-run tactics in the past, after all."

True as the accusation may have been, Prel seethed silently. The thought had occurred to him, of course, but it seemed his foe was one step ahead of him—for now.

"Well, it appears that we're at an impasse then. You have a pleasant night, Mr. Verco." The hooded stranger strode past Prel, nodding curtly as he went.

"Wait." He wasn't about to let him walk away and be forced to start the search anew. Prel reached out and placed his hand on the man's shoulder, while with the other he reached to his belt and removed one of two bags full of small diamonds. He turned reluctantly and held the bag out for the man to see.

"Half now, half when I have the necklace. Final offer." *And a knife in the back if you so much as think about crossing me...*

His erstwhile business partner took the bag, peered inside for a moment, then jerked his head. "Follow me."

He trailed the stranger at a distance as he led him through more dark alleys towards the city walls; he wasn't comfortable being led around like this, so he kept a constant eye on them.

"So, how do you come to own such a valuable artifact, anyway?" he asked, trying to not seem too curious.

He was very curious, though; there was no doubt about that. The necklace had been a particularly vexatious item for him, as he'd had only one chance in the past to acquire it when he was much younger, and he had nearly succeeded. But the owners at the time, a husband and wife whose names he'd long since forgotten, had complicated matters, forcing him to beat a hasty, messy retreat with blood on his hands but no necklace to show for it. Though he had left no witnesses to identify him, it was nevertheless an invisible blemish on a criminal career full of successes, and even though he'd long since forgotten most of what happened, that failure still lingered at the fringes of his mind, forever taunting him. Since then, the piece had dropped out of sight completely, try as he might to hunt it down again.

"Do you answer people when they ask for your secrets?" the hooded man asked without looking back. "Several people had to die for me to get my hands upon it. Let's leave it at that."

Prel inquired no further. As irritating as such an answer was to him, he couldn't deny that, had the roles been reversed, he would have said the same thing. They wanted to be evasive? So be it.

From that point on, they traveled in silence, neither man having anything more worth saying to the other.

They snuck past the city guards via a secret sally port and crept along the wall to the main road heading away from the town into the surrounding farmland. To anyone watching, the two men would have made for an intriguing study in contrast—one man tall and self-confident, striding down the middle of the road, bathed in the bright moonlight without a care in the world, and the other small and hunched, sticking to the shadows.

After an interminably long walk, the pair arrived at a dark farmhouse. The curtains were drawn and a calm quiet hung over the place, the sounds of the night eerily absent. No wildlife could be seen or heard, and the tree line nearby stood thick and foreboding. The stranger unlocked the front door with a key drawn from within his cloak and they entered. The fire in the fireplace was still burning dimly, its embers barely clinging to life.

Once inside, the stranger put a few logs on the sputtering fire then bent over to warm himself. He threw back his hood and undid his scarf, taking a deep breath. He gestured for Prel to join him but Prel ignored him, instead pacing the floor like a caged animal. He was already on edge, having traveled this far from the meeting point, and while his 'business partner' hadn't tried anything yet, he still by no means trusted him. His gaze flicked from door to door and window to window, ready to jump at the first sign of trouble.

Out of curiosity he snuck a glance at the stranger, scrying his face for clues to his identity. He was middle-aged, unkempt, and had a long, thin face with hollowed cheeks. All told, he was utterly unremarkable, and yet something about his eyes seemed vaguely familiar. . . . Before he could remember any more, though, the recognition was gone again, and so Prel forced his mind back to the subject at hand.

"Alright, where is it already?" he demanded impatiently, tired of the charade.

The man just shook his head. Expelling a sigh, he got back to his feet and pointed to a door down the hall.

"Right in there." He crossed to unlock and open it; keeping his distance, Prel followed behind, peering in over the man's shoulder.

At the far side of the room, under a wide window bordered by open curtains, stood a small table. Sitting on top, perfectly positioned in a pool of bright moonlight, was the necklace, prominent inside a small wooden box.

The sight of the beautiful piece of jewelry, its emeralds sparkling gently in the candlelight, was absolutely intoxicating. Prel could barely contain himself. It was more beautiful than he had remembered it being, and yet the sensation he felt watching the light dance off it was just as incredible as he remembered. He was so close to finally achieving his life's mission. All he had to do, all he wanted to do, was go forth and take it at last.

Nonetheless, he still smelled a rat. He looked over at his companion and jerked his head towards the necklace.

"Alright, go and get it then. I ain't paying this much to play fetch."

The stranger shrugged and walked over to the table; Prel watched his every move, checking for any subtle sign of a trap laying in wait. He saw nothing though, so while his business partner's back was turned, he pulled his dagger and made his move, rushing as stealthily as possible across the floor, determined to run him through before he had to chance to react. There was no reason he should have to pay some rookie for something so precious if he was gonna turn his back to him like that, after all.

He was nearly across the room when he heard a sharp CRACK! Prel instinctively ducked, but he had barely moved when the floor beneath him disappeared. On his way down he thought he caught a laugh from the man, who hadn't even turned to see what had happened. Prel felt weightless for a moment before the ground rose to meet him. There was a surge of immense pain, then . . . blackness.

Prel awoke in a world of hurt. His vision drifted in and out of focus, his head pounded something awful, and his face was damp with what could only be his own blood; reaching up to wipe it off, he felt a sharp pain from what was likely a cracked rib, maybe worse. He tried to stand, but immediately collapsed when his leg gave out from under him, the pain nearly causing him to black out again. Looking up, he could see the hole he fell through perhaps twenty-five feet up; a trap-door hatch that hung from the opening swung gently. The face of the stranger appeared as he looked down upon his fallen foe.

The man's face shone faintly blue as moonlight played across it. Prel summoned the strength to unleash a tirade of curses upon him, but the words stuck in his throat as the stranger's face began to blur and shimmer. Prel wondered if it was his head injury or a trick of the light, but soon it was indisputable that this was no trick.

Looking down at him now wasn't a meek, shallow-faced man anymore but a young woman with long black hair and sharp, elegant features. The only thing that remained the same were those bright, violet eyes. He realized suddenly where he had seen those eyes before: they were the exact same as those of the woman who'd owned the necklace all those years ago, and there the spark of recognition burst into flame as it all came rushing back to him.

"No . . . you . . . you're dead," he croaked, shaking his head in disbelief. If Prel Verco had believed in ghosts, he would have been terrified.

The young woman smiled wickedly. "Yes, that's a very easy mistake to make. My mother and I share a striking resemblance, wouldn't you say?"

Her mother. . . . A chill ran through him.

"It's funny how superstitions and traditions can grow from distorted memories. The magic users of old here were masters of illusion and deception, light and shadow . . . except moonlight, which rendered them powerless, hence why they would hide their faces at night. Fortunately, the old ways didn't die out completely, and from them I learned a trick or two, as you can see. And what better place to put such skills to use? It took years for me to find your weakness, figure out the proper lure for the trap, but once I found it, everything else just fell right into place."

She disappeared for a moment before returning, holding the necklace for him to see. It looked even more stunning in the moonlight, the emeralds glittering so brightly and clearly; Prel momentarily reached for it without thinking before the pain brought him back to his senses.

"My parents thought this was just a lovely necklace, but apparently to you it was something worth killing for," she said, her voice as cold as a winter's night. "I hope it was worth dying for, too."

"I've survived worse," Prel called out defiantly.

The girl just smiled and scoffed. "If I'm feeling charitable, I might come by to check on you in a few days, if you last that long." With that, she took one last look at him before pulling the hatch back up and barring it shut, leaving Prel in near-total darkness.

As his eyes adjusted to the inky blackness, the injured man considered his options. As hurt as he was, he was confident it wasn't serious enough to kill him, not quickly, at least. What's more, as deep as the hole was, from the looks of the walls there appeared to be rocks and crevices that he figured he might just be able to use to climb back up. Already he could feel his leg hurting slightly less than before; if he allowed himself a little recovery time and was careful, he'd be out of there in no time at all. Once he was, he'd allow nothing or no one else to stop him from finally seizing his prize.

'Oh, I'll teach her not to mess with me alright, last thing she'll ever learn...'

Struggling to his feet, he felt around for handholds before he heard something that froze him in place. A soft whispering seemed to be coming from the walls themselves. Turning to look, he soon wished he hadn't. All around him, the shadows had come alive, moving and shifting in concert, and they were closing in on him. Desperately he threw caution to the wind, grabbing for whatever holds he could reach, but to no avail; one hand slipped, his leg gave out, and he fell back into the swirling shadows beneath him. As the darkness closed in on him, it dawned on him that, at long last, his luck had run out.

LEGITIMACY

BY JESS MONNIER

Jess could be living in Nebraska, California, or Japan, depending on where the Air Force takes her, her husband, and her dog, Dizzy. She loves reading and writing fantasy, science fiction, and blends of the two, and has wanted to be an author since she was twelve years old. On any given day, though, you're more likely to find her playing board games with her husband and friends than writing, which is perhaps why it has taken so long for her to get published.

* * *

Wris studies the crowd that surrounds their procession, her stomach in knots, the rhythm of the march carrying her forward. Between the guards around her, the rain of flowers thrown by cheering citizens, and the aura haze generated by the press of so many people, Wris can't make out the details of any one person, but still her stare rakes the throng. She catches occasional glimpses of dark aura pits dragging at the brighter haze, but there are too many bodies jostling all around her to pinpoint their source.

Motion and the heat of someone's touch at her elbow send Wris nearly out of her skin, but it's just her guard Eba, grinning and gesturing toward her hair. Wris reaches up into her cloud of curls until her fingertips brush against the stem of a flower; it must have landed on her and gotten caught, and she's been so distracted she didn't even feel it.

She pulls the flower free, her stare catching on the soft pink petals. She should make light of it, but with her heart pounding against her ribs and her palms sweating, she can't find the levity or the words. The flower falls from her fingers to be crushed under the tread of the procession and she returns her sweeping gaze to the crowd.

There—another aura pit pulling at the bright swirl around it. Wris draws in a measured breath, squinting through the aura haze. It would take incredibly dark thoughts to weigh down the blur of auras made light by celebration. Could it be someone loyal to the usurpers?

Eba's voice cuts through the background roar and her concentration: "Is something wrong?" Wris's focus shatters, but it doesn't matter; the march of the procession has already carried her too far to make anyone out in the crowd. She lets out a sharp breath and turns to meet Eba's concerned look. "Are you okay?" the guard asks.

Wris nods and plasters on a smile to hide her anxious swallow. "Thought I saw something." She nearly has to shout to be heard above the crowd.

The slight pinch between Eba's eyes and the softness of her smile say that she sees right through Wris's facade, but she only gives a shallow nod and turns her gaze forward again. Wris's stare follows hers unbidden, drawn to the imposing monolith of the palace: black clay brick topped by three brilliant copper domes. The procession marches inexorably toward it, beaming faces looking at it with pride, but Wris's gaze skitters away. She starts to scan the crowd again, but it's useless. If she's honest, she knows she can't pin the shapeless fear throttling her chest on potential assassins in the crowd. Instead she peers through the guards, seeking comfort or at least purpose in the sight of Kaya, but finds only fleeting glimpses of her back through their swaying, clinking ranks.

A mistake. There's nothing to see but flashes of the ceremonial garb of the Incarnacy. Back in this city after so many years, and without the anchor of Kaya's familiar face, those ceremonials bring nightmare memories roaring back. A bed soaked in blood; strained, dying breaths. Before that, her mother's whispered pleas as she closed Wris into a wardrobe:

Don't make a sound, love, just stay here, don't move, hush now—

The procession passes out of the main thoroughfare and into the courtyard fronting the palace, carrying Wris onto the grounds. The courtyard that once welcomed her home now yawns open like an abyss, dragging her forward.

Don't make me do this, don't hurt me, I'm with child, I've done nothing to you, please—

The palace doors swallow the front of the procession—two rows, five people deep, of Kaya's guards, then Kaya with more guards flanking and following her—and then it is Wris's turn to take her first step into the palace in more than sixteen years.

Her mother's voice fades. She is not here. Even if she has reincarnated by now, the likelihood that she'd be born into a life that would lead her back here is miniscule—and truthfully, Wris is not actually sure she would recognize Mama's reincarnated aura if she saw it.

The procession stops before the thrones that still stand proud at the far end of the grand reception hall. They have an audience interspersed between the columns lining either side of the room: rebels who swept the palace in the night. Did the usurpers who ruled the last sixteen years feel the same fear that Wris did the night her childhood was taken from her?

It's not a comforting thought.

The Incarnate's Guard parts before the thrones, leaving Kaya standing across from three of the usurpers and the guards that ensure they remain kneeling, heads bowed before the rightful Incarnate. Well, soon-to-be. Probably.

Wris shifts, running her sticky palms across the linen over her thighs. The ornate ceremonial shawl marking her as Awakener, the highest Auramancer position in the Incarnacy, feels heavier in this place. It isn't the one her maman wore; even if they had thought to take it when they fled that night, it would have been torn and bloodied beyond repair by the wounds that killed her. Wearing it has felt awkward or ostentatious before, but here in the palace where her maman fulfilled the role of Awakener far better than Wris ever could—this is the first time it has felt utterly wrong.

Ahead of her, Kaya stands straight-backed and dignified as she regards the usurpers awaiting her justice. She has grown into her role with such grace. Sixteen years old is at least four years too soon to be burdened with Awakening, but with both Incarnates killed in the insurrection, she's expected to Awaken and step into the role of Ascendent Incarnate all at once, and as soon as possible now that the palace is secure.

Kaya's aura brings both truth and lie to her confident posture. There's a flicker to its edges that shows her nerves, her doubt—but it is also anchored solidly at her core, the sheen of determination lending her almost a glow.

"You have ruled with stolen power for sixteen years," Kaya says, the room's acoustics adding resonance to her voice. "Today your tyranny comes to an end. It is my people who have suffered the most beneath your fist, and my people who will judge you." Her tone shifts minutely as she addresses the guards. "Keep them secure until the trial is arranged."

The guard in the center nods and reaches down; she and the guard on the prisoner's other side yank him to his feet. The usurper staggers slightly on his way up. He looks to be only just beyond his prime, and far from frail. The other guards follow suit with the remaining prisoners and file them toward a side door. Each of the prisoners struggles to match pace to a different degree, but they shuffle along, auras clinging to them like a tight, dim film. They've had practice masking their auras—and Wris not enough practice picking up these sorts of details.

Kaya gestures for someone to approach, and Commander Asongo crosses toward her from the side opposite where the prisoners exited. He stops in front of her, bowing his head and touching the knuckles of his fists together at waist level until she releases him with another gesture. "How may I serve you?" he asks.

"How many were killed or wounded last night? On both sides."

"We had one severe wound, and two of their staff were killed in the struggle," the commander answers. "Some other minor wounds, but nothing requiring extensive attention from a physician."

Relief washes through Wris. Only two deaths; she'd feared there would be more.

"Treat the dead respectfully and deliver them to their families," Kaya says. "They will be allowed an audience with me after the Ascension, should they wish it; I will consider their grievances and consult the wisdom of the Incarnacy."

"Yes, Our Wisdom," Commander Asongo says, bowing his head again and obeying the dismissal in her tone.

The title creates a tension in Kaya's shoulders that Wris wouldn't notice if she didn't know her so well. That hint of doubt amplifies Wris's own. The young woman takes to her role with such ease, though; surely that is evidence that she truly bears a soul of the Incarnacy. Today, in particular, she fully looks the part. Wris forces herself to take in the gilded ceremonial shawl and skirt over Kaya's linen dress and the Incarnal headdress that complements her intricate braids, separating this image from the memories that nearly paralyzed her minutes ago. Unease still writhes along her spine, but she takes in the regal air Kaya projects and uses it to smother her uncertainty.

Once Commander Asongo disappears through a side door, Kaya turns to Musambe. "I would meet with my advisors. Please arrange it."

"Of course, Incarnate," Musambe says. "I will have them gather in the council chamber in an hour. Until then, I suggest you retire to your suite to rest and prepare."

Kaya doesn't move, hesitation in her posture.

"Ah." Musambe gives her a fatherly smile. "Of course. You don't know the way. Awakener Okoru, can you show the Incarnate to her suite?"

Wris's breath stutters in her throat, her last memory of the Incarnal suites flashing against the darkness of a blink. She opens her mouth, hesitates. "I'm not sure I remember the way," she lies. "I was four when . . ."

"That's right," Musambe says without missing a beat. He turns and touches Kaya's elbow. "I will gladly guide you myself." Wris suspects he saw straight through her lie to her distress; at any rate, he doesn't suggest that she follow.

Which leaves her standing in the receiving hall as it slowly empties, members of Kaya's court filtering out to begin the tasks that will characterize their new normal.

Wris should go. Do something. Ask after her new room. Find something to drink. But she doesn't move for long moments, until finally Eba clears her throat. "Awakener Okoru?" Eba asks, her concerned gaze so maternal that Wris's gut twists.

But gravity pulls her stare away from the guard, back in the direction of the Incarnal suites.

"Wris," Eba says, and the familiarity of it wrenches something loose within her. The older woman's hand finds Wris's elbow and guides her away from the center of the throne room toward the relative privacy of one of the ornate pillars along the side. Wris blinks away heat only to find it trailing down her cheeks. "It's hard, being back here." Eba's voice is gentle and knowing. "I should have thought. Both of your parents . . . "

Wris nods, more warmth spilling down her cheeks, but she can't meet Eba's stare because it's so much more than that.

She needs to go back to that place, but she's not strong enough. Reliving her maman's death might break her, but it's the only way she can think to be sure. She found Kaya following distant memories of that night, and she hasn't been able to stop the questions since.

She suspects—knows—that she will find answers in that room, but she can't force her feet to carry her there. So she takes a deep, shuddering breath and turns toward the gardens instead, shooting a fragile smile at Eba that she hopes will paint the lie she wants to project, wishes were true: that she has gathered herself after a moment of weakness. That everything is fine.

* * *

THERE IS no comfort to be found in the gardens. Maybe one day memories of playing hide and seek with her mother or plucking a bouquet for her maman will be a balm to her grief, but right now, with the setting sun casting twisting shadows through the leaves and guilt squeezing at her heart, Wris can hardly breathe.

Eba follows like Wris's own shadow. She tried to dismiss her—"The palace is ours now, I'll be safe"—but the guard would hear none of it. Her presence isn't obtrusive, and in truth Wris forgets she is there half the time. The other half, her frustration is misdirected and pale compared to the dread suffusing her body.

Finally, the overwhelming perfume of the flowers beginning to raise bile in Wris's throat, she can take it no longer. She has momentum now, and the Incarnal suite should be empty while Kaya meets with her advisors. Wris strides out of the gardens, following the pull of that cursed room; sometime in the last hour, it planted a hook beneath her diaphragm, and now it draws her inexorably forward.

The murals covering the walls leading into and throughout the suites fascinated her once, but now they blur as she passes. The relief work writhes with shadows that defy the steady glow of the gas lamps set into the walls at even intervals. Her mind playing tricks; she ignores it and plows forward, attention straight ahead.

A warm grip slips around her upper arm and Wris jumps, a startled cry bolting from her lips as momentum swings her around to face Eba. "What are you doing?" Eba asks, concern and confusion mingling with the faintest hint of accusation in her voice.

"I—I have to see it," Wris says, hoarse.

"See what?"

"Where they died," she whispers.

Eba hesitates, eyes glinting as she studies Wris's face. "Are you sure —" But Wris clenches her jaw, her brow knitting together. Eba watches her a moment longer before nodding. "In the Incarnal suites?"

"Incarnate AvCet's bedchamber." The words come out small, like a child's voice, and Wris swallows hard and gropes for the impossibility of control and release. She is spiraling, caught like driftwood in a whirlpool, but she can't fight it. She needs the answers she'll find once she's swallowed.

Eba nods sharply. "Come, then." She turns, taking the lead, and Wris finds that there's comfort in following rather than making her own way. Eba greets the guards at the entrance to the Incarnal suites, exchanges words that slip through Wris's focus, and then they are past the doors and moving toward the bedchamber at the western end of the suites. There, Eba once again handles the exchange with the guards. Wris knows their names, but can't summon them right now. An image of the shorter of the pair playing with a giggling daughter springs through her mind and then vanishes, pushed out by the enormity of being steps away from the stage on which her worst nightmares played out.

Wris's stare falls to the floor as they open the doors. "I'll be right outside," Eba says. That she doesn't need to barter for privacy should be a relief, but Wris has no space for anything under the oppressive crush of fear, doubt, and grief. She steps across the threshold and waits until she hears the doors shut before lifting her gaze.

The bruised sunset sky, cut up and distorted by the elaborate glasswork of the balcony doors, dominates the room. Phantom movement jerks Wris's attention to the right, but it is just the long shadow cast by the bed.

It isn't the same bed, but she can see it all the same. The Incarnate, his dying breaths wheezing through the room. Her maman—Oma—heaved onto her side beside him with one of his hands grasped between both of her own.

Wris sinks to her knees at the foot of the bed, burying her forehead against the edge of the mattress. Her breaths shake and struggle through her throat, her face heats, but she does not cry. Against the dark of her eyelids, she relives that horrible memory:

It was dark, lit by a wavering lantern in the hands of a frantic chamberlain, but not dark enough to disguise the stain of blood over Oma's side and stomach. "I've brought your daughter," someone said. "The other Auramancers are—are dead. They . . . killed them all. Even the children. But I found little Wris in the wardrobe . . . but your wife . . ."

Oma looked at Wris, a pained expression tightening her face. She released the Incarnate's hand long enough to weakly wave her over. The comforting weight of someone's touch left Wris's back, instead pulling her away from where she clung to a familiar leg, then lifting her and helping her to crawl into the hollow between Oma and the Incarnate.

It was wet, and smelled bad, but then Oma's arms were around Wris, her hands once again clasping the Incarnate's. "Pay attention, little one," Oma croaked weakly. "Remember your exercises." She swallowed, heaved a breath, and then rattled onward. "Follow my aura to the Incarnate. Drift. Drift."

Terror made everything sharp. Wris couldn't fall into her exercises. Instead, she noticed how weak the Incarnate's aura was, how it seemed to be trailing away. And Oma's—hers felt wrong, too. Thin, drawn out.

Oma was doing . . . something. Wris wasn't sure what. Her aura twined with the Incarnate's and flowed—or no, it trickled—toward . . . somewhere. Wris tried to follow. It helped, in a weird way; solving a puzzle instead of remembering—

Her breath hitched and she focused on Oma's aura.

Even as they faded, the auras moved with purpose, wound together. It was weird, not like walking or riding a horse, and the timing was all off, but it felt like they traveled somewhere *far*. She followed their auras a long way, her own all stretched out to reach.

She didn't recognize it at the time; it wasn't until she was ten that she put words to what happened. But Oma's aura guided the Incarnate's to one of two seeds of life. Twins, still nestled in a stranger's womb. And then the connection Wris had followed snapped, yanking her back to that bloody bed, where Oma and the Incarnate were both still and the world stank of death. She turned to shake her maman, confused, growing increasingly frantic, until a familiar woman tried to pull her away and her silent tears turned to shrieks and sobs.

Now, she rocks against the bed, her crying muffled but for sharp, irregular sniffles and gasps. The memory doesn't fade; Wris still feels its grip tight around her, suffocating, but slowly she adjusts to the pressure. To the new shape imposed on her aura by its weight.

It's worse than the memory of the most terrible night of her life. That would be bad enough, but on top of that, it's a decade of insecurity and worry realized.

Being here again, it is impossibly clear: Kaya isn't the Incarnate at all. Two souls sought out those twin seeds of life that night. The familiarity of Kaya's soul is not, has never been, that of the Incarnate.

It is that of Wris's maman.

* * *

WRIS STARTS at the sound of the Eba's voice in the hall. The words are muffled, but it sounds like Kaya is back. Wris bolts upright and wipes the tears from her face just before the door opens, Kaya's voice preceding her: "It's alright, give us some time."

She's backlit by the lamps in the hall, but Wris can just make out Kaya's expression: a weary smile that gives way to confusion, then concern. Kaya shuts the door behind her. "Why are you in the dark?" she asks as she fumbles with the lamp affixed to the wall.

Wris glances toward the balcony doors, where the last vestiges of daylight have gone. The moon looks strange through the whorls in the glass.

The bloom of light from the lamp draws Wris's gaze back toward Kaya, who meets her stare with concern pinching her brow. That dear, familiar face. Wris shifts her perception, studying Kaya's aura with new eyes. Oma. How could she have missed it?

"Wris?"

The words climb Wris's throat, jumble in her mouth: *I was wrong. You're not the Incarnate. You're my maman—I missed you—what do we do?*

But she doesn't say anything. How is she supposed to break this to Kaya? She needs to know—of course she does—but this will upend her whole world. It will dredge up Kaya's own worst memories: her twin sister on the ground, throat painting the floor red, killed by a father so loyal to the usurpers that he would rather both his daughters die than risk the return of the Cet Incarnacy. They barely stopped him from killing Kaya, too.

Kaya breathes a soft sigh and walks to the bedside table, pouring a glass of water from a pitcher there that Wris hadn't even noticed. "Come sit outside with me and have some water," she says, gesturing toward the balcony. "You can talk about it if you want to, or we can just sit."

Wris hesitates a moment longer, pulling her perception out of her Auramantic sense, and then finally nods. "Thank you," she whispers before she heads for the balcony. She pauses with her fingers on the handle, a memory flitting through her mind: sitting with Oma and Incarnate AvCet on the balcony, belly full from lunch, laughing as she beat the Incarnate at marbles.

She lets out a shaky breath and finally turns the handle, stepping out into the moonlight. Kaya's footsteps sound behind her as she follows. It's the same table and chairs on the balcony, and the same view of the Cet skyline, though she has only ever seen it in daylight before. Distant sounds of celebration drift up from the city below, citizens still reveling in the triumphant return of the Cet Incarnacy.

Except that's a lie. The Incarnacy really is gone, and they have no better claim to this place than the usurpers did.

Kaya presses the glass of water into her hands and gently draws her toward one of the chairs to sit. Once Wris sits and takes a sip of water, Kaya pulls a chair next to hers and sits down too. "Eba mentioned . . . what happened here," she says. "I'm here if you want to talk about it."

Wris remembers her maman gently waiting her out when she was upset. *We'll talk when you're ready*. A hysterical sound escapes her throat, something not quite laugh but not quite sob. If—when—she tells Kaya . . .

Will she be disappointed?

No. No, it doesn't matter if she will be disappointed, or angry, or afraid. She has to know. They have to figure this out. Cet's future hangs on what they do next.

So Wris sucks in a deep, shuddering breath and looks at Kaya. Gathers her words, and the strength to say them. "You died here," she begins. "I had to come back here to really remember."

By the light of the moon, her voice pitched soft, Wris tells Kaya the truth of who she is.

THE SWORD IN THE SLATE GARDEN
BY MICHAEL A. EPANCHIN

Michael has loved writing fantasy and science fiction all his life, the stranger the better. In addition to writing and reading, he loves cooking, history, politics, and games of all kinds. He's a historian and teacher living in Northwest Georgia with his lovely wife and three children.

* * *

Restralia dreams of home sometimes. At least, she thinks it's home. The place in her dreams feels like how home ought to. It's warm and soft, without loneliness or hunger or confusion. It is, though, some-place else. Somewhere apart from here and now.

This place is sharp and cold, with splintered wood and dripping dew, with insects buzzing around her scaly flesh and shrill fowl chirping in the remote hours of the day. Most times it was hard waking from a dream of home but at least she did so in the comfort of the night.

It's so bright now. Why would she be awake at such a late hour? She writhes uncomfortably on her bed of leaves and twigs, only partially shaded from the worst of the morning sun.

"Mortimer," she murmurs. "Come here, Mortimer."

Silence. Mortimer must be asleep still. Just look how late it is. The sun is nearly overhead. "Lazy, bitter bird," she mutters. "In the times I most need him, why must I find myself alone? He'll hear of this later."

She forces herself to sit, lumbering then to her feet, unfolding, stretching, until she can nearly reach into the higher boughs of a nearby tree. She needs more sleep and her head hurts. The grove is still and quiet, but bathed in unwelcome light piercing down from above. Her eye finds that ancient slab of slate, still in shadow, still bare. Something about it stirs a cold anger. She cannot remember or understand why. All she knows is that the stone ought not to be bare.

But as her senses stir, she realizes that it is the air that forces her to wake. It is different today, filled with a strange smell. Strange but familiar, touching upon distant memories she can no longer reach.

"There's a man here," she says, an incredulity in her voice. "Why is there a man here, Mortimer?" It has been so long, perhaps years. Longer, maybe. But she cannot recall. Time as she understands it spirals around her, twisting and coiling into itself. Sometimes it's as if she chokes on it, and the memory then slips away. She will have to ask Mortimer.

She stretches again and begins her slow trek toward the smell, out into the woods where dappled midday light scratches at her skin, hot and irritating like mosquito bites.

The man is not difficult to find. His smell is loud, acrid smoke and sweating meat, and he is poor at hiding. She soon spots him, crouched amidst the undergrowth that obscures his form. He hides behind a shadowed pile of stones, slate and smooth, watching something distant among deeper trees, a bow poised in his hands. His attention quickly shifts. Like him, her presence is never quiet.

And then he starts to scream.

The arrow that pierces her shoulder, now oozing hot black blood, is stone-tipped and cold. And while the pain of it forces her to clench her jaw and gasp a huge, fetid breath, she is more astonished at the audacity of the man to attack her with no provocation.

She roars. It's a monstrous bellow, carrying far into the forest, where small animals and birds now flee. Her eye is on the hunter, and his skin pales as her gnarled body unfurls. From the hidden places on her back, thin, boneless appendages slither out and form a pale plumage that frames her body.

The man runs, securing a lead on her before she can bring her legs to move.

But he cannot get far. Her steps take time to quicken as her stiff muscles loosen. At her most determined, she is faster than him too. And she knows these woods well, by some old instinct if not by memory.

As she gains on him, she can hear his panting breath and smell the fear in his sweat. One appendage lashes forward, snapping at him like a coiled snake. It is not to kill or to maim, but to frighten. To distract. This is how she hunts, when she must. By now, she knows she has won and will smother him. She cannot remember her prey ever escaping once chased this closely.

But in her cloudy mind, Restralia also knows that she is not cruel. She does not wish to harm him.

She knows something about these creatures, if only barely. They are not like rabbits. They speak to each other, as she speaks with Mortimer. They live together in warrens of their own making, using forest wood and woven reeds. And long ago, so very long ago, perhaps even slate stone. Mortimer once told her that, she thinks, or it was part of a dream.

Her maneuver works. The man yelps as the appendage crashes into a fallen tree just off from his path, and he staggers. His foot catches in a hole hidden beneath a bed of withering and rotting leaves on the wet forest floor. His body twists, but his leg does not, and when he finally lunges forward, Restralia hears the sounds of his fragile body tearing, his shrill cries echoing in the silent woods. She slows as she nears him, her one wide eye, now fully acclimated to the searing daylight, glaring down on him.

"Why did you shoot me, Man?" she says. It has been a long time since she's spoken their tongue, and she isn't sure if her words are correct. But she forms them as best she can.

His face is stricken, reddened and contorted in pain. Through this mask, though, the man appears similar to another one she has seen.

She cannot recall, and it is just the faintest impression that comes to her.

"I asked you a question, Man. Speak, or I will treat you as an enemy."

But Man does not speak to her. And Restralia realizes she has underestimated the pain he must be experiencing.

Her anger drains and she is left feeling hollow and all-too-aware of how weary she is, and of how fragile this small creature is. Were she to leave him here, surely he would die. She reaches to him, grasping his body and lifting it into her arms as if he were a child.

"Mortimer. We have a guest today."

* * *

MAN IS LAYING on the bed of twigs and leaves in the grove, his broken leg now cleaned and splinted, his breathing even and slow as he sleeps. When the gentle touch of moonlight falls on the grove, Mortimer finally wakes, fluttering in with sleepy golden eyes. He glances between Man and Restralia several times before hooting at her.

"He attacked me," Restralia says. "Look!" She points at the arrow wound. Mortimer's eyes narrow and he cocks his head to one side. "Then he fell and broke himself."

Mortimer calls to her, insistent.

"What? No, he is helpless, Mortimer. It is the right thing to do."

Man now writhes in a restless sleep, the discomfort of his leg seeping into his dreams. The sleeping root must be wearing off. His brow is cold with sweat, and he speaks, though she cannot understand his words. Not quite. But the sounds of them linger.

"He seems familiar," she says. "Has a man come recently, Mortimer? It is difficult to remember. Everything is so hazy."

The owl hoots again, his answer vague.

". . . Killed her," Man says, then mumbles, before speaking again, clearly, and now louder. "You killed her."

Restralia tilts her head to watch him sleep. She must have met him before.

But she cannot recall. Here, the nights blend together and time passes in cycles of season and light that merge together like shapes in a mist. What is different from one season to the next, or one night to the next?

But Man does not see time that way. Somehow, this is clear to her, though she cannot say how she knows it. Man and his ilk see time as an arrow, always moving forward, always piercing new thresholds. And they remember.

Restralia wants to remember as Man does, and so she waits.

The moon hangs wide and low, shining a cold light on the grove, when Man wakes. She is drawing in the earth, her appendages absently scratching patterns and images with fallen shards of trees. He takes long minutes to realize where he is. The root will leave him groggy and confused.

"I am not your enemy," Restralia tries to say. She speaks slowly, with utmost care, as if unearthing something delicate and valuable.

Yet Man's response is not as she expects. She expects fear, yet with his jaw clenched, and a vein throbbing on the side of his head, Restralia sees something else.

Mortimer calls to her, as if reading her mind, confirming her suspicion. "Why would he be angry, Mortimer? What have I done?"

"You killed her, demon! You killed my daughter!" He shouts it at her, and his eyes are lined in red, as if he only sees blood.

He looks down, and then something changes and she sees the dirt on his face streaking with water. She remembers crying. She remembers there was a time when she wished she could cry, when she was new to this garden, and the cold kept her quivering through day and night. But that must have been ages ago.

"I killed?" Restralia says, but it doesn't sound right. "Mortimer? I do not remember killing one of these creatures. You know me, my friend. I would not kill if not needed."

The owl calls from above, then flies down into the bare light of the grove, only just visible now, his brow bent and eyes staring imperiously at Restralia. He speaks again.

"A child? I would never!" She turns back to Man. "How dare you accuse me of something so terrible! Tell me this story of yours, Man. I wish to hear it, for I know it is false."

He is silent for too long, and when he finally speaks, his voice is soft and cold. "Demon lies. I saw you in the village that night. I saw you take her. Others did too."

Restralia's legs weaken and she is glad not to be standing. What does Man mean? Why is he accusing her of such things? Does he not know that it hurts to hear?

"Mortimer, is it in the nature of this creature to tell lies? To accuse others of terrible things?"

The owl's voice is soft in reply, soothing now rather than insistent. His own language swells in her mind like the tide, and she feels her anger recede.

Mortimer is correct, she realizes. She can see the signs of that barbarism. A cruelty she had forgotten.

He wears the skin of animals, some who live in this very forest. On parts of Man's body, she sees fur. Elsewhere she notes the pale look of smooth bone, and the ruddy finish of animal hide, supple and shining with polish. It is one thing to eat from the forest to live, and another to wear as ornaments the lives that dwell here.

He wears a talisman too, something of metal that shines like Mortimer's eyes as it catches the watery light. And at his hip, something had been hidden by the cloth and fur that covers him. Now she wonders how she could have missed it.

It is the sword. The one that belongs here. Seeing it feels like a fire catching in the underbrush. She feels its point as if it strikes her.

As if probing at her thoughts, Mortimer calls her attention to it, urging her.

"He is the thief, then," she says, coldly. Her rumbling voice shudders. "He took it from us, then? You're right Mortimer. You're always right."

Perhaps Mortimer is even right about the fate Man deserves.

"It would be easy, Mortimer. I could snap him like a fallen branch and leave him for his people as a warning. Would that do us good, Mortimer?"

Mortimer hoots again, and Restralia's appendages flutter, waiting for release. But she holds them back.

"You are always so wise, Mortimer. But I disagree here. If I kill this thief, the rest of these creatures will come for revenge. They are bitter things, aren't they Mortimer? Short-sighted and proud. You say so yourself."

The owl is silent and she notices Man watching her. He does not seem fearful or angry anymore. "You're right. Others will follow. We always come, demon, to hunt you. We will forever come here to rid your evil of this place."

"Evil?" she says, affronted. "I live in peace in this forest. It was you who attacked me." An appendage gestures to the still-sore wound on her shoulder.

"I speak of my daughter, whom you murdered. When they learn you are alive, they will seek vengeance for Restralia and for me."

The sound of her name is a bell, hollow, deafening in her ears. Her body is numb, and even as Mortimer hoots at her, urging her forward, she merely waves a hand. "Shush Mortimer." She hears the owl's voice as a distant call now, and she ignores him.

She gestures to herself. "Restralia," she says. "That is me."

Man hisses back, his anger darkening. "Do not say her name. You have no right. She is not your trophy!"

She touches her chest again. "I do not remember many things, Man. I remember night and winter, I remember sorrow. And I remember my name. I know myself, and I know that I have not killed any of your people."

Now, Man laughs and it sounds bitter and miserable. "What does it matter? All of this must be some punishment. Some divine joke. How else should you be here, taunting me with her name, when I killed you? I killed you, demon, to take my sword!"

When he pulls it free from the scabbard at his belt, something in her changes. Something wells behind her eye, as if she were to cry. But there can be no tears now.

She stands, and her appendages thrash above her, rustling branches and slamming mace-like mounds of flesh into the ground. Sometimes they act on their own. Man's face changes in an instant.

She reaches, taking Man with one huge hand, and glaring into his now truly fearful eyes. He is like a doll to her.

"That sword belongs in the garden, Man," her voice is like far thunder, rumbling and growing, and her appendages now turn to Man, poised. "I should kill you for stealing it, and leave your broken parts all over the forest. Would that be good, Mortimer? Would we have justice, then?"

Something crashes, splintering. She feels the branches as they bounce from her body. She is so close to doing it. It would take so little effort, just the slightest flinch and it would be over. Even in silence, she can feel the owl's urging presence.

But in Man's misted eyes, she catches the briefest glimpse of a monstrous skull covered in scaly hide, a single giant eye rimmed with red veins, a slack mouth revealing sharp ivory teeth and a dark maw beyond. It has been so long since she saw herself, and it never seems right. She sees too well sometimes.

She lowers him down. Her anger is still there. Perhaps it is always there. But then, as now, it cannot repair all that is broken.

"Keep your story for now," she says bitterly. "It does not matter if I kill you or not. You will not survive out here long on your own. And believe what you will, Man, but I am not the monster you think me. I will take you to your home, safely. On my word. In return, you will tell me this story."

* * *

THE SKY IS obscured by a tall thatched roof, narrowing nearly to a point above a room that, she thinks, is large by the standards of these creatures. Along the walls are sun-bleached skulls of animals. A deer. A boar. A bear. Then there is a fine-looking leather shirt with bulky shoulders, and a bow made of a distinctive mottled wood, flaring at the lower limb.

She draws a flower in the dirt of the floor with a stick. She has only just seen the flower for the first time, and she is proud of it. She looks about, and sees others here too. A man and a woman, though they sit far apart in the room as the cold gusts through the portal that keeps the night at bay. The woman wears gray, and sits nearest the hide-flap, looking beyond, her eyes silver with hints of moonlight. Restralia calls to her, but from her mouth comes no voice, and the woman cannot seem to see her.

She looks now to the man instead, eager to show him the flower. He is sitting near enough to the fire for light more than heat, a long-bladed sword with a pearly finish laying across his lap. Fire flashes in his dark eyes and as she approaches him she slows, feeling the warmth sapping from the hearth and a fear creeping in. She speaks to get his attention too, but as his eyes shift away from the blade to her, she sees them weary and reddened, the man's mouth gaping with sharpened teeth.

Mortimer's voice, like a knife, wakes her. Man is awake, the sword brandished in his hand.

He raises it, face contorted in rage or hatred or pain, and moves to strike her. But he stumbles, unable to keep balance on his broken leg, and his arms fall, the blade burying itself in the soft earth.

"I suppose it was pointless," he says.

Restralia grunts as she stands. She thinks it gets harder each day, and all her body aches in the effort. There is little comfort, whether laying or sitting or standing.

"I tended your leg," she says. The Man's language feels easy now. "I promised you safe passage to your home. We have traveled two days now without incident, and still you try this? Still you wish to kill me?" She sighs, though she isn't sure how the low rumble must sound to Man. "Mortimer, bring Man something to eat while I rest." The owl, still awake and alert from the disturbance, takes flight.

Man is silent, but he eyes her with less hatred than before, she thinks. Caution, maybe. "I cannot trust you," he says, a moment after the owl has left.

Appendages flutter about behind her, above her, reaching up and into the branches absently to probe and search. She feels it like a shrug. "It doesn't matter. When I take you back to your place safely, you will know. And if I wished to kill you, I could have already."

"You should not trust me, either. I try to kill you, and you help me?"

"We are different," she says at last. "I do not enjoy killing. I would not do it at all, in fact, if I could survive without."

She wakes in the early night, and leaves Man under Mortimer's care by the stone ruins to hunt. It doesn't take long for her to find a coyote and return with it dead and cradled in her appendages. She mourns it, but knows that it will become part of her, as one day she will become part of this forest. She eats it, unconcerned for the looks of horror that Man gives her as she does.

When she has finished, they travel.

She holds Man as he might hold a child, her body upright and tall, her appendages poised around her. This is the third day traveling in the forest and, as she had the two nights before, she walks until near dawn.

Man's body tenses in her arms with her steps. He moans with discomfort, sometimes sucking in air at the sharp pains. She doesn't like the sounds he makes, and she shivers each time, as if she can feel the pain herself. But there is nothing she can do to help him, besides what she already does.

Mortimer is with her throughout. He helps by calling out shifts in the path ahead and by reminding her which way to go. It is her home, but the forest is treacherous sometimes, and even with him, she must stop on occasion and look around to find her way.

But without him? She would be lost without Mortimer, in so many ways. Without her only friend, these last years would have been very different.

Here, the ruined stones are more common, one so large that it occludes the night sky, creating something like a cave in the middle of the trees. Vines and lichen cover most of them, but in the places where the gray is bare, it is still smooth. Untouched by time.

She watches Mortimer here, happily aware of the owl's joy. He seems to love these places, relishing in them, settling upon one stone block before fluttering over to another and perching there. She wonders if they remind him of his home. She thinks it odd that he has never told her of his home, in all their years together.

She lowers Man gently onto a soft, wet part of the ground where he can rest a moment. She checks his leg, and then his skin. It's warm. Mortimer flutters near her and calls.

"His skin is warm, Mortimer." The owl remains silent. "He needs food."

It's too late to find good game here, as the sun is now touching the far end of the trees, but there are other things worth eating in this part of the forest. One of her appendages finds a fruiting bush with berries. She knows they are safe, and delicious. And, best of all, this bush is heavy with them. She gathers as many as she can, and brings them back to Man.

His brow is wet, and he stares unfocused into the distance. When she arrives, he turns from her to look at them and his eyes widen. "You found magberries?"

"I don't remember what they are called. Only that they are safe and I love them. I bring them to offer you, Man. See? Maybe you can trust me."

He eats them slowly at first, then faster. She eats some too. They aren't enough to fill her stomach, but they nourish her in some other way. A memory lingers, just beyond the fog, and she thinks for a moment that she must have eaten them when she was new in the forest.

"I haven't seen them in years," he says. "My daughter loved them."

He is quiet then, until he sleeps. That isn't strange, but it feels different now, and he watches her for some time. Restralia has trouble sleeping again too, and she stares at the ground as her appendages scratch something in the soft earth with branches and sticks.

She thinks of the cruel words Man says, and what he has said she's done. She doesn't understand why she forgets. She can barely even remember her grove. It is home to her, but all she can see in her mind is a dense gray fog where it ought to be. What else has she forgotten?

As she readies for sleep, he still watches her, his heavy lidded eyes falling also to the earth at her feet. There, she sees a flower, though she doesn't recall its name. Her eye meets his, and she wipes away the drawing with one huge hand.

She watches the sunset after waking again, and the forest's amber glow fades. They are not long on the trail, after, when Man speaks to her, more calmly than before.

"Do you still wish to hear the story?"

Restralia lumbers, her stride long and slow and she turns her eye from the path ahead to the man cradled in her arms. "Yes."

* * *

"IN MY VILLAGE, we speak tales of these deep woods. The elders tell of a magic grove that houses a sword wrought by the gods long ago, a weapon to turn the tide in a great war. It is said that a demon guards the blade, and that any man brave and wise enough to take the blade from the creature will lead us to a golden future. Others found the sword, as the stories go, but that was many years before me, and the sword always returned to the woods.

"I searched for it, as many young men did. But we all failed, year after year. We returned home, and went on with life. I wanted a family, but I was neither a skilled wrestler nor hunter. Neither was I hand-some nor of the eldest family. It took me time to find a woman who would marry me, but eventually I did. In time I came to love her, and together we had a daughter. Her name was Restralia."

He stops talking for a moment, taking long careful breaths as if steadying himself. She wants to urge him to continue, but knows it is better to stay silent.

"They were my life. I loved them and served them with all my spirit for three years. But we struggled to survive, pushed to the edge of the village when I was unable to hunt enough game." He chuckles, and a faint smile crosses his fevered face. "I suppose you saw why just a few days ago."

He struggles with a long breath. "I only wanted to do well for them, so I went back into the forest. My wife thought me foolish and we fought over it. She did not think I would return, and worried for our daughter. I ignored her.

"I traveled for days into the forest without avail. But just as I was about to give up, admit she was right, and go home, I found the sword, and the demon. It looked identical to you. Nearly.

"I was ready to fight for the sword. But the creature was unfocused and indifferent. It wailed mournfully as I fought it, but did not fight back. When it was dead, I moved to take the sword but a voice came to me as I did. It told me that the sword was mine, if I wished, but that I must exchange for it that which I most cherish."

He stops then for awhile, perhaps lost in some unpleasant memory. She wonders if the swaying of her slow, lumbering walk has put Man to sleep. He feels hot in her grasp, his writhing movements weakening. But Restralia does not say anything. This is his story to tell.

"I was young and brash. A fool," he continues. "Looking at the pearly blade for the first time, I could think of nothing else. I could not imagine anything mattering more. Looking back, it's hard to understand the workings of my mind then. But I cannot change my past. I took it. And when I returned to the village, I was met with great fanfare. I was the greatest hero of an age. The first to find the sword in decades.

"Everything changed so quickly. Soon I was the leading elder on the village council, the youngest in memory to hold the position, and the most respected man of all. We moved to a larger home, we ate better than we ever had. But my relationship with my wife grew cold and distant.

"I took comfort from others in the village. Praise from the men, attention from the women. It was no secret that I strayed from her in those days. I took other women to bed, I drank and hunted more than ever I had before. And we fought, all the time. It was lonely in many ways, despite all the attention. I drifted, and in doing so I left my family behind. It was as if I brought a curse upon us."

Restralia does not stray from her path, staring ahead while her mind drifts elsewhere. She feels Man's reddened eyes on her.

"It seems obvious now. Obvious and foolish. Am I so mad with fever to see you this way?" He shivers, and Restralia cannot help but think his death near. "You don't remember me?"

"You are familiar," Restralia says. "Somehow. But it is always difficult to remember."

He closes his eyes. "I cannot trust myself, not with this chill."

And he sleeps.

Mortimer perches on one of Restralia's upper appendages, hooting with some alarm. "I am going as quickly as I can, Mortimer," she says.

But Mortimer's insistence grows only stronger. "I know he is ill. But I will not give up on him when I have promised him help."

She feels the owl's claws gripping her in disgust. Mortimer is, if anything, a stubborn and ornery thing when he doesn't get his way. And she knows, in the end, that he is only looking after her safety.

When Man wakes later, he is shivering and his eyes are dull. She tries to examine him as he lays on the soft, cool ground of the forest, noting how splotchy and cold his skin is.

His eyes focus on her. "I was dreaming. My little girl was alive. Not killed, not kidnapped, but cursed. Could such a thing be? Oh, Restralia. Long nights I watched her dreaming eyes flutter, hoping that in there she found something I could not give her. Now I find solace in my dreams."

He reaches for her face, his touch gentle on her dry and scaly flesh. "It was a dream, wasn't it?" He pulls his hand back. "Why did you take her name from her?"

"I do not remember," she says. "It is my name. It is the only one I know."

"Then I am sorry. Words are small things. But they're all I have left to give you."

"Sorry?"

"For everything. For all I have done, for all I haven't done, you ought to leave me here. It is fitting I should die in these woods." His hand reaches for the pommel of the sword.

Mortimer is no longer upset, but neither is he calm as he usually is. But his grip tightens on her shoulder and, when he speaks, it is like the black blood that oozed from her shoulder. She listens to him carefully.

"Then you regret taking it?"

His eyes close, and she wonders if he's drifted away again. "I should. I do. Yes."

Mortimer grips again, his voice slower still as he speaks. "I can take it from you now, and I will return it after taking you to your place. We are close now. The sword belongs in the slate garden."

His eyes come into sudden focus. "I said I regret it, but it is mine now, and it's all I have."

The words come out of her mouth easily, as if another speaks through her. "What if it could heal this curse? All your woes vanished."

Man's face is as stern as it can be, as he lingers at the edge of death. "Even gods cannot bring back the dead. I have told you my story, creature. I was wrong about you. I admit that much. But now our bargain is complete."

She has no more words either. They stop to rest, but neither can sleep. Not well. She sees Man tossing and turning, whimpering with fever. She brings water to him, to drink, to wet his skin. She lingers until the morning heat touches her, and she drifts off into an unpleasant and dreamless sleep.

Then Mortimer is shrieking, a deep and horrible sound, monstrous. She feels the arrow pierce her body and she knows it is her voice, and not his.

* * *

HER MIND THICK WITH FOG, Restralia is slow to rise, slower still to adjust her vision to the bright sun of mid-morning as the hunter's poisons course through her. At first, she only sees blurred shapes against the brilliance. Four, maybe. But they are not focused on her. Three are holding Man, carrying him away into the thicker woods where she struggles to tread.

Another arrow strikes her in her long abdomen and she roars, her panicked voice thundering so far afield that she hears birds fleeing distant arbors.

"No, take me back," Man says. His cry is hoarse, and her vision has cleared enough that she can see him struggling against the others who carry him. "I was wrong! She's alive. She's alive, you fools! Take me back!"

Thick blood, black as pitch, oozes from her wounds as she pulls herself to her feet, her eye on Man and his desperate, grasping gestures toward her. They vanish into the trees, and she thinks, for a moment, that it is over.

"Go back with your people," she says to herself, her voice almost too quiet to notice.

Another arrow strikes her in the leg and she turns to see the lone remaining hunter. She steadies, pulling herself up, and her appendages whip out as razors, wide and ready, a pavonine silhouette of bitter armament in the glary morning light.

But the hunter does not back down at her furious display. Instead, he pulls another of his stone-tipped arrows, nocking it on his bow with honed alacrity. She hears him muttering under his breath, a curse perhaps, or a proclamation. "This will be the final one, demon," he says. "Then the blade will be mine." There is bright hunger in his eyes, his black hair unflecked by gray.

Beyond in the wood, she still hears Man's wild cries, and even though she understands his mind to be confused by the chill, she is saddened by it, and feels a singular urge to glimpse him again.

The hunter looses the arrow. But now an appendage whips around with a mind of its own and seizes it, shattering its shaft into falling splinters. The others come just after, whipping and piercing at him, swift enough that Restralia can barely see the hunter's face change from hunger to regret. Sometimes they act on their own. It is too easy, for such a horrible thing. But she kills if she must to survive.

Man's voice is far now, and fading, and though she wishes to follow, she feels light headed as the black blood continues from her wounds. She does not follow. She cannot.

And then, she thinks, why would she? The others will care for him as they know best. Restralia knows little of such things, always depending on Mortimer.

As if summoned by her thought, the owl's talons tear into her flesh again, now in a fit of anger beyond anything she can recall. The owl glares at her in firm disapproval, his golden eyes glowing in the shade.

Her mind is too slow as she turns her head to him. "Why? Why hurt me?"

Mortimer's eyes smolder, tightening with his talons. She hears him in her mind. "Why would I do that? We promised him safety. And more, Mortimer. He is special to us, I think. Can you not feel it?"

His voice becomes insistent, a deep hooting sound that seems to circle around her among the trees. "What are you talking about?" she says. "What enemy?"

The owl claws into her again until she can endure it no longer. Her appendages turn on him, swatting here and there, and then striking. The owl shrieks surprise, and then catches flight, fleeing into the golden forest.

"You can come back when you want to be polite again!"

The owl calls to her from somewhere, his voice seeming to easily reach her through the tangled, thorny branches.

"You'll get over it," she says back.

Alone, she ambles through unfamiliar woods, fearful that the hunters will come for revenge. She wanders until the moon slices through the treetops and directs her to the sounds of water. The forest feels different here, dense and old, as if none had stepped through this place for a long time.

She finds a brook that winds as a snake's form traversing small gaps in a maze of tall slate rectangles burrowing out from the forest floor. She drinks and washes her wounds, and finds a soft patch of dark earth to lay on. As she drifts off, she stares at one of the old stones, scarred by numerous well-ordered marks. They are short lines, as if scratched by a dagger or talon, one after the next like tallies.

* * *

THE WALL HINTS at a memory she cannot reach. She is always on the verge of remembering, but never quite. Who she is. What she's doing here. She struggles now even to remember how she came to this place, this old ruin of some long forgotten time. What sorts of creatures, she wonders, made this place?

Maybe she used to know. Now she doesn't, and she doesn't understand why everything in her mind is like mud, impossible to grasp and always sliding away down slopes to some dark place below.

When she sleeps, her dreams tumble about in her head, only fragmented images and sounds. But within them, a soothing voice speaks to her. A familiar voice. It reminds her who she is.

Then, like thunder, she wakes, and the fog has cleared. She feels rested, like herself.

"Mortimer?" she says, standing. "Where is this place?" She smells the air, she feels along the pockmarked stone. Her friend does not reply, but she thinks she knows her way home.

Restralia walks for several days, the smell of the forest growing familiar and comfortable. Though she is pleased to find her garden, and the place where she sleeps, she then notices the bare stone, perfectly smooth and gray. And then she recalls the sword, and it feels as if someone important has left.

Then comes a day when Restralia wakes, when the sun is still orange and low in the sky, to a strange smell. She knows, somehow, that is a man.

He carries a leather pack high on his back, and walks with the aid of a stick. On his hip, he wears a sword. The sword.

A small form flutters above amidst the trees, settling on one to watch. Restralia narrows her eye, then widens it upon sight of her friend.

"Mortimer? Where have you been all this time? And why is a man here?"

The man frowns. He speaks at her, but she has difficulty understanding, until she hears one word, like the blazing fire of a lighthouse on a foggy night.

"Restralia?"

"Yes," she says. She gestures to herself. "Restralia."

"I remember. I brought the sword back," he says, and she understands him now. "It's time."

Restralia's eye fixes on the sword. "Give me the sword?" she says, her voice tremulous.

"It took me months to recover. But I thought of you every day. I was certain I was mad for some of the time, but the voice came to me again. I knew then, in the sober day, the truth. So here I am. I told the council I would no longer lead them, and gave my home to another."

"The . . . sword . . . " she says again. Her appendages come to attention, attracted to it as snakes lifted by some alluring melody.

"Yes," and he removes it from its sheath. It is not lovely as Restralia expected, and instead other feelings stir that she cannot quite understand.

"The voice told me that I could return the sword, and lift your curse. You . . . you can be free, Restralia."

Her appendages flutter. "Free?" she mutters. "Mortimer, what does the man talk about?"

Mortimer comes down from his high place to perch upon the stone at the heart of the garden. His golden eyes move from Restralia to Man and back. His voice is stern and clear in her mind. She listens.

"It is a dark feeling, Mortimer, my friend. Dark and uncomfortable and strong. Anger, you say? Why must I be so angry, Mortimer?" Her hand shakes as she speaks now, realizing that the feeling inside is not dimming over time as the bright moon does in the middle of a clear night, but grows colder and sharper still.

The voice continues. "The curse remains," it says. "It will always remain. The enemy will be made to suffer." The voice speaks again and again. She doesn't understand what Mortimer is saying, but she knows what she must do.

Her form rises, appendages turned outward, pointed at this man and the sword he carries that belongs in her home. She imagines, with more clarity than she can recall imagining anything, the violence that will come.

"This blade has been my companion for many years," he says, weighing it, shifting it from hand to hand, turning it over such that Restralia must squint against the searing light reflected in the metal.

Both turn to behold the owl when the voice speaks. "Forever, the enemy will be made to suffer. Now, place the sword back on the altar. Place it there, and she will be freed."

Man hesitates, but moves to the plinth, sword in hand. Mortimer watches, still as the stone upon which he sits.

But Man stops to appraise the sword in his hand again, seeming to admire the pearly finish, the gleaming silver on the crossguard, the old leather on an ancient grip.

"The voice promises much in a single moment of contrition. Too much. How can it be so easy to reverse all the pain I've caused? It has taken me too long now to realize that it exists, this exists, only to torment us."

The anger, once focused as moonlight, is wild now, burning through her chest and her mind. She cannot imagine anything so vividly as vengeance on this thief, whose greed has done so much to her, to her garden, to her friend. She knows, in a moment, that her misery is his doing. But she cannot do it, not yet. She holds herself at the very edge.

Man's voice is soft now. "I can only beg forgiveness every day from now on. And I will, though I do not deserve it."

"What is he talking about, Mortimer?" Her voice is barely restrained, held together as she is, only by a growing confusion. But her friend offers her nothing. Instead, she only hears his voice, now repeating itself again and again, colored with a swelling anticipation.

Then, silence.

Man swings the sword at Mortimer, and there is a cracking sound like the final moments of a tree's burning. Where an owl had been on the stone now only a smear of black sludge remained, steaming in the cool air. Man releases the sword, but it does not clatter to the stone or the earth, and instead floats, its polished sheen turning black, and bursting into thick and acrid smoke.

Restralia roars as a pain she has never felt grips her every bone. She can hardly keep her balance, appendages thrashing through branch and leaf above. She falls, and the pain only grows, blinding her vision, numbing her body in the final breaths before death.

She is sure she is dying now, dying because the sword has been destroyed. She knows now that her life, everything that she is, has always been tied to it.

But she opens her eyes, and the light feels different. It comforts rather than burns. Her thoughts are clearer too, and memories begin to fill her mind as if it were a basin. She is suddenly aware that she is naked in front of her father, and she pulls her knees into herself, covering her body.

He seems not even to notice, not through the tears streaming down his face. But when he does, he reaches into his bag and pulls out a familiar gray dress.

She sees it in her mind, in the house from her dreams, worn by the woman that lived there.

"How long has it been?" She sounds so different now, small in her own ears.

"Eighteen years."

"And mother?" Her voice wavers.

He hesitates. "She passed two winters ago."

"You left me here eighteen years," she says, with more sadness than anger. "And I will never again see my mother."

"I searched." He looks down, avoiding her eyes. "Others thought you gone, and no longer came with me on the hunts. But I went on my own for many seasons. But we lost hope too, for the forest was empty."

"If you thought me dead, why are you here now?"

"I . . . " he speaks, but struggles to form the words. "I came to find the demon who took my daughter. I came for revenge . . . or to die."

She could not help but smile. "And yet you found neither."

He looked up to her, his eyes reddened and raw, and smiled back. "I seem to fail in all my efforts."

"You have saved me now."

"You would not need saving if not for my hand. I can say nothing else. Forgive me, Restralia. I would trade all my life for just another moment in those days before this curse. Yet I know that cannot be so."

Her mind, clear as lakewater now, remembers home as it was, not as it appeared in her dreams. The memories confuse her as she looks at his face, streaked with dirt and tears, summoning feelings of both warmth and fear. Sometimes he is stinking of beer there, and his eyes burn with anger that makes him seem like another person. She turns away, her eyes drifting to the altar where the black stain writhed on the stone.

She cannot understand all he did then either. But nor can she understand herself so clearly. She knows that same anger now. She reaches a hand to him.

"We have something better," she says. "We have new days."

ALL FOR YOU

BY ODESSA SILVER

Odessa has been stuck in her imagination since a child creating strange ideas and weaving them into stories. Often fusing fantasy and science with darker themes, her stories tend to dig into all aspects of human nature. Worldsmyths moderator, logo creator, and strange Brit who doesn't actually like tea.

* * *

It was going to be the perfect day. Blue skies, a warmth that buried deep into your bones; the kind of day you don't forget. Clara wouldn't.

She stood on the shit-splattered pier, the seagulls above screeching and laughing, eyes on the tray of half-eaten chips sat precariously in her hand. I hoped one of them would dive for her. I could see it now, that look of surprise on her perfectly-sculpted face, chips flying in all directions. But no. She moved on.

It was easy enough to blend in with the throngs of people milling around, one step behind an old couple watching the waves rolling in and out, avoiding a group of lads swearing loudly, chugging cans of cheap cider. Every one of them enjoying the summer sun and their time at the seaside, but not her.

I moved away now, linen shirt flapping in the soft breeze, loose sand slipping in my shoes. I hated the beach, the way everyone flocked to it ready to cook themselves to an unhealthy red glow. I was only here for her. Mimicking her path, watching with care as she continued down the pier.

Soft sandals pattered on the sea-beaten wood. *Clunk, clunk, clunk.* Those lithe legs were getting closer now, bronzing in the sun, brushed by the delicate fabric of her skirt. Red curls bounced against the creamy white blouse which fit her all too perfectly, and it made my stomach twist. She was just as I remembered before her funeral. Well, almost. Her hair had been ginger back then; and now it really was red.

Silly Clara, thinking she could trick me again, trying to keep me away with lies after lies after lies. Back then she told me she didn't love me. I'd seen through that. Her father hated me; she was just trying to keep the peace. Of course I'd forgiven her. I wasn't cruel. I loved her after all. My Clara. Sweet and kind and a fucking liar.

I'd ignored the obviously fake documents I'd been served. There was no way Clara would put a restraining order on me. No, not me. Her father had a hand in it again, always the meddler. I should have taken her away from him back then. We could have pushed him away together, escaped together, been together forever.

But no. It wasn't to be. I'd found her again after all the lies, after the fake funeral, and she'd moved on. A three-bedroom house, husband who worked away, cosy little affair on the side, and her oh-so-perfect job. I'd seen her side piece, a tall man with impossibly black eyes. I followed them up to the woods, winding through the villages, getting further and further from the beach. They'd fucked in that car. I saw it. She didn't really try to hide it, and that's when I knew it was for me to watch. The sky had been dusky and the trees shading them from view, mostly. But she knew me, knew that I always picked the parking space closest to the exit.

By then I'd already sent her three bunches of flowers. Roses of course: her favourite. I didn't want to scare her away, especially after the funeral. We couldn't let her father intervene again. But he was old now, so maybe he just needed a push in the wrong direction. Falling down the stairs with a *thump, thump, thump*. Maybe he wasn't right in the head—after all who fakes a funeral and buries a person who's still alive?

I'd gone to the funeral, laughing in the face of his fake restraining order. He'd spotted me, eyes glassy and unfocused. Crocodile tears, just like the rest of them. Boohoo, our daughter is dead.

I wasn't sure if he'd worked out who I was when I walked right up to him. I looked a bit different back then, dying my hair red to match Clara and wearing one of her blouses that I'd stolen, a black silky one. I loved the feel of the material on my skin, and I could still smell her scent on it. She was giving me a hug from wherever she was hiding, and we were fighting her father. Her mother took one look at me and burst into tears, hissing how everything had been my fault, how I'd not been in prison long enough. Stupid bint, look at your husband, not me. I was protecting Clara. You got me locked up for taking care of your daughter.

No matter what they did though, I would always return to Clara. And here I was now, watching her every move, ready to whisk her away and live in happiness once again. But first, she needed to know I was angry at her. For the lies, for letting her father be cruel to me. I could still feel his fingers wrapped around my throat as he tried to kill me. *Shame about the arthritis mate*, I'd managed to say with a crooked smile. *Can't strangle anyone with those fucked up hands.*

From the pier, Clara moved towards the car park, stopping to dump her half-eaten chips in an overflowing bin. Her sparkling black Audi sat proudly away from all the rest. Taking my advice even now. Always take the spot near the exit, in case you needed to escape.

I now sat on a nearby bench ready to watch everything unfold, pausing for the occasional lick at the melted ice cream now running down my hand. Chocolate, her favourite. I was getting giddy as she got closer and closer. The stage was all ready for my entrance. Button click, car door opened. I had to hide the smile forming as she slammed the door, gagging so hard she threw up, spraying half-digested chunks of potato across the car park.

I jumped up, dumping my ice cream on the sandy floor, and approached her.

"What the fuck?" I heard her spit between retches.

"Are you alright there, love?" I bent down to pick up her fallen handbag, scooping the contents back in quick and placing it next to the car.

Blue eyes stared up at me. They were once black, like her father's; she must be wearing contacts today.

"Thank you but I'm . . . fine. Upset stomach."

Did she recognise me? I couldn't tell. Maybe she was playing it safe. We were in public after all.

"Want me to fetch a drink? There's a co-op round the corner."

"No, really I'm fine." There was a tightness around her face, her lips pulled back in a half-grimace. Poor thing. "Thanks for the offer."

I paused. "What's that smell?" I asked innocently.

"F—"

As she threw up again I wanted to reach out and hold her hair, stroking it gently as I tell her everything is going to be fine. Her car, maybe not. I mean, the fish would have been bad enough if I had bought it from the fishmonger this morning, but I'd slipped three-day-rotting fish into her back window. With the sun up high, it'd easily raise the inside temp into the 30s, and I expected getting the juices out was going to be great.

"It's fine," she gasped out, wiping dripping spit on the back of her hand. "My husband will be here soon."

Husband, or bit on the side?

I smiled. Fine. I'll return later. Maybe this was too much all at once? With the fish, the sun, the discarded pregnancy test. I'd slipped that into my pocket while putting everything back in her handbag. I hadn't seen the result yet. I'd check once I returned to my car, finding out if we're going to be parents or not.

"But I want to make sure you'll be alright."

"I said I'm fine." Clara stared at me now, eyes quickly flittering to the space beside me.

"If you say so," I said, giving up for now. I didn't want to scare her. I was too excited to read the test anyway.

I left her groaning on the floor and hurried to my car. Slipping into the front seat, ignoring the searing leather, I pulled out the test. It was one of the fancy ones like they advertised on the telly. This one also had the blue *pregnant* written on it.

I really would have to wait until later to see her. She'd need to go home, tell her husband, tell her other lover. They'd fight, cry, stomp on out the front door, but I'd be there for her. My Clara. I would never abandon you.

I didn't want to wait. I wanted her now. Maybe I should get her a gift? The others would hate this pregnancy but I would love it, love her, love the baby.

I jumped out—pausing only to check on Clara, who was now screaming at her husband—and headed into town, wandering past the packed chip shops filled with tourists queuing into the street. There were too many today, blocking the paths. Kids were screaming and running out into the road to escape their flustered mothers. Others flooded the arcade, swarming the 2p droppers, waiting for the next crash of coins of their win. I saw them now, jumping up and down in the hopes the movement would send the coins wobbling off the edge. So young, so naive.

The crane games at the front were filled with huge plush figures as always, the children beneath them singing a choir of *But I want Pikachu mummy!* Everyone knew those things were rigged, and hardly worth the time.

Although. Maybe if I turned up at Clara's house with a teddy, she'd be thrilled. I could tape the pregnancy test to its hands to let her know I knew. Pushing my way through the sea of squealing children, I found an unoccupied crane game. Coin in, arm moving, I clawed at thin air a few times before it struck fabric. The stupid game still held my prize hostage. A swift kick to the side of the machine and still it sat goading me.

"Oi!" A security guard came over, face crumpled in a scowl. "Pack it in or you're out."

"I ain't doing anything."

Behind me I heard the clink of a coin hitting a machine. I spun around to find a smirking teen hogging the controller.

"Hey."

"You weren't using it," he said, sending the machine's arm wobbling towards my prize.

"I'm standing right here." He ignored me as the machine flashed and played a tune as the plush hit the prize chute. "Hey, that's mine."

Scoffing, he grabbed the teddy and held on tight as I reached for it. "Fuck off mate. Get your own."

I wasn't going to back down. I stamped on his foot; he yelped and loosened his grip for a split second. I took my chance, gripping it tight, and legged it out to the streets as the guard yelled after me. No little shitbag would stop me getting this teddy for Clara and our child. Everything was going to go great. I couldn't wait.

* * *

NIGHT FELL SLOWLY. My anticipation was growing. I'd sat down the road for a few hours, watching her house. The husband had left an hour ago for his night shift. I'd given Clara a little longer; I knew she'd be excited to see me too, but I had to time this right. I pulled the teddy from the passenger seat, pregnancy test taped tightly to its paws. The tape had deformed its head a little but I was sure she wouldn't mind. Not when she saw me.

Her house was a corner plot surrounded by high fences. So nice and quaint. They wouldn't stop me. I waltzed over, pulling her house key from my pocket —I'd made a copy of that too— and locked the front door. Just in case. I couldn't have her running away from me.

I made my way around the side of the house, stopping only to reach up and unlatch the gate. With my thick boots, I stomped right through her neat flowerbeds, kicking up flowers and crushing the delicate petals. She'd worked hard for this house and I'd never dream of taking that away from her—just the small things. Across the miniature courtyard wound a manicured wisteria vine, weaving around a trellis that lead right up to the window I would enter from. I, her Romeo, would climb up, and she, my Juliet, would be ready for my loving embrace.

The moon tried to betray me, holding back its light. It was out to get me like the others were. Despite its feeble attempts, I still found the wood beneath the foliage and caught hold. Up and up I climbed to the open window calling my name, begging me to rescue my Juliet.

Shimmying through was easy enough, but the landing was far from desirable. I'd fallen on my arse, legs akimbo on her bedroom floor. I pulled the teddy from my shirt where I'd stuffed it for safety and placed it on her bed, facing the door for when she entered. The stairs clattered as she stormed up.

"You better not be—oh." She froze, blue eyes wild, terrified, empty. "W-Who . . ."

I grinned. "Who is this?" I pointed to the teddy and pat his head. "The kids call it Pikachu. It's for you, both of you, see. I found the test."

The door slammed on its hinges. Perhaps this wasn't going to be as easy as I thought. I rushed to reopen it calling to her, "It's alright, Clara, your father isn't here. It's just me."

"Get away from me!"

"Clara."

"Fuck off." She squealed and shrieked, thundering back downstairs. "I'm not Clara."

Why wasn't she listening? Were her father's lies still in her head? I followed, needing her to listen. Down I followed, backing her into the kitchen.

"Come back, I just want to talk." I tried to sound calm and careful but I could feel the frustration bubbling beneath the surface.

"Yes, hi, police please—"

"Don't you dare!" I yelled, rushing towards her grabbing after the phone.

She had her back to me, fingers clamped around the mobile. I had seconds to stop her. No time to play nice. I shoved her into the back door, her face slamming the glass. It was enough to send the phone bouncing on the tiles sliding towards the fridge. I snatched it up and threw it into the full kitchen sink. No police.

"Look what you made me do," I hissed as she cowered on the floor. "I was going to be nice to you. I even brought you a present." I paused. "But I suppose you can still make it right again. Just forgive me for earlier. I know cleaning the car will be a nightmare, but you had to be punished."

"I d-don't know who the f-fuck you are. Leave me alone."

"Don't be like that," I soothed, closing in on her. "You don't need to pretend now, truly. It's just you and me. I locked all the doors. Nobody can interrupt us. I know why you did it, why you pretended to be dead. But I saw all the things you were doing, letting me know you still cared. I even saw you in the woods."

I placed a hand on her head, fingertips rolling down her glossy hair.

"You sicko."

Clara sprung to her feet, pushing me away, hurrying anywhere else but here. How could she? I loved her. She loved me. We were going to be a family all together. She needed to be punished some more. To make her see.

"You told me you loved me," I yelled at where she once stood. "Was that a lie too? Like the funeral?"

I hunted through the house for her, stepping over strewn paperwork and broken glass. She wouldn't get far from me.

"Please, give me five minutes? Don't make me hurt you again. I don't want to. I love you, Clara, I never stopped loving you. Even after everything you did. It's all your fault but I can forgive you."

I peered into the study, checking under the desk, behind the door, all for nothing. I stopped, listening for footsteps. I smiled as I heard the *creak, creak, creak* of the floorboards above.

Oh, Clara. You'll regret this.

It took only moments to reach her on the stairs, grabbing her deliciously-soft wrist. I could snap it so easily. I wanted to.

Frozen in place, the shock robbing her of any senses, I could see the fear and fury in her eyes. She wanted to fight back. Yet here she was at my mercy.

She screamed again and I clamped a hand over her mouth. "Shush, calm down now, my sweet. I just want to talk, alright?" Clara nodded. I smiled. "Good. Now, let's return to the bedroom."

Yes. That's right. Surrender to me.

Step. Step. Step. We'd reached the top of the stairs. Her wrist was still tight in my sweaty palm. I hovered closer, breathing her scent. I wanted to taste that ripe fruit being crushed beneath me. One little bite. What harm could that do? Pinning her tighter, I pressed myself against that lithe body of hers. She tried to wriggle free, but I wasn't letting go.

With a muffled cry, she buried her elbow into my stomach. I gritted my teeth and tried to hold on, but she was quick. Spinning, she shoved against me with everything she had and backwards I fell, head bouncing off the stairs, body following after. Pain lanced through my skull, bright and searing as I landed in a heap at the bottom, the room spinning round and round.

Another scream and I looked up to see something falling, hard and heavy, *bang, bang, bang*. My hand flew to my head as it landed with a crash, smashing into pieces and clattering down on me. I groaned in pain, pulling my bloodied hand away.

"I get it," I said, trying to push everything off of me as I stood. "You're mad at me. I pushed you off the cliff, you pushed me down the stairs. But we're even now right? Now we can move on?"

Clara wasn't at the top of the stairs.

Hobbling, I pushed through the pain and hurried back up.

"Come on Clara. That's enough now. Look, you've made me bleed." My hand left a bloody print on the door as I pushed it open. "Time to patch me up."

I saw as Clara scrambled out of the window, red curls catching on the handle. A shriek, then nothing. I rushed to the window.

"No, no, don't hurt yourself."

Below in the darkness lay Clara, half-buried in a bush and still. No, no. You can't do this to me. I told you before only I was allowed to hurt you. I clambered up into the window, swinging my leg over. Still Clara didn't move.

I'm coming, my Juliet.

I lowered myself quickly, feet reaching for the trellis once again. Brick. Only brick. I froze for a second as I hung limp from the windowsill, feet scrambling at nothing. Where's the trellis? I couldn't—

Sweaty fingers slipped on the sill. Air whooshed by as I plummeted. A sickening crack.

"Oh god."

Eyes open. Vision blurred. Clara pulled herself from the bush, untangling from the trellis now on the floor.

It hurts.

I couldn't find the strength to open my mouth.

She did it. She must have moved the trellis.

Footsteps stomping away from me. My love, leaving me here. She's going to get help. Of course. My love would not betray me.

Coldness seeped in, exhaustion called to me. I'm just going to sleep for a minute until she returns . . .

SMALL REBELLIONS
BY FREYA BELL

Freya Bell is a Canadian writer residing in Alberta with her husband, cat, and dog. As one of the admins of Worldsmyths, Freya has helped shape this anthology alongside her co-editors, all driven by her love of speculative fiction. Find out more at www.freyabellcreates.com

* * *

"You do not belong here," said the dead dragon to the battered child.

The child hesitated, hands grasping the hem of her dirty dress. "I know," she replied. "Mother says the volcano's peak is cursed."

"So it is, child." The dragon settled his skeletal forebody down onto the ash that filled the dormant volcano's hollow cone. He tilted his head to regard her. "And what brings you here? You are alive." His voice turned bitter. "This place is better left to dead things like me."

She stood at the head of the path that led down to the island below and met his empty gaze with one of uncertain defiance. "I just wanted to see what Mother was hiding up here. She has so many secrets."

"That," the dragon gestured with a claw for her to come closer, "is an understatement. With how many curses that woman tosses around, I'm surprised any part of her life *isn't* kept secret." He curled his bony tail around his forelegs like a cat and laid his head down so he was at her height.

The child sat down on a low stone opposite him, stifling a moan as she put weight on the welts on the back of her thighs.

"Are you cursed, then?" She fiddled with the frayed hem of her dress as she gazed into the empty sockets of the dragon's skull.

The dragon scoffed and gestured at the serpentine length of his body, the turning loops of bone twisting around the shattered peak of the volcano above them. "Do I not look cursed to you? I am bound to this place, my soul trapped as my remaining vitality slowly drains away. Any who bleed on that witch's altar will suffer the same fate when they die."

The child rubbed her work-coarsened hands up and down the scars and partially-healed cuts that climbed her arms. "She did this to you," she stated.

The pebbles at her feet tumbled and knocked together as the dragon growled, air rumbling from his phantom lungs. The child clapped her hands over her ears in surprise and the dragon subsided, growl softening into a bitter laugh.

"I see your mother in your face, child. But luckily, I see none of her in your soul." He barked another laugh, as bitter as the first. "And lucky for you, too. You never would have survived this long if she sensed a rival."

The child hugged herself, knowing his words to be the truth.

"What do I do? I don't want to be a skeleton. I just want. . . I want to be free of her." Her hot tears spilled onto the ash.

The third laugh was gentler, the bitterness softened by pity. "Something I doubt you have the guts for, girl. Matricide is not for one so young as you," said the dragon in a slow voice.

The girl tilted her head and left a grimy trail across her cheeks as she swiped at her tears. "Ma-tree-side? What is that?"

"It is when one kills their mother." The dragon's voice was as cold as the grave. "It is the only way for us two. Kill her, and free us both."

The child blanched and hugged herself tighter. "No, no, no. I can't. I can't!"

The dragon pushed himself up from the ash. "What loyalty do you owe to a woman who bleeds her only daughter dry? To a woman who beats you, treats you like a slave, makes you sleep on a splintery floor while she sleeps in a plush bed? Aye, I know how you live, girl. My ears are sharp, I've heard the screams. What love could you possibly have for a woman like that?"

"I can't," the girl whimpered again.

"Can't, or won't? Do you want to end up like me?"

"I'm afraid of her!" cried the girl, surging to her feet.

The dragon hissed and darted his bulk forward until his shadow loomed over her, cutting her off from the moonlight. "More afraid of her than dying?" he boomed.

"You don't understand! She would kill me slowly, drain me, make me hurt."

The dragon's head wove back and forth across the cone of the volcano as the bulk of his body uncoiled from the peak. Wicked claws cast sparks against the stone as he rasped his way down the steep face above her. He held up a wrist and the moonlight shone off manacles. Chains as thick as her waist trailed off them into the shadows, where a hidden altar stood. She leapt away as the dragon reared above her with a snarl.

"You think I know nothing of a slow death?" He tugged at his chains, and the altar began to glow with a sinister purple light. "You think I know nothing of the pain she likes to inflict on those who oppose her?"

The child tried to back away, but the dragon darted around her and cut her off from the path down the volcano. He lowered his horns towards her, each taller than she was, and advanced, giving her no choice but to step backwards. With each step, the altar's malevolent presence grew. Echoes of pain cried out through the veil of ages: the dragon's pain.

Her mother's touch was clear. The girl's eyes adjusted to the shadows, revealing the blood stains that not even decades of rain had been able to touch.

The dragon closed in on her, turning his head so one blank eye socket was level with her face. His voice was deadly calm. "Aye, child. I know it is not death you fear, but the dying."

Her welted thighs hit the lip of the altar, and she cried out. The dragon showed no pity and advanced further.

"The dagger. Take it. Take it and end her before she can end you."

The child looked over her shoulder and there, on the stained bowl cut into the rock of the altar, was an obsidian blade. Its facets caught the moonlight, reflecting it back at her in a pretty manner completely at odds with its sinister purpose. She picked it up by its leather-wrapped handle. It was identical to the one her mother used to extract blood for spell work.

She dropped it. "I can't. It's an evil thing."

The dragon's head whipped towards her. "More evil than what she has done to me? To you?"

The child took a step away from the altar. "I can't, I don't know the spells."

The dragon withdrew against the side of the volcano's cone, and gave her a sidelong glance. "So you would leave me here then. Allow me to be drained of every last shred of vitality, left to power that witch's foul spells."

The child examined her bare feet. Scars crisscrossed the tops of her toes, remnants of a spell gone wrong. She knew better than to interfere with powers she couldn't control.

"I can come visit. Keep you company?" suggested the child in a small voice.

The dragon opened his jaws wide in a mocking laugh. "What would I do with your company, child? At least when I am alone, I can sleep. I can forget, for a short while."

The child nodded. She knew the value of forgetting. She shifted, moonlight glinting off the obsidian blade, drawing her hand towards it without her awareness.

An inkling of an idea crept through her fear.

"Dragon. . . " said the child, hesitating. "Blood is power, isn't it? Blood is used for a binder. It can be used for unbinding."

The dragon froze, taking in the scars on her arms. "Her power is your power," murmured the dragon hesitantly. "But without knowing the spells. . . "

The child bit her lip and hesitated before answering. "Mother says magic is about belief. And I know I want you to be free."

His empty gaze followed the length of chains from the altar to his wrist, then trailed up to the bright moon. He was silent for several long moments, as still as a statue.

At last his head snapped towards her. "Can you do it? Can you unbind me?"

The child squeezed her eyes shut, heart breaking at the plain longing in the dragon's voice.

"I will try," said the child.

The dragon surged forward, one wicked claw inches away from her chest. "Do not think this a game, child. Do not give me hope. I cannot. . ."

The child squared her shoulders and grasped the dagger. "I will do it."

"Even knowing that my last act before passing on will be to devour your mother, to crunch her bones between my teeth?"

The child squeezed her eyes shut. "I. . ."

Above, the seabirds called to each other in their sleep from their nests in the rocky peak. She opened her eyes, the stars reflecting off the tears caught in her lashes, blurring her vision. The stars were free, and the birds. No one could touch them. Why not her, too?

"Yes," she breathed.

The dragon made a sound like a cut-off laugh, land lowered himself back onto the ash to curl up like an obedient hound. He gestured towards the altar.

"Begin."

The child took a steadying breath and turned back to the altar. The deep purple glow writhed as if it could sense her intentions and sought to escape her. Sweat trickled between her shoulder blades as she raised the obsidian dagger. With a practised motion she brought it down, the keen blade barely kissing her skin. She flinched at its familiar sharpness.

Blood, bright in the moon's light, trickled down her wrist into the shallow bowl of the altar. The purple glow deepened and edged into dark redness that pulsed in time with her swiftly-beating heart.

The child raised her arm high above the bowl, clenching and unclenching her fist to keep the blood flowing. Just like how mother had taught her.

Once a small pool had gathered, she eased her grip and turned to face the dragon. The pain beat at the back of her mind, but the strangeness of the scene before her pushed it away.

The child could feel the intensity of the dragon's gaze, but in this moment he looked like a carved toy left behind by an irresponsible child. Moonlight played over the planes of his skull, unruffled by the warm sea-and-flower scented breeze blowing up from the lower island. Lights from the neighboring island twinkled in the distance over his spiny shoulder, and if she concentrated, she could just hear the crashing of the waves on the beach far below

It was so lonely up here.

A rock slid loose and crashed somewhere along the path below them, breaking her reverie. She raised the knife once more and inhaled shakily. She took one step forward, then another, and another. The dragon stayed perfectly still as the girl lay her bloodied hand on his manacle.

"Hear me, spirits," said the child in a tiny voice. She took a stuttering breath and glared at the scars on her arms before trying again. "Hear me, spirits. I don't have the secret words of my mother, and I don't know what I can promise you besides my blood, but I ask that you attend me now. I ask that you unbind this drag—oof."

The air vanished from her lungs as something heavy struck her stomach. The dragon wheeled around, chains clinking, and recoiled.

The witch stood at the head of the path, hands on her hips as several head-sized rocks levitated around her. Her eyes flicked from the child to the dragon, face too calm for the murder they held in them. The dragon backed up until he hit the wall of the mountainside, head weaving as he vainly searched for an escape.

The mother strode over to the child who lay on her side, lungs gasping for air as her broken ribs creaked. A merciless toe prodded her, and elicited a pained gasp from the girl.

The mother looked down at her daughter with impatience. "Look what you've made me do. I know small rebellions are expected at your age, but this? Sneaking out for a stroll I could understand, but trying to undo one of my best spells? Ridiculous. And you." She turned to the cowering dragon. "Why aren't you asleep?"

"The girl woke me up, Master, when she entered the cone." He dipped his heavy head, and if he had eyes, they would have been lowered.

The mother snorted and turned to the child. "And what exactly did you think you would find here?" She waved her hand to encompass the volcano's peak. "A feast in your honour? I forbade you from this peak for a reason. Stop snivelling and get up. I didn't hit you that hard."

The child pushed herself up to a sitting position, bleeding arm held tight against her broken ribs, her other hand still clasping the now-forgotten dagger.

The mother tapped an elegant finger on her red lips, sauntering towards the dragon. "Now what to do with you? You've been so very disobedient."

Bones clattered as the dragon trembled. "Put me to sleep, Master. I promise not to wake up again without your permission."

The mother sneered. "Just like that? No, I don't think you've learned your lesson yet." She raised her hand and flicked the levitating stones at him. The dragon snarled and snapped at the air as they shattered against him, breaking off shards of bone, but he made no move to defend himself.

"Mother, no!" cried the child. She pushed herself to her feet with effort, fresh tears leaving clean streaks down her ash-dusted cheeks.

"Silence, girl. At least he knows his place. Stand there and watch unless you want to be next." She raised her other arm and a deep purple glow enveloped the dragon. She clenched both fists. The dragon shrieked, then it fell to the ground, writhing in pain.

"Stop hurting him!" The child grabbed at her mother's sleeve but was shaken off with a snarl and a shove. The child fell to the ground, elbows striking the hard earth with numbing force. The mother crossed her arms across her chest and the dragon arched his back, claws scrabbling in the air as he keened in pain.

His cries drilled straight into the center of her being. The fear the child felt melted away, replaced by a fiery hot desire to protect.

The child interposed herself between the dragon and the mother. "STOP."

She shoved the mother in the chest with both hands.

Both hands.

Spouts of blood spurted into the air as the obsidian blade bit with ease into the mother's chest. Mother and daughter exchanged identical looks of shock as together they fell to their knees. The mother grasped the blade and pulled; the dagger came out with a wet sucking noise. Hot, sticky blood soaked the front of the child's dress as Mother pawed weakly at the wound, trying in vain to stop the flow. Her hands twitched, hovering over her mother's reddened chest.

The mother wheezed, blood filling her lungs, eyes wide with fright. She shuddered and the child jumped and pressed her hands to the wound.

"Mother, I'm so sor— I didn't mean— I didn't want—" Even in her babbling she couldn't voice lies to her mother. Bloody spittle bubbled on her mother's lips, but the child couldn't understand her futile attempts to speak.

Behind them, the dragon's chains clicked open and fell to the ground with a loud clatter as the price of blood was paid.

A white blur flung her into the air as the dragon shoved her aside, bruising her already tender ribs as she landed on the altar. The blood from the bowl soaked into her ruined dress, mingling with her mother's lifeblood while the girl looked on in horror.

The dragon took one long look at his prey before he lunged.

Bones crunched as he seized the mother in his jaws. Hot blood poured out of his skeletal throat and his mighty claws churned it into foul mud as he chewed.

The child could only watch, thoughts numb and distant as the dragon spat the remains into the mud and pranced on them, bones rattling with his glee. He crowed in the language of the sea dragons, but the child didn't care because she couldn't understand.

At last the dragon stilled. A bright cerulean glow bathed his bones and gathered in his eye sockets as his hold on the mortal plane weakened. The glow intensified, and he turned his attention to the moon and breathed in its pure white light. The dragon shuddered, bones trembling. He fell sideways as he shook free of his bones, which collapsed into a messy pile.

But the dragon still stood, transparent and shining. He looked as he had in life, pale blue and serpentine, with deeper blue fins sprouting from his cheeks and eyebrows.

He looked over his shoulder, giving the child a deep bow of respect before approaching the edge of the cone. With one last glance of gratitude, he dove off the volcano's side and dropped towards the ocean below. The waters parted without a splash, and his glow disappeared below the waves.

The child sat in silence, alone. Night birds called and chirped from the trees that covered the lower slopes, and the waves still crashed in the distance. She raised her head and across on the neighboring island, the lights were blazing, despite the late hour. Bright too were the lights on the fishing vessels heading towards her island, no doubt coming to investigate the screams and strange lights.

The child sat on a low rock opposite the dragon's empty bones and fiddled with the hem of her blood-soaked dress, waiting for the fishermen to arrive.

OF THE BEAST
BY IRENE BOWIE-JOHNSON

Irene lives in the Blue Mountains of Australia and gets to enjoy stunning views daily. Half the time she writes about magic, manners, and mayhem. The other half she writes about soldiers, space ships and star travel.

* * *

The fourth landing was in sight when Bernice saw Lord Calver kill his manservant.

She was resting on a ledge above the landing, putting the cap back on her canteen of water and stretching out the moment. She'd told the others she'd pause to take a drink and get her breath back. As soon as the cap was back on the canteen she'd need to start moving again.

It was the yelp of terror, echoing up from the landing below, that made her look down. Lord Calver was holding his manservant by the front of his shirt, their figures dimly-lit silhouettes. They'd strayed dangerously far from the wardstones their Guide had powered to light their way. At first, Bernice thought the manservant had stumbled and Lord Calver meant to save him, but she dismissed the thought when Lord Calver let go of the shirt, flattened his palm against his manservant's chest, and pushed him almost casually over the edge into the void.

The manservant fell, pulled back over the ledge by the weight of the bags on his back. His cries echoed upward, rippling through the vast silence.

Bernice glanced at the other pilgrims, but they'd seen nothing. Vintus, the Xancheran, and Rin, the Al'veran monk, were still climbing down the steep vertical pillar that joined the third landing to the fourth. Their attention was focused on the shallow handholds and footholds carved into the rock, slippery and smoothed out by the hands and feet of a thousand pilgrims before them. Their Guide was nowhere in sight. When he'd reached the landing, he'd disappeared around a corner and hadn't reappeared. Bernice assumed he was taking care of nature's call.

The Xancheran and the monk looked around as the manservant's cry faded into silence, in time to see Lord Calver's outreached hand stretched out as though to save, not kill. They hurried their descent, and within moments the Xancheran's voice echoed up from below, asking what had happened, his questions heavily accented and stilted as he hunted for the right words in the common tongue. The monk said nothing. Rin was an Al'veran and had sworn a vow of silence for the pilgrimage. It seemed even the death of a fellow pilgrim was not enough to make him talk.

Lord Calver's response was too low for Bernice to hear but she could tell it wasn't the truth. The Xancheran was all sympathy, his hand going to Lord Calver's shoulder in an offer of comfort. Lord Calver endured the touch for several seconds before he shrugged it off and stepped away.

Bernice closed the cap on her canteen and hooked it back onto her belt. Turning around, she slid her feet into the smooth round hollows carved into the rock and started the climb down. The image of Lord Calver pushing his manservant over the edge played on repeat in her mind. Why had he done it? The question was a burden she didn't want, one she was being forced to carry against her will. Bernice poked around the edges, following the shape of it, but hesitated to explore it in full. If Lord Calver wanted his manservant dead, better to leave well enough alone.

Bernice reached the landing just as Lord Calver repeated the story for the Guide. The Guide had lit a new wardstone near the ledge. Many of the wardstones along the pathways were carved directly from the rock, however this one was a sphere, set on a triangular plinth. Bernice knew there would be empty plinths dotted across the landing, where the sphere could be moved to if light was needed somewhere else.

'He said he saw something in the dark,' said Lord Calver, an edge of impatience in his voice at having to tell the tale again. 'Whatever it was terrified him. The man backed himself to the edge of the ledge before I knew what was happening.'

Bernice stopped a safe distance away. She watched Lord Calver as he talked. Nothing she knew of him explained why he'd push his manservant into the void.

She considered the few things she did know. She'd known him for less than a week and in that time, he'd been brisk and demanding, rarely speaking, except to share his concerns about the pace they were keeping or to help coordinate the camp at night.

His manservant had kept even more to himself. He'd made it clear from the start: he was there to carry bags, cook for Lord Calver, and keep watch. Nothing more. He wasn't a true pilgrim and didn't want to play at being one. Bernice had seen the Elduric talisman he'd kept tucked into his shirt and wondered if it had troubled him, to be travelling somewhere his god couldn't see.

'Did he say what it was he saw?' The Guide asked the question as though he expected it to be answered. His tone of voice reminded Bernice of Father Oredon's when members of the congregation came to him with their problems. It was a warning and a reminder. you might want this to go your way, but remember: I don't serve you.

'He was muttering something about yellow eyes,' said Lord Calver.

The Guide nodded slowly. 'And you didn't see anything?'

Lord Calver shook his head. Sharp and frustrated. He wanted the conversation to end.

Bernice found herself looking for signs of what he'd done in the set of his jaw or the depth of his eyes.

He hid his guilt well. It was hard to find, but it was there in the way he was trying to escape the conversation with the Guide and in the subtle shake of his hands before he crossed his arms over his chest and tucked them away.

Bernice wondered what he feared. Was it simply being caught? Or was it the judgement of the gods? She pursed her lips. She somehow doubted the gods' justice would haunt him as it haunted her.

'Whatever he saw... it wasn't real,' said Lord Calver. 'There was nothing there.'

'Perhaps,' said the Guide.

'Demon?' The Xancheran suggested.

Bernice shivered. Everyone knew demons lurked in the darkness beyond the protective glow of the wardstones that ringed each town and gave them light. They hovered above the darkest pathways between the landings, and devoured any travellers foolish enough to walk the paths without a Guide. It was possible to survive beyond the wardlights for a time, although Bernice had never heard of anyone spending more than a few hours in the dark, and no one could live there forever. The wardlights not only warded off demons; they brought the landings to life. No food could grow beyond their light. The ability to power them was the reason Guides were so valued. With only one in one hundred able to summon light, it was a rare skill that was deeply prized.

At the start of the journey, the Xancheran's suggestion might have been easy to dismiss. Demons were rare in the high strata of the landings, where the pathways were short and the towns clustered together, sometimes with less than a stone's throw between one landing and the next. In the low strata, however, the paths were longer and the darkness between the landings was deeper. Everyone in the lower landings knew not to stray too far from the wardlights. This deep in the substrata, demons were never far away. It was said they were drawn to the temple and they came in the thousands to lay siege to the gods.

'It could be a demon,' said the Guide, his voice calm and steady. 'Although, I've never known one to take a pilgrim from the path.'

Bernice took a breath and shook off the fear, sharper than any emotion she'd felt for a long time. It wasn't a demon. She knew it wasn't a demon - she'd seen Lord Calver with his palm pressed to his manservant's chest right before he fell. Besides, they had a Guide travelling with them to protect them.

'He was carrying the last of the food,' said the Guide. 'We might have nothing to eat tonight.'

'I have.' The Xancheran gave a reassuring nod. 'Inshirumsum.'

The word meant nothing to Bernice, and the Guide furrowed his brow as well. Lord Calver shifted, impatient to leave. She hoped the Xancheran understood they were talking about food and was offering something edible.

As though the Xancheran's words were a signal, the group disbanded. The Al'veran monk left to start a fire in the fire pit at the centre of the landing and fill a pot with water from his water-stone. The Xancheran went to sit beside him, opening his pack and digging through it for the last of his food. Lord Calver disappeared to the other side of the landing, hidden from sight.

The Guide stayed.

Bernice wondered what the Guide would say if she told him she'd seen Lord Calver push the manservant off the ledge. He might believe her, but that wouldn't matter. When she'd joined the pilgrimage, she'd been told Lord Calver was a baron, cousin to the queen and a retired army general. The Guide was in command while they walked the pilgrimage, but Lord Calver had the power in the world beyond.

Bernice said nothing.

The Guide was the first to speak. 'He was carrying your bags.' His voice was low and filled with sympathy.

The others seemed to have forgotten, but the Guide had looked out for Bernice more than once on the pilgrimage already. His kindnesses prickled at her skin, like material knit from xanthan fur. Warm and irritating, but ultimately welcome when one had only ever been cold, lonely, and unloved.

Bernice looked out at the void where the manservant had fallen, her bags on his back along with his own. They hadn't even reached the first landing when Lord Calver had decided she was a liability and had snapped at his manservant to take her bags so she could keep up with the pace. He hadn't said she was fat and unfit and shouldn't have come on the pilgrimage, but it had been implied. His manservant hadn't been happy, and Bernice had received several resentful looks over the situation. She'd tried to say thank you. Her overtures had been met by a stony silence.

'There wasn't anything important in them,' said Bernice, still looking down. This deep in the void no landings glowed in the distance. There was only darkness, as far as she could see. The dark of the void; held back from consuming them by the wardstones their Guide imbued with light as they travelled.

Her answer was only partially true. The bags had contained her grandfather's will, the only document that identified Bernice as the rightful owner of the narrow and dusty townhouse her grandfather had owned in Exedon. It was a dark and gloomy place, with faded carpet, unfashionable wallpaper, and cabinets filled with curios along every wall. It was lonely and uncomfortable and the only place she'd lived since her parents died when she was twelve.

Bernice had left it behind without regret and dreaded the thought of returning. She hated the townhouse in the same way she hated the fact she had her mother's eyes. It was a fact of life she wished she could be rid of but could never imagine changing.

Without the will, Bernice would have nothing to her name except her memories and the sins she was praying would be forgiven. It was a terrifying and liberating thought.

...

The next morning, Bernice was woken by the Xancheran calling Rin's name. The monk was on his back and wasn't moving, even when the other man shook his shoulders and begged for him to wake.

'Won't wake,' said the Xancheran, when he noticed Bernice was sitting up and watching him. 'Sick.'

Bernice went over to them. The monk was sweating. When she put a hand to his forehead she could feel a fever burning through him. A dark red rash curled around his throat like a collar. It was distinctive but unfamiliar to Bernice. Her knowledge of fevers was limited to the ones her mother had let burn through her unchecked when she was a child.

The Guide and Lord Calver, woken by the noise, came to find out what was happening.

'He was well last night,' said the Guide. He glanced at the Xancheran and then back at Lord Calver. 'Perhaps the food—?'

Lord Calver shook his head. 'No, this is different.'

The Xancheran looked between them, mouthing the word 'different' and then touched his forefinger to his lip in the sign of a silent prayer to Tully.

Bernice wondered what the Xancheran was making of this. It was said demons could make men sick as well as lead them to their death. It would be natural for the Xancheran to believe the monk's illness was linked to the manservant's death the day before. Only Bernice and Lord Calver knew any better.

'He needs a healer,' said the Guide. 'We don't know enough to help whatever this is.'

Lord Calver nodded and knelt to take the monk's temperature for himself.

His voice had been curt, as though the monk's illness was an irritating distraction, but his hand was gentle as he pressed it against the monk's forehead. It didn't look like the hand of a killer. Bernice looked down at her own palms, curled on her lap. Plump fingers and no jewellery. Black dirt from the climb crusted under her nails.

'The Temple is on the next landing,' said the Guide. 'There are healers there.'

'We'll have to carry him down,' said Lord Calver. His gaze travelled from the Guide, who needed to be able to move freely, to the Xancheran, who had complained of being sore from the climb every night, and finally to Bernice, unable to carry her own bags.

He sighed and looked over at the Xancheran. 'Bring me your blanket.'

Bernice helped the Guide pack away the camp while Lord Calver and the Xancheran made a sling to tie the monk to Lord Calver's back. Bernice picked up one of the bags.

'You feel well?' asked the Guide.

Bernice nodded and glanced over at the monk. She knew what the Guide was thinking. If the illness afflicting him was one that could pass to another person, they'd all been exposed. She felt the knowledge settle deep inside her, yet another burden to carry. The knowledge brought with it fear, but it was dull. As though there was some part of her deep within that felt she deserved to get the disease. She flinched away from the thought as soon as it rose in her and turned back to packing the bags.

'If you need anything, let me know,' said the Guide.

Bernice glanced at him, gripping the Xancheran's pack tightly to hide the shaking in her hands. The Guide's gaze was soft and friendly.

Bernice looked away. She could feel the temptation to lean into his kindness. He was compassionate and gentle and she was cold. Like a starving cat, staring through a window at the warm fireplace, wanting to get close enough that it burned. She wondered what he'd say if he knew who she truly was. If he knew why she was here and what she'd been running from when she'd left to seek her gods.

'I'll be fine,' she said.

...

The descent to the last landing was longer than any of the others. The Guide went first, imbuing wardlights down the length of the pillar of rock to guide the way. Lord Calver went next with the monk on his back, followed by Bernice and then the Xancheran carrying Lord Calver's bags as well as his own.

Things seemed to be going well until about halfway. Bernice felt it before she saw it. A nauseous, sick feeling filled her stomach, and she was hit with the sense memory of eating a rotten apple when she was a child, starving and forcing it down her throat because her mother hadn't fed her for days and her belly was gnawing at her ribs. The slimy, musty sense of it filled her mouth and nose. Bile clawed up her throat. She closed her eyes, only to open them to the sight of a dark shadow moving above her, sliding down the pillar, formless and unidentifiable except for two yellow slit eyes. The sick feeling in her stomach intensified and fear raced through her, freezing her muscles until she was unable to even take a breath.

Above her, the Xancheran gave a yell and lost his grip. He fell past

Bernice as the shadow grew closer, coming right toward her. Bernice closed her eyes and gripped the pillar tight, holding on with all her strength. She felt the shadow wash over her, breaking on the barrier created by the wardlights, unable to get through. Below her, Lord Calver and the Guide also cried out, and a piercing light flooded up the pillar as the Guide strengthened the wardlights he'd set on the way down. Within moments the demon was gone. As quickly as it had came, it disappeared.

'Is everyone all right?' the Guide called.

'The Xancheran—' Bernice choked on her answer.

'The Xancheran fell,' said Lord Calver, matter of factly. 'He let go when it came. Fear, I think.'

There was silence down below. 'We will say a prayer for him when we reach the landing,' said the Guide.

Lord Calver said nothing. He just started moving down.

Bernice stayed where she was for several heartbeats. Part of her was sure she couldn't go on. She started moving again when the wardlights around her dimmed and she realised it would be worse to be left behind in the dark. If the demon came back, she'd be the best target, alone and unprotected. With her hands cramping and her knees aching, she climbed the rest of the way down.

...

Bernice didn't slow down until she reached the last landing. Unlike the other landings scattered along the descent to the temple's entrance, this landing was lined with wardlights, already imbued with light to welcome the pilgrims at the end of their journey.

The Guide and Lord Calver were standing at the bottom, waiting for her.

'He fell over there,' the Guide gestured to a part of the landing beyond the glow of the wardlights. Bernice wasn't sure if she imagined it, but she thought she could see a dark shape among the shadows. 'We checked the body. Broken neck. He died on impact.'

'We said the prayers,' said Lord Calver, his voice flat.

'We didn't think you'd want us to wait.' The Guide's voice was gentler.

Bernice nodded and looked away from the shadows. 'What was it?' she asked. 'The thing.'

The Guide's mouth tightened, and he shook his head. 'I don't know,' he said. 'I've never seen anything like it.'

'Yellow eyes,' said Lord Calver. 'Whatever it was has been following us since yesterday.'

Bernice looked at him and wondered once again what she'd seen from the outcropping above the landing. If the demon was real, what had happened when she'd seen him push his manservant over the edge?

'Come on,' said the Guide. 'Let's get inside. It will be safer there.'

The Guide led the way through the wardlights and along the pathway that was the only thing tethering the temple to the other landings that made up their world. As they approached the door, carvings in the stone came into focus. On the temple doorway a carving depicted the five gods fighting serpent shaped demons. The gods were carved to resemble humans, wearing armour and wielding rays of light. Overhead there was a circle with rays of light coming from it too.

Bernice had read about the temple carvings. Father Oredon had found her an eager pupil when he talked about the temple. He'd told her there was a great debate about the single circle above the temple door. One side of the debate claimed it was a mythological light source called the sun. A light that burned so bright it could illuminate all the pathways of the world. The other side of the debate said the sun of legend was a folk tale. They said the circle depicted a great wardlight, like those that ringed the foreign city of Xanchera.

At the temple gate, the Guide knocked on the doors. They were vast, twice the height of a person and wide enough to take in four people abreast. Set into them was a single smaller door, the size of one person. It was this that opened.

'Elric,' said the man who opened the door, greeting the Guide as a friend.

'Riven,' said the Guide. He stepped forward and clasped the priest's arm in greeting. 'You look tired.'

As soon as the Guide said it, Bernice saw that he was right. The priest looked worn thin. His long brown hair was oily and limp around his forehead and he had dark shadows beneath his eyes.

The priest nodded and stepped back, letting the Guide's hand drop from his arm. 'It is not good, Elric,' he said. 'There is a sickness in the temple. You should take your pilgrims back to their homes.'

The Guide shook his head and gestured to the monk on Lord Calver's back. 'We need help,' he said.

'A fever with a rash?' The priest gestured at his throat.

The Guide nodded. The priest sighed, and his shoulders fell. 'Then the illness has escaped the temple and you cannot return. The High Priest has commanded that no one touched by the illness may leave. You should take your friends to the infirmary.' He stepped back, holding the temple door open. 'There may not be much help for him. The healers are overwhelmed. Still—they will do what they can.'

The Guide led them into the temple. Beyond the door was a vast atrium filled with irregular columns that stretched high into a shadowed ceiling. The columns were carved ornately with patterns that looked like knotted rope covered in strange serrated ovals. Only a small portion of the atrium was visible. Wardlights had been set out in a single pathway leading between the columns and into the distance.

'Normally, it wouldn't be so dark,' said the priest. 'We have been conserving our energy since the illness came. You know the way to the infirmary?'

Their Guide nodded and they set out along the path of the wardlights. 'On feast days, the entire atrium is lit,' said the Guide, gesturing to the vastness of the room. 'I have known thousands to gather here with room to spare.'

Bernice didn't know what to say. She stayed silent along with Lord Calver as they passed through a door at the side of the atrium and into a small dark corridor beyond. The lights there were dimmer and warmer. The Guide led them down the corridor, turning left and right at regular intervals, even as the corridors split and branched and the maze of lights led away in other directions. 'Here,' he said as they reached the end of a corridor. He pushed open a door and led them in. 'The infirmary.'

...

The infirmary was filled with hundreds of patients. There were beds along the walls and pallets on the floor. Dozens of healers moved among the sick, followed by acolytes dressed in black and carrying bowls of water and clean cloths.

An acolyte came to them as they entered and led them to an empty bed. 'One of the sisters passed this morning,' they said, before they left to tend to another patient.

Lord Calver put the monk on the bed and stepped back. Bernice sat down in the single chair beside the bed. It creaked as she sat but held steady. Lord Calver sat on the edge of the bed opposite and stared at the monk. The bed's occupant behind him didn't so much as stir.

'Will he live?' Lord Calver asked, his voice low and rough.

'I don't know,' the Guide replied. He looked over at Bernice. 'You'll be cared for here. I need to go and let Father Warren know about the Xancheran's body. Wait for one of the healers to come and help you. They'll make sure you're both okay.'

Bernice nodded. She wanted to beg the Guide not to leave but swallowed the words.

With a nod, the Guide turned and left.

Lord Calver looked at Bernice. 'Just us, then.'

Bernice looked at him and realised she no longer wanted to carry the burden he'd forced on her when he threw the manservant off the landing. She had weight enough of her own to take before the gods, without carrying his as well.

'You killed him, didn't you?' she said. 'Your manservant.'

Lord Calver's expression grew unnaturally still. 'You saw,' he said, his voice rough.

'Yes,' said Bernice.

'Why didn't you say?'

'Would it have done any good?' Bernice looked down at her hands, curled in her lap. 'You're a lord of the realm. Even if the other's had believed me, you only needed to say the word and you'd have walked free.' She looked back up, catching Lord Calver's gaze. 'No matter what, your manservant would still be dead.'

Lord Calver stared at her. 'I'm not—' He cleared his throat. 'I'm not going to justify myself to you.' The words were harsh, dismissive. He stood up abruptly and looked out over the infirmary. 'I'm going to get help.'

He stalked away. Bernice watched him go and wondered what had brought him here. A lord, a general, a murderer. In the distance, he waded through the crowd of the infirmary and then disappeared entirely, going through one of the side doors. She replayed, once more, the moment he pushed his manservant over the edge of the landing. She wondered what he'd thought in that moment. If the demon had tapped into something deep and dark inside him and he'd found some secret relief in sending his manservant over the edge.

Around her the healers hurried from one patient to the next, followed by their acolytes who only briefly left their side to gather more supplies or remove the bodies of those who had passed away.

Bernice sat quietly and let the noise and atmosphere of the infirmary wash over her. She felt like a speck of dust, suspended in the air, unmoored from the things that had once anchored her to her life. She thought of her grandfather's house and the town she'd never return to. It wasn't a sad thought. She'd lived in the house for over a decade, but it had never been her home. Her grandfather had treated her more like a nurse and housekeeper than a member of the family, and she'd never made friends or had anyone else to care for.

It had been a lonely life and, despite everything, she was thankful she'd chosen to join the pilgrimage. She'd used to imagine the journey, sitting in church on holy days and listening to Father Oredon speak of the gifts given by the gods. She'd dreamed of simply getting up and walking out of her grandfather's house, joining a pilgrim group walking the path to the temple. She'd never dreamed of arriving, only of leaving everything else behind.

Beside Bernice, the monk shifted on the bed uncomfortably. Bernice reached out and put a hand to his forehead. His temperature was rising. The rash on his chest had spread down his arms, and she could see it peeking out from beneath the sleeves of his shift.

Bernice sat back down and looked out at the infirmary again. Beside her, the monk shifted and moaned until, eventually, he fell silent.

She looked over at him but didn't bother reaching out to touch him again.

With no reason to stay, she stood up. On her way out, she found one of the acolytes hurrying back to their healer with fresh cloths and told them one of the beds was no longer needed. The acolyte nodded, looking flustered and red in the cheeks. Bernice looked down at their collar and saw the tell-tale spread of a rash creeping across their skin. She thanked them for their time and left the infirmary.

...

Out in the corridor, Bernice followed the brightest wardlights deeper into the temple. She met no one to stop her or ask her what she was doing.

Eventually, the path of wardlights led her to the temple shrine. The room was large and well-lit. It was larger than the cathedral Bernice had attended while living with her grandfather. Larger even, she suspected, than the Archbishop's cathedral in the capital. It had rows of seats facing a great altar at the end of the room.

The altar had been carved from the stone itself. Like the temple doors, it depicted a famous scene from the battle between the gods and the serpent beasts. The gods were carved on either side of the altar. They appeared human and were wearing robes so finely sculpted that each fold of the cloth could be seen. They had their heads raised and their arms overhead. Inside their hands were bright wardlights, glittering with power. The demon they were fighting was between them, its body winding its way around the altar and its head raised high over the room, its mouth open to devour the gods below. The eyes of the demon glinted in the light spilling from the wardlights: two yellow gems set deep into its rock skull.

Bernice knelt in front of the altar and prayed. There was no response. Bernice looked up. Whatever answer she'd been hoping to find, it wasn't here. The holiest of holies was an empty room.

She sat back on her knees and looked at the gods carved into the rock—Agnetha and Tully, the sister gods of light. The great defenders against the dark and the first among equals in the pantheon she'd worshipped since birth. Whoever carved these images had done a good job. Agnetha and Tully's features were polished with loving detail. Bernice found herself looking at the flare of their noses, the snarl of their mouths exposing their teeth and the wildness of their eyes. As she stared, she saw for the first time the fear and desperation on their faces.

Around her, the air in the room began to close in until it felt claustrophobic and stifling.

Bile rose in her throat. The same sensation she'd felt when the demon appeared outside flooded through her. The air felt foul and thick as she drew a breath and dragged it into her lungs. It tasted of rotten fruit and the sharp iron tang of blood. Bernice coughed, and it was like trying to breathe in while drowning in a pool of stagnant water. She fell to her hands and knees and fought back the memory of being locked in her bedroom until her tongue became so swollen in her mouth she'd become desperate and drank water from the basin of water on her washstand. It had tasted like sickness, and she'd paid the price later, but she'd survived.

She looked up at the altar, at the fear on her gods' faces and at the demon poised over them, ready to devour them all. The wardlights glinted off the demon's yellow eyes. This room had not been built for her gods. Wherever they were, it wasn't here. This shrine had been carved for the demon at its centre.

Bernice tore her gaze away. She looked to her right and saw a body hidden by one of the columns. It had collapsed on the ground like a ragdoll, thrown through the air and left behind where it fell. She crawled to it on her hands and knees. She knew it was Lord Calver before she turned it over. He'd been sitting in the pew near the column when he'd slit his wrists. Had it been the realisation this was a place belonging to demons that sent him over the edge? Or simply the emptiness of the room? It could destroy you—praying to an absent god.

'He couldn't stand the guilt,' said a voice behind Bernice. Masculine and smooth. 'He enjoyed it, you see—the moment he pushed his manservant over the edge. It ate at him. The knowledge he felt joy in the killing.' The foulness of the room subsided enough for Bernice to drag in a single deep breath.

Bernice turned to look at the man behind her. He was dressed in black robes over a black silk shirt and trousers. His hair was long, and half-pulled back at the top of his head; it gleamed where it fell in waves to the small of his back. His skin was porcelain-fine and his features were perfectly proportioned—a strong nose and full mouth. It was his eyes that gave him away. They were gleaming yellow slits.

Bernice moaned in fear and stared up at him, as speechless as the monk had been before he died. Her tongue felt thick and heavy in her mouth. Immovable.

The man stepped forward and crouched down to look her straight on. 'You timed your pilgrimage poorly, my dear Bernice,' he said, almost gently. 'It's taken thousands of years for us to gather the energy to break free, and here you are. On the day we finally succeed.'

He looked over at the slumped body of Lord Calver and gave a nod in its direction. 'It was his sacrifice that did it. We only needed one more death to break the bindings tethering us to this place.'

The creature stood up again. Bernice swallowed and looked away, trying to turn her face from the demon and the statue that dominated the room. The creature laughed.

Bernice felt tears running down her face as her chest heaved in silent sobs.

The creature strode toward the altar and stopped in front of it. Bernice could hear the soft scuff of its feet and the gentle rustle of its robes.

'Look at me, Bernice,' it said, the command in its voice impossible to refuse.

Bernice looked up, her cheeks still wet.

The creature looked down at her. 'I'm going to give you a chance,' it said. 'Oh no—' It raised a hand in warning, commanding her to stay silent. 'It's not because you deserve to survive. The opposite, really.' It gazed down at her, and there was no more softness in its face. No more pretend gentleness or fellow feeling.

'I'm going to give you a chance because you have been a true worshipper at my shrine,' it said. 'You have prayed to me every day with your fear and your anger. For years now, you have given me rich offerings of bitterness and resentment. You are one of mine, Bernice, and, for that, you will be given this chance.'

Bernice tried to look away.

It caught her gaze and held it, pinning her to the ground. 'I know you, Bernice, and all the things you've done. I know you stood outside your parents' door when the roof caved in and listened to them screaming and crying, asking you to go for help. I know you stood there and I know you did nothing.'

Its words were like lashes peeling Bernice's skin from her, leaving her bloody and naked on the floor.

'I know the doctor told you your grandfather was healthy enough to live another dozen years, so you purchased powder for killing rats and fed it to him day by day until he withered away and died. I know you, Bernice. I know only minutes ago you sat by Rin's bedside in the infirmary and watched him die, doing nothing to help. Bernice, you cannot hide what you are. Not from me.'

Bernice choked and tore her gaze away from the creature's eyes only to have them catch on the yellow gems of the serpent statue. She felt seen for the first time in her life, as though all the layers of her—the skin, the flesh, the muscle and the bone—had been stripped away, leaving only the essence of her on display. She was a crippled, broken, and unworthy thing.

The creature raised its hands and the wardlight held by the god Agnetha floated down into its grip. 'Take this wardlight,' said the creature reaching out to Bernice. 'It will be enough light to take you safely back up the landings to Exedon. Tell them what happened when you get there. You will be our prophet to the people. You can let them know their death has been reborn and is coming for them soon enough.'

Bernice slowly stood, struggling to get her legs under her as she fought a battle against gravity. Her pilgrim's robes clung to her like poorly fitted sheets, stained and dusty from the floor.

She reached out for the wardlight but the creature pulled it away, holding it just beyond her reach. 'There is one condition,' it said. 'I offer you this gift only as long as you are true to yourself. Stop for no one. Give no one aid. You are our prophet, and only you will survive. Everybody else's life is forfeit to me.'

Bernice's eyes widened and she shook her head in denial.

The demon stared back. 'No?' it asked, as though amused. 'Do you think refusing will bring redemption?' It gave a cold smile. 'You should know by now you don't deserve redemption for what you've done.'

Bernice flinched away as the final, flimsy membrane protecting her from the truth of herself was torn aside.

Her mother and grandfather had formed her. That was true. They'd sketched what she was to become in bruises on her skin. But she was the one who'd painted in the details. It had been her choice to let her parents die while the cries of the rescue teams echoed from the streets. She'd bought the poison to feed her grandfather and had never once hesitated to serve one with his morning tea, even as it weakened him and he withered away.

Bernice trembled. She realised what she had always known deep inside. There had never been forgiveness waiting for her here. Only judgement.

'If you don't take it, no one will,' said the demon. 'I will not make this offer to anyone else. It's you or no one, Bernice. Make your choice.'

She thought of Lord Calver, who couldn't live with the burden of having killed a single man. Weakness or bravery? She didn't know. She only knew her own burden had been carried for so long it had become part of her. It had dug so deep that it had changed the very shape of her soul and she'd grown calluses to help numb the pain. She'd thought she could put it down and leave it behind with her gods but she realised now it had been false hope leading her on. The realisation would be enough to break her, if she wasn't broken already.

The demon had removed the calluses but nothing could ever remove the things she had done or the way her choices had twisted her —moulded her—into shape.

She wasn't Lord Calver. She was an uglier, more pitiful thing and she wanted to survive.

She reached out her hands.

The creature smiled and gave her the wardlight. 'Off you go now,' it said, with a casual flick of its hand. 'Time to leave.'

...

Bernice left the shrine, her feet carrying her away on instinct. The wardlights along the walls had all flickered out, their warmth consumed by the passage of whatever evil lurked within them. There was noise ahead, and Bernice followed it until she came to the atrium and emerged into chaos. She hugged the wardlight the creature had given her to her chest. It was warm and alive under her hands, its goodness worming its way into her chest and rebuilding some small part of what the creature had torn apart, enough for her to feel sick with horror at the sight that greeted her.

The priests and priestesses had been taken without warning. Bodies lay heaped across the ground. Overhead, great serpentine shapes circled in the shadows among the columns. Clawed feet dripped with blood and knife-sharp tails left deep gouges in the pillars as they passed. Those temple priests and priestesses who were still alive were being herded one way and then another as the demons drank in their fear and desperation.

Bernice walked past them toward the doorway on the other side of the atrium. As she passed, cries for help echoed off the walls. She kept her eyes on the doorway and didn't look around. With every cry she ignored, a new burden of guilt was added to the load she carried. No longer dull or distant, the feeling burned her like a brand, sinking through her flesh and etching scars on her bones.

Bernice had protected herself for years, keeping her feelings at a distance. Telling herself she'd be a different person, if only she could escape the grasp of her mother. If only she could leave her grandfather and the prison of his townhouse behind. But she was a creature of her own making and deep inside she'd known from the moment she'd shouldered the burden of her pilgrimage that she'd be held solely accountable for her sins. As those around her died and she did nothing to help them, she knew one day she'd be held to account for this as well.

Overhead, demons turned to look at her with sickly red and purple gazes, but none of them tried to stop her. She'd been given passage from this place, and they weren't going to stand in her way.

'You.' Near the doorway, the priest who had welcomed them to the temple lay against the wall in a pool of rapidly spreading blood. He was still alive, and she could feel his eyes on her as she came closer. 'Was it you?'

Bernice didn't look at him and didn't answer.

The door opened. She was about to step through when a voice behind her called her name.

'Bernice.' The voice was familiar. Bernice turned and saw the Guide, Elric, several columns away and hurrying toward her. His curly brown hair was matted with blood on one side, and he was limping on his left ankle, but he was alive. Bernice stared at him and felt an echo of the same warmth that had bubbled within her at the campfires along the pilgrimage. Elric had been kind to her. He was the only person she'd ever known who had cared enough about her feelings to sit with her and ask if she was okay.

His wide brown eyes caught hers, and she saw relief in them that she was alive. Relief and hope. He had seen the open door, and Bernice didn't need to hear him speak to know he thought they might be able to escape together and survive the slaughter of the temple.

He slowed a little, lulled into a false sense of security.

Behind him, a silver-grey demon raised its head.

Bernice heard the demon's words echoing in her mind. *Stop for no one. Give no one aid. Everybody else's life is forfeit to me.*

Two pathways laid themselves out in front of her, as clearly as if she was standing at a fork in the road. Hold the door open, help Elric escape and in doing so condemn herself to death. Or leave the temple now and save herself.

Hugging the wardlight to her chest, Bernice chose.

OF FULL MOONS AND MOONSHINE
BY MARTY KESLAR

When Marty Keslar is not writing fantasy, she works as a tour guide in
Salem, MA and as a freelance theatre technician. Raised as a dancer,
her hobbies encompass a wide variety of activities including knitting,
sketching, painting, playing Dungeon and Dragons, and researching
Irish folklore. Marty can be found enjoying life with her cat and her
fiancée outside of Boston.

* * *

"Grandpa! You promised us a story."

Patrick McGillicuddy grinned wryly at his twelve-year-old grandson, Michael. Putting an empty tankard down on the table, he said,
"That I did, but have you come prepared to listen?"

It warmed Patrick's old heart to see the boy nodding, even if it was
only once. Patrick turned to his nine-year-old granddaughter Mary and
raised an eyebrow. "And have you got time for your grandpa's tales?"

"Yes," Mary gleefully sat in a chair, her eyes shining in her excite-
ment. "Grandmum Sheila told us you had seen the fairies long ago. Can
you tell us that one?"

"Sheila told you about the fairies, eh?" Patrick chuckled. "I suppose

I can tell you about that. Though I have a question for you two. Do you believe in the good folk?"

Mary nodded but Michael only shrugged, and Patrick wondered briefly if his grandson would have reacted differently if the story were about trains or wars. The old man raised a kind eyebrow. "You doubt, Michael?"

The boy shrugged again as he slumped into another chair. "Well, I haven't seen them."

Turning to the small table beside him, Patrick filled his tankard with his famous home-brewed moonshine. Taking a sip, he relished in the taste. It was almost the same as his father used to brew but somehow a touch better than his old man's. Throughout his long life he had never tasted anything quite like his own recipe for moonshine.

Patrick sat once more in his large armchair and ran a thumb over the worn cap of his cane. "You might see the good folk if you walked through the crossroads on the full moon."

Leaping up from her chair, Mary ran to the small window. "Really? It's the full moon tonight! Can we go?"

Laughing, Patrick placed his tankard back on the table. "Sheila would box our ears if we did something so foolish. But I can do something better."

"What's that?" Mary asked, turning away from the window.

The old man lowered his voice into a theatrical whisper. "I can tell you about the time I talked with the queen of fairies."

Michael rolled his eyes. "Fairies are only stories you old folk come up with to keep us from having fun outside."

"And if I told you that I saw them with my own eyes?" Patrick asked, taking another swig.

Michael hesitated. "You swear?"

Nodding solemnly, he replied, "By the saints above us, I swear I saw the good folk."

"Oh enough of this," Mary said, walking back to her chair and settled into it. "Tell us the story!"

Thumping his cane lightly against the floor, Patrick launched into his tale.

"When I was a young man, nearing the end of my apprenticeship years, my mum, that would be your great grandma, bid me go to my friend Ryan's house."

"Was Ryan a fairy?" Mary whispered.

Patrick grinned. "Far from it. A more solid lad you've never met. He didn't believe in the fairies either. Rather like Michael here."

His grandson looked ready to protest this notion but Patrick tapped his cane on the floor again. Seeing his grandson start down the path of discarding the world of wonder and beauty for the more mechanized world of logic and purpose broke Patrick's heart. Holding his grandson's eyes in his gaze, his inner resolve settled. "All I ask is that you listen."

After a moment of consideration, Michael gave a slow nod.

Smiling, Patrick continued. "My mum had entrusted me with the task of giving a fresh cheese to Ryan's mum. That would be Mrs. Callahan, it would. As Mum handed me the bundle, she reminded me that while the road was fair in the day, it was perilous after dusk. But I barely heard her warning for in my youthful enthusiasm, I estimated that I could get to Mrs. Callahan's and return well before the shades of dusk fell."

"But did you?" Mary asked.

"I'm getting there, young Mary. I started off bright and early. My mother had given me my old father's hawthorn walking stick. Even though he had passed on, God bless him, we thought a little bit of his protective spirit resided in that old hawthorn stick."

Michael snorted. "Really?"

Patrick raised an eyebrow. "Yes, we did. Whenever my mum or I had that stick, no harm befell us. Even if we fell from a cliff or slipped near a bog, we came to no harm."

"Do you still have it?" Mary whispered in awe.

Patrick grinned. "Of course I do."

"Can you show us?" she asked.

"It's right there," he pointed to a rather worn but trusty-looking walking stick leaning against the corner of the house. Mary's eyes widened and even Michael looked at it curiously.

"Now, if you keep interrupting me, I'll never finish. So hush with your questions until I'm done, eh?" Patrick grinned to lessen the sting of his words.

Mary settled in her chair again and Michael's eyes wandered to the window. Patrick sighed a little as he watched his grandson.

"So, there I was," he continued, "walking on the road to Ryan's house with my trusty walking stick in one hand and the fresh cheese in my satchel. The journey there caused no alarm, though I must say the back of my neck prickled as I passed the old oak trees at the cross-roads. You know the ones. That crossroad appeared so peaceful but I didn't trust it, so I clutched my walking stick and hurried through. It felt as though eyes watched me and I fairly flew the rest of the way."

"So you didn't see the fairies then?" Mary asked, disappointment creeping into her voice.

"No, I didn't," Patrick replied. He lowered his voice and added, "But I will tell you that I felt mighty queer having those ghostly eyes staring at me. I made it to Ryan's house and it was a merry meeting. I gave Mrs. Callahan the cheese and while Ryan and I tusseled playfully as we did when we were younger, Mrs. Callahan made a plate of some bread and cheese for a small meal."

Patrick leaned in closer to Mary and Michael and said in a lower voice, "But when I prepared to leave, Mrs. Callahan looked out the window, and what do you think she chanced to see?"

Mary bounced a little. "The sunset!"

"Exactly. As I put on my coat and grabbed my trusty stick, she pulled me aside. 'Patrick,' said she, 'I don't like the idea of you going out after dark like this. The perils of the crossroads are dangerous tonight for us mortal folk.'

"'You mean the fairies are there?' I asked her.

"'Tis the full moon. They hold their court there and it isn't wise for mortals to be caught in their mischief.'

"I stood up straight. 'I have my walking stick. Pperhaps I can walk around the crossroads and not use the road.'

"Ryan's mum shook her head. 'That is even more dangerous, for the will-o-the-wisps are likely to bring you to your doom. You must stick to the path and run through that crossroads like the hounds of hell are at your heels. Don't stop until you are far away from that crossroad.'"

Mary interrupted. "But why is it so dangerous?"

Patrick smiled wryly. "It is dangerous to disturb the fairies at their sport, for they don't like being interrupted. They have the power to change me into anything they want, or to take my cows, or my mum, or make my life miserable in a hundred different ways. I know you wish to see the fairies, Mary. But listen to more of my tale."

Mary settled once more, listening intently.

"I now had my mum's warning of walking after dusk, and also Ryan's mum's warning about the crossroads. Clutching my father's walking stick tightly, I hoped his spirit was indeed with me as I walked the path towards the crossroads.

"As dusk fell around me and shadows began to linger, my nerves tightened. I'd walked this path a hundred times in the day, but there's something about the darkness that gives a familiar landscape new terrors."

Michael scoffed. "You were scared?"

Patrick shifted in his chair. "I was. Only a fool wouldn't be. As the night creatures started making their noises, I crested the hill and the full moon's light illuminated the crossroads before me. I watched them for a good while, making note if anything crossed them. I saw two hares dash across, but that was it. Glancing off to the surrounding countryside, I saw the little will-o-the-wisps. I knew not to follow those for they led to the bogs. There wasn't anything else for it; I had to run through the crossroads. Both Mum's words and Mrs. Callahan's words stayed close in my mind as I cautiously stepped towards the place where the two roads crossed. The full moon reigned in the sky as I inched closer. Every sense clamored that I was being watched. My heart began to race and I clutched my walking stick tight as I prepared to run.

"But before I could take a step, a woman's deep voice rang out through the clearing.

"'Who dares enter my domain?'"

Mary gasped. "The fairies!"

"Who's telling the story, eh?"

Patrick tapped the cane against the floor. Mary grinned and settled in to listen some more.

"The fairy that spoke was not just any fairy. As I started to run, I tripped spectacularly and landed at the feet of the most beautiful woman I have ever beheld. I can still remember her red dress, her long, raven-black hair, and her piercing silver eyes. I felt trapped as those eyes examined me from head to toe, her lips tightening into a straight line. I scrambled to my feet and held my trusty stick in front of me, hoping against hope that my father's spirit could protect me from this strange woman."

"Was she the queen of fairies?" Mary asked.

Michael rolled his eyes. "Well, he did say he would tell us the story of meeting the queen of fairies."

"It could have been one of her ladies in waiting," Mary shot back.

"It was indeed the queen of fairies. Now hush your noise," Patrick interrupted. "But there was another fairy with her, a cheerful fellow, though he did rather delight in making sport of me."

"Who was that?" Mary asked.

Patrick hesitated, wanting to reprimand Mary for interrupting once more, but then his eyes settled on Michael. Maybe, just maybe, he could bring back the childlike wonder to his grandson's eyes. Michael had always loved stories involving one particular character when he was younger. Patrick whispered the name, as if a magic spell. "Robin Goodfellow."

"Robin was there?" Michael gasped. The boy straightened in his chair, eyes widening.

Seeing his grandson suddenly gain interest in the story gladdened Patrick's old heart. "Aye, that he was. He was the one that tripped me and laughed as I tried to regain my composure. I didn't like being laughed at, so I bristled a little as the queen and Robin conversed."

"First the queen asked how any mortal could be so foolish as to cross her, and Robin replied, 'Ah, but this young man appears to have been wanting only to pass through before I tripped him up.'

"Before I could say anything in my defense, my trusty stick began to feel a bit warmer in my hands and I had a small voice in my head tell me to stay silent. I stared at the stick in wonder. I felt as if my father stood with me as dozens more fairies stood at each of the paths leading from the crossroads. I tried to keep my wits, but with being surrounded by the good folk, listening to the taunts of Robin Good-fellow and trembling at the feet of their queen, I didn't know if I would survive that night! The full moon indeed found me at a perilous place. Now, if you ever find yourself in a similar predicament, always remember this: speak as few words as possible. The good folk will take whatever you say and twist it."

Both children nodded. Patrick smiled to see that Michael began to listen more thoughtfully. "So, I don't remember all the words that the fairies said, but I do remember Robin saying, 'And the foolish mortals always wish for things that lead to their ruin.'

"'A wish, a wish!' the other fairies began chanting, and the queen's eyes sparkled as she turned towards me. 'Young mortal, do you wish something from us?' They chanted and sang, and suggested the most outlandish wishes for me to choose from. They offered me the moon, the stars, riches beyond understanding and more. They began to dance around me, and while I do like a good dance, this was the most wild dervish I had ever seen. Their howls and laughter mocked me from all sides as they whirled around me.

"I clutched the walking stick and thought of my father. My old man had always been a sturdy presence in the home. When he was alive, we always had plenty of visitors coming over for my father's moonshine and good stories. Ever since he died, Mum and I could never find the recipe and so the visitors had come less and less. I could tell Mum was getting quite lonely, and I even missed those days. The stick warmed in my hands once more and suddenly I felt a warm hand on my right shoulder. Hesitating, I reached for that warmth with my left hand. Once my hand touched the ghostly one, my father's words spilled out of my mouth.

"'I want the best recipe for moonshine!'"

Michael's eyes bugged. "Your famous moonshine!"

Patrick nodded. "Aye, the very same. As I stated my wish for moon-shine, the fairies stopped their frantic whirl and froze. A hundred pairs of eyes stared at me, though the most intense belonged to the silver eyes of the queen. After some silence, Robin Goodfellow started laughing and I turned bright red."

"The queen looked rather strange as she said, 'You wish for the best recipe for moonshine?'

"I had regained control of my tongue, at least and answered her aye.

"'Very well, mortal,' the queen replied. 'You shall receive the best recipe for moonshine. But be warned, you shall never profit a penny from it.'"

"What?" Michael cried out.

Patrick shrugged. "Every wish has a cost. This was mine. That I could make the best moonshine, but I have never tried selling it. I am sure the fairies would laugh if I tried." He glanced at the tankard he drank from and took another swig.

"Once the cost had been named, the fairies laughed and danced once more, and I took a cautious step. When no one stopped me, I bravely trotted along the path and, once reassured that none of the good folk would chase me, I began running. The laughter and their singing lingered in my ears as I ran the rest of the way home. My mum looked caught between reprimanding me for staying out so late and gratitude that I made it home safe. I meekly took the cuff to the ears and we both reverently put the walking stick in the corner. Without it, I'm sure that I would have fared much worse at the hands of the fairy queen."

Mary and Michael turned to look at the walking stick in wonder. As they stared, Patrick's wife, Sheila, walked in.

"Telling your stories again, Patrick?"

"Aye, macushla," Patrick said. "Though this one has come to its close."

Mary turned to her grandmum. "And it was the most marvelous story!"

"I am glad you liked it, young Mary," Patrick said. He stood and filled another tankard with the moonshine. Placing it on the windowsill, he said, "I leave this as an offering to them, and in proper thanks for letting me get home that night."

"Can we offer something?" Mary asked.

"Of course," Patrick said. "They particularly like some oatmeal with fresh butter."

Sheila shook her head. "There is no oatmeal, but I do have some cheese. Come, Mary." She helped Mary find some and arrange it on the windowsill to Mary's liking.

As Sheila and Mary fussed with the arrangement, Patrick turned to his grandson. "Do you believe me?" he asked softly.

Michael bit his lip, not looking at his grandpa in the eye. "Did that really happen?"

The old man sat so he could look in Michael's face. "Cross my heart and hope to die. All I said truly happened."

A tiny bit of hope returned to the boy's eyes. "And you saw Robin Goodfellow?"

Patrick nodded.

Michael hesitated, then said softly, "Could I offer something to the fairies too?"

Feeling his heart swelling with pride, Patrick grinned. "Of course you can." He then helped his grandson pour some honey into a small saucer and place it on the window.

Sheila smiled. "Come along, Mary and Michael. It's time for bed."

The two children thanked Patrick for the story and chatted excitedly as they scampered off. Sheila quickly tidied the small room.

"Patrick, do you think it is a good idea to be telling these stories?"

Patrick grinned. "It's time for them to be learning their family history."

Sheila chuckled. "I suppose if they find themselves in a similar predicament, they'll wish for something similar."

As Sheila banked the hearth, and Patrick snuffed a candle, the old man chuckled. "Well, I know if I ever am stuck in a similar position, I'll be wishing about potatoes."

Patrick and Sheila chuckled as they left the room.

The full moon shone upon the windowsill, reflecting off the plate of cheese from Sheila, tankard of moonshine from Patrick, and saucer of honey from Michael. As a cloud crossed the moon, Robin Goodfellow arrived. Looking about, he chuckled, and grabbed the cheese off the plate. He greedily snatched the honey, then beheld the tankard with a grin. Swigging down the moonshine, he laughed merrily and stole away into the night.

THE RAVEN'S CROWN
BY ALLY KELLY

Ally (Allison) Kelly is a new writer living in eastern Connecticut, USA, in an apartment with her kitten, Merlin. Ally has been writing stories since she was young and has grown fond of the fantasy genre over the years. Creator and head admin of Worldsmyths, Ally is extremely excited to celebrate Worldsmyths' ongoing success as an online writing community and as a publishing company, and this next anthology. Find out more at www.akfantasywriter.com

* * *

A dark cloud drifted across the moon as Ciaran, third-born son of King Emyr, strolled the shadow-marked gravel pathways of the palace garden and turned toward the ballroom. He breathed in the scent of new blossoms and buds in the garden, savoring the cool night air against the heat of the packed ballroom with its candles and multitude of nobles.

His sisters, Rosaleen and Zaira, swayed outside the glass doors in puffy pink and purple dresses that looked as though they'd swallow the girls whole. Zaira was on her tiptoes, whispering something into her older sister's ear.

Ciaran grinned, coming up behind Zaira. He wrapped an arm around her waist, picking her up and spinning her around a few times. His sister, only ten years old, laughed, wrapping her arms around her brother's neck.

"Ciaran!" she cried out, mirth shining in her eyes.

"There you are, Ciaran," Tiernan, his eldest brother, said.

Ciaran turned, still holding Zaira in his arm. Clad in their soldier uniforms, his older brothers Tiernan and Declan had stepped outside the ballroom doors, both with their hands clasped behind their backs. The kingdom's crest, a green dragon wrapped around the trunk of a white tree, was embroidered on their chests.

"Father's been looking for you," Tiernan warned.

"I think he's noticed you haven't danced with any of the courtiers yet," Rosaleen said.

"Who would want to dance with clumsy Ciaran, anyway?" Declan sneered with a laugh.

Ciaran glared at his brother and resisted the urge to roll his eyes, placing Zaira back down. He looked over through the glass doors. Women clad in elegant ball gowns of every shade spun around the room to the orchestral music, accompanied by dashing noblemen wearing foolish grins. He wanted no part of it.

"I do!" Zaira pulled on her brother's arm. "Will you dance with me, Ciaran?"

"Of course I will, Zai," he promised with a smile, looking back down at her.

"We all better get back inside. I think Father plans on making a speech," Tiernan said. He turned to Ciaran and grinned, clapping a hand on his shoulder. "Come on, Ciaran. It'll be over before you know it."

"Not if Mother has anything to say. She'll have another ball announced in a fortnight," joked Declan. They shared a laugh, and Tiernan led the way into the ballroom.

Queen Léan had arranged this ball to celebrate the homecoming of Ciaran's father and two brothers from the north. A masquerade open to the entire city made for a fine distraction from the distant threat of war brewing in Elisora. Both Ciaran and his siblings had protested. His brothers cited security reasons; Ciaran simply didn't want to attend, but he'd feigned support for their cause. It had been of no use, though, once their father had gotten involved.

Ciaran remained where he was as the guards opened the doors for them. Zaira paused, looking over her shoulder at him.

"Aren't you coming, Ciaran? You owe me a dance!"

She looked up at him with wide, green eyes, and he smiled. "Of course I am. There's just something I have to do at the aviary first. It won't take me long, I promise. You go on in."

"What about what Father said this morning, about not going anywhere alone?" Zaira asked.

Ciaran paused, remembering the warning their father had given that morning. King Emyr had placed the guards on high alert. Officially, this was for the security of the guests. In reality, the increase in patrols and guards was due to spy reports that Morwyn, queen of the wild fae, and her forces were nearing White Arbor's borders. An open ball made a tempting target for assassins, and King Emyr had warned his children to stay close to the palace until further notice.

"That's nothing to worry about, silly," Ciaran laughed. "Now hurry and go inside. I'll be right behind you."

Zaira nodded and followed their siblings back into the ballroom. The guards shut the doors, leaving him in the garden's silence.

Ciaran weaved his way through the garden and toward the aviary that sat at the edge of the palace grounds. The grounds were surrounded by high stone walls covered in green moss. In the center sat a water fountain with a stone statue of a dragon in its center. The statue's likeness, Cathan, king of the dragons, had passed on the last of the Drachenwald trees to their court some years ago, both to protect and to use as the court's source of magic. From that day forward, the symbol of a green dragon represented the southern court of White Arbor and every year the kingdom celebrated the Festival of Dragons. The stories of Cathan, the dragon king, had been Ciaran's childhood favorites.

Ciaran walked past the fountain, running his hand through the water as he continued to the aviary, but he paused when the clanking of armor and heavy boot steps approached. Ducking swiftly behind a statue of his father, he let them pass to turn toward the palace proper, his presence unnoticed.

Once he was certain of his solitude, Ciaran slid out from behind the statue and back onto the pathway. The royal aviary was housed between two stone walls with a gate on the opposite side, leading outside the grounds.

As he approached, he pulled off his raven mask, taking a moment to admire the finery. It was a simple but elegantly-crafted mask. Its long silken black feathers matched his dark hair. He traced the long black beak thoughtfully.

Laughter from the ballroom echoed in the distance and he considered going back, if only to avoid one of his father's long lectures.

Dismissing the thought, he placed the mask on a stone bench to his left.

Darkness settled over him. An icy shiver moved down Ciaran's spine, and he looked up at the sky, waiting for the moon to reappear once the dark cloud had passed. Pulling his cloak tight around him, he reached for a torch hanging off one of the high garden walls, muttering an incantation. His familial magic welled up within him in answer. Yellow flames crackled to life, casting dancing shadows on the ground as he stepped toward the aviary.

Ciaran cautiously let himself into the building, making sure no servants were nearby. He opened the door and stepped inside.

Six sets of yellow eyes stared back at him from within the cages hanging from the ceiling. Ciaran unlatched one cage, allowing the raven within to walk out. Fehin hopped out onto a branch beneath his cage, raising a claw in greeting to the prince. Ciaran smiled, reaching for a tether hanging from a hook on the wall.

"Hello, Fehin," Ciaran greeted him. "I hope your evening is going better than mine."

The raven stomped his claws on the branch, turning his head from one side to the other.

"This is the third ball my mother has thrown in the last month alone. I think I already have a blister on one foot," Ciaran continued with a sigh. "I wish I could just fly away from here. No more balls, no more boring meetings. Just me, the sky, and the clouds."

"You wish? I wish someone would let me through this gate. I'm late to the ball!"

Ciaran whirled around, looking through the bars of the aviary, his eyes wide as he tried to place the unfamiliar feminine voice. A woman wearing a long black dress beneath a purple, sparkling cloak covered in gems stood behind the walled gate, peering through it with large, round eyes. Long, blonde hair pulled into twists and braids fell against her shoulders and she wore a silver circlet crown with a purple jewel in its center.

"Who are you?" Ciaran asked carefully, trying to will his pounding heart back to its normal rhythm.

"My name is Maeve, daughter of Lord Daesyn. Are you Prince Ciaran?" the woman asked.

"I am," he answered. "What are you doing here?"

"I was invited to the ball, but I'm afraid I've arrived a little late. One of the carriage horses slipped his shoe," she answered.

Ciaran frowned, trying to put a face to her name. He knew most of the courtiers by now, since he'd seen them so often in the last week. But he didn't recognize her.

"Forgive me, I'm afraid I don't recognize your name, Lady Maeve," Ciaran said. His frown deepened as he looked behind her — not even a servant nearby. "Where is your escort?"

"My escort?" Maeve asked innocently. "Oh, I told him to stay with the carriage. I was sure I could find my way here . . . besides, it seems I've found an escort on my own." She gave him a soft smile.

Ciaran shifted uncomfortably. He *did* need to get back to the ball before his father realized he was gone. That she'd come without even a servant or escort to accompany her to the garden entrance was odd, though.

He turned back to Fehin, who still sat on the branch, and removed the tether from the raven's ankle. He waited for the raven to enter his cage once more, then locked it.

"If you wouldn't mind waiting outside the ballroom, Lady Maeve, I'll return to the palace and ask my mother—I'm sure she'll be able to confirm you're on the guest list." He stepped out of the aviary, locking it behind him before walking back through the gate leading back into the garden.

"Please don't leave me out here all by myself, Your Highness," Maeve begged, her eyes soft. "I'm so very thirsty. Perhaps I can get a drink while you check with your mother."

Ciaran paused in the walled entrance, listening to Maeve's voice as she pleaded with him.

When he touched the latch, Maeve placed her hand on his arm through a single bar, and he supposed then that she was right—it would be incredibly rude for him to leave her all by herself. If she turned out to be on his mother's list, he would never hear the end of how bad he'd make them all look. And what would happen if they were caught out here by themselves? He certainly couldn't deny allowing her to get a drink while he spoke to his mother.

Maeve's hand found its way up his arm and rested on his chest. The movement wasn't lost on him; he glanced down at her hand and swallowed, shifting uncomfortably. He turned his body toward the gate, allowing her hand to slowly fall away.

"I think that would be fine," Ciaran said after a moment.

"So you're inviting me in?" Maeve asked.

Ciaran nodded and opened the gate, allowing her to walk through. As she strode past him, a light purple glow appeared in her eyes as their gazes met. Ciaran blinked, trying to shake it from his vision—maybe the low light was playing a trick.

As they walked along the stone path, Ciaran tried to think of a conversation topic. "Tell me, Lady Maeve, where are you from?"

Maeve smiled. "I don't really have a home," she answered. When he frowned, Maeve continued. "At least, not a permanent one. I travel a lot, you see. It's hard to call one place home."

Ciaran nodded. White Arbor was the only home he'd ever known; he'd been to the other courts, but he'd never truly gotten to explore the lands of Elisora. The idea of traveling, of meeting other people, and exploring their cultures sounded far more interesting than his own life.

As they approached the ballroom doors, he turned toward Maeve. A light purple glow appeared in her eyes as their eyes met again. He blinked, trying to shake it away—that was twice now he'd seen it. The glow was still there. Something was wrong—very wrong.

Purple swirls of magic appeared in front of him, blocking the doorway. Ciaran stepped back, his jaw dropping in horror as Maeve appeared in front of him. Her once-blonde hair had faded into curly black locks laying against a matching gown and Ciaran realized who it was—Morwyn, queen of the wild fae.

Before a single sound could pass his lips, Morwyn raised a hand and purple ropes of pulsating magic poured from her fingers. They wrapped around Ciaran, cutting off his breathing. He lifted into the air, crushed and constricted. The tendrils of power contracted, and something happened to him. He was shrinking, legs withdrawing into his body as arms shortened and sprouted feathers. He tried to scream, but an awful croak was the only sound he made before losing consciousness.

* * *

CIARAN WOKE up to find the world looked strange. Colors weren't what he expected. Red almost glowed, light yellows faded into gray. Still groggy, he tried to rub his eyes, but instead of fingers, he found something soft and silky . . . feathers?

What's happened to me? Somebody help!

Ciaran's vision blurred as he tried to focus on his surroundings, his feathered chest heaving in and out as he focused on steadying his breathing. He tilted his head downward and realized there was something long wrapped around his ankle—a tether, like one for training the ravens.

Black eyes stared at him from the ground. He hopped backwards in a panic, before stilling. It was his raven mask.

The long black feathers were a cruel mockery of his current state. He pecked at it in reflexive fear, scoring the black paint of the beak. Footsteps sounded behind him and he spun around.

Long purple tendrils reached toward him from above, wrapping around his small body and levitating him into the air. He lost his breath as his wings tucked against his body and he froze, as still as the statues in his mother's garden, unable to even turn his head.

"Now, now," Morwyn said, taunting. His body remained unmoving in the air as he reached her eye level. "Fighting it won't do you any good, dear prince. Besides, you'll want to be on your best behavior for the king. You have an image to present, after all."

Ciaran tried to glare at the queen—could birds even glare? He didn't know. Her magic lowered him onto her left shoulder, and though it loosened its grip and allowed him to breathe normally, he still couldn't move. The queen pulled the tether from where it hung off his foot and fastened it to her finger, giving it a quick tug with a satisfied smirk.

The queen walked toward the glass ballroom doors. Before the guards could announce her, a blast of wind threw them open. The music paused and the dancers followed, lowering their masks to look toward the queen as she stepped into the center of the room.

Ciaran tried to see his family with his limited vision. Declan and Tiernan stood to the side of the dais near their father, while Rosaleen and Zaira stood on the opposite side, near Queen Léan.

King Emyr stood as Morwyn entered, his eyebrows furrowed together as he carefully observed the intruder. Ciaran's brothers both reached for the swords hanging at their sides and moved to stand by their parents, but King Emyr stayed his hand, silently warning the boys to hold off.

"Lady Morwyn, to what do we owe this pleasure?" King Emyr asked.

"Everyone else seemed to be invited to this grand party of yours, so I thought I'd join in," Morwyn answered, taking a few steps forward.

"How did you get past the palace wards?" Queen Léan asked.

Morwyn smiled. "Why, I was invited, Your Majesty."

"By who?" King Emyr's words echoed throughout the ballroom, worry trailing in his voice.

"Your son."

Hand-shaped smoke pulled Ciaran from his perch on Morwyn's shoulder, holding him tight in its grip. Once more, his body shifted and contorted, transforming him back. The hand placed him on the ground, forcing him to his knees.

The dancers stepped back, gasping and whispering as he sat there trying to get his bearings. Ciaran glanced down at his hands before looking at his family. King Emyr stood from his throne, his body towering over Ciaran even from the floor. His mother's jaw dropped in horror. Ciaran looked at his brothers, gazes emotionless. His sisters hovered close to each other, tears threatening Zaira's eyes.

"What is the meaning of this?" the king demanded.

"Father, I'm sorry. I didn't mean to. I was tricked—" Ciaran was cut off as he transformed again into a bird.

Morwyn stepped forward, bending down to pick Ciaran from off the floor and place him on her shoulder, stepping back into the center of the room. Ciaran tried desperately to call out to his father, but Morwyn's magic was far too strong and it forced him to remain still on her shoulder.

"Change my son back and I might allow you to live," King Emyr threatened.

Morwyn laughed. "I don't believe you are in a position to make demands, King Emyr," she said. "I, however, have some of my own. As I said, I was invited by your son. He made a wish, you see. He wished to fly away from his responsibilities."

Morwyn turned toward the crowd of people, slowly circling around before looking back at the king. "Surrender your kingdom to me, and fulfill his dreams."

"Never! I will never surrender my kingdom to you, nor will I allow you to have my son," King Emyr said. "You have no true power here. Now, free my son and be gone."

"Suit yourself," Morwyn said.

The queen silently raised her hands as purple magic billowed from the tips of her fingers, creating long swirls of magic that slithered to the floor. A blast of wind blew through the ballroom, slamming the glass doors shut. The candles hanging in the chandeliers high above from the ceiling flickered and blew out, leaving the ballroom in darkness.

"Guards!" King Emyr called.

The dancers gasped, stepping back from where the queen stood as the guards rushed forward to encircle her. Morwyn's eyes glowed purple again, and long, violet strands appeared from her fingers once more, slithering along the floor toward the crowd of people.

Ciaran watched in horror as Morwyn's magic crept through the crowd, slowly making its way toward his family. Dancers fell to the floor, clutching at their throats as they gasped for air.

* * *

THE COLD STONE floor touching his cheek woke Ciaran as the scent of smoke filled his nostrils. He coughed as he breathed it into his lungs, then groaned and opened his eyes. He rolled on his side and up onto his knees but, before he could stand, two guards standing on either side pulled him up from the ground by his shoulders.

As the smoke cleared, Ciaran looked around, frowning. His legs and arms ached like they'd been pulled together into his body. A fuzzy image of black feathers flashed in his mind as he stared down at his hands, remembering the silky texture. His heart pounded in his chest as he looked around at the bodies littering the floor.

"No . . . " he whispered, struggling against the guards. *This has to be a dream.*

Morwyn stood at the top of the dais. Ciaran watched as she attempted to sit on his father's throne. He couldn't help but smirk as his family's magic did its work, throwing her back from the dais and onto the floor with a loud thump. Morwyn grumbled angrily under her breath as she stood back up.

"You," she said, turning toward him. "Why can't I sit on your father's throne?"

Ciaran's smirk deepened. "Only someone from my family line can rule," he answered. "Guess you didn't think of everything, did you?"

Morwyn chewed her lip. She walked back toward the throne, stepping around the bodies, and stopped at the bottom of the steps. She looked back at him, smiling. His smile faded, his heart pounding in his chest. He'd said too much.

Morwyn used her magic to lift the crown from King Emyr's head, still wet with blood. The guards pressed hard on his shoulders, keeping him from moving as the crown levitated slowly toward him. Ciaran tried to squirm in their grasps as it paused over his head. A drop of blood fell from the crown, sliding down Ciaran's forehead.

"No!"

The crown lowered onto his head. Ciaran tried desperately to reach up and knock the crown down, but it was no use. Morwyn's magic grasped him once again and he lifted into the air. His body was carried toward the throne, hovering for a moment before the magic forcibly sat him down.

"You, Ciaran, third born prince, son of King Emyr, sit upon this throne as King of White Arbor," Morwyn said. "Consider yourself lucky, little prince. Your life has now been spared. You will serve as my pet for the rest of it."

Magic appeared from Morwyn's fingertips once more, and Ciaran changed into his raven form. His father's crown hovered above him as he shifted. When the transformation was finished and he sat on the soft cushion of his father's throne, the crown lowered again, circling him as it fell to the pillow.

Ciaran tried to calm his breathing but panic had pinched his throat shut. Every thought was a jumble, words becoming fuzzier with every moment.

It's . . . my . . . fault.

THE GORGON SLAYER
BY EMMA SCHOUTEN

Emma has grown up in the French countryside despite being Dutch, but decided to start writing stories in English just because she could. Her time is divided between welcoming guests at work, writing stories at home and reading books everywhere. And her five cats, of course.

Aglaia's cloak swept across the ground as her hurried steps took her from the village. Her eyes fixated on the path; her fingers tugged on the hood's frayed edge. Even as a rustle broke the silence, she never looked up. She didn't need to. She knew the way.

Tonight, however, felt different.

In the clear sky, a large full moon rose in the company of stars. It bathed the village in its silver light, though it cast long shadows too. The hope and the fear of what might happen before the sun rose again, personified. Aglaia's heart beat wildly in her chest; her entire life, she had been told never to go out on a night with a full moon. On this night, the Barterer came to the crossroads, granting wishes for those brave enough to stomach the consequences. And the old wives' tales had always come with plenty of terrible consequences.

It was the reason full moon nights were feared. To fear the day, however. . . There was nothing worse.

Aglaia couldn't stand it much longer. The fear of leaving her home suffocated her. Worry and uncertainty drove her and her mother crazy each time her father and brothers left for their work in the forest. As the sun set, their eyes turned to the door, praying it would open. The utter relief flooding her when it did was exhausting, and all the while they pretended not to hear the desperate cries coming from a neighbor's house.

Something had to give.

The final straw had come when her brother Chares had failed to return home only four nights ago. She could still hear her mother's desperate heartbroken sobs.

Her breath came out in white puffs of air. Temperatures had dropped in the hours since sunset and the cold bit at her exposed fingers and the tip of her nose. Her fur cloak kept most of her warm, but Aglaia wished she had thought to take her gloves.

A trivial thing in the grand scheme of things. She balled up her hands and pushed on.

At the village's edge, Aglaia hesitated. The village and the forest were one. In her mind, she had never separated them. But now? One was safe. The other was not. That her mind now noted them as two separate entities frightened her. The path continued for a hundred yards before reaching a crossroad.

So close, yet so far.

Aglaia steeled herself and forged ahead though her eyes remained on the ground. *What you cannot see cannot hurt you.* Aglaia hoped that was true. The woods rustled, night critters out gathering supplies before winter. The evergreen pines gave little indication of the changing seasons but Aglaia could taste it in the air. Winter was fast approaching.

"Well, well, a young lady out for a nightly stroll?"

The male voice that broke the silence startled her badly. Her hood fell back as her head snapped up. All warnings left her mind.

The man slouched against a pine mere feet from the crossroads, legs crossed at the ankles and hands shoved into pockets. His light eyes met hers as his thin lips pulled into an interested smirk. His clothing was dark and, had he not spoken up, Aglaia wouldn't have noticed him even if her focus hadn't been on the road.

The man crossed the distance between them in two strides. Lowering his face to hers, he raked his eyes across her features.

"Terrible things hide in these woods, you know." He cocked his head to the side. "Aren't you scared?"

Wetting her lips, she shook her head. This brought a smile to the man's face. Moving around her with a spring in his step, he inspected her more closely. Could he hear her erratic heartbeat? Did he know it was a lie?

"I think you *are* afraid," he stated. "But it's all right. A white lie for confidence; I won't judge. Now, young lady. What brings you to the woods this late?"

"I have come to make a wish." She waited, then added, "With the Barterer. Are you the Barterer?"

Again, the man cocked his head inquisitively. "Why yes, I am." He bounced on his feet, stepping into her personal space anew. "Why would someone as pretty as yourself desire to make a wish? Surely there must be a slew of men who would make the wish for you."

Aglaia kept quiet. She could make her own bargain, could bear the consequences herself. Everyone in the village did their part; this would be hers. For a second, however, she worried he wouldn't bargain with her.

Even in the dark, the Barterer's eyes lit up at her silence. "Oh, a determined little thing, aren't you? Big enough to make her way into the woods under a full moon, big enough to make her own wish. Are you certain you aren't afraid? There is still time to turn back."

"Of course, I am afraid. Everyone is afraid. But why should another have to face their fear and not me? Why should I be exempt?" Aglaia jutted her chin up and dared him to turn her away.

The Barterer gave a booming laugh. "Very well." His eyes glittered as he stepped back and spread his arms wide. "What do you wish for?"

She cleared her throat. "A terrifying creature roams these woods. We're afraid to leave our homes. We barely go out to hunt and to gather. People leave in the morning and never return; *my brother* is among the missing. There is talk of leaving for good but it would mean traveling through the forest for days, which is just as scary. Something must be done."

"Tell me about it. It's been terrible for business," the Barterer sighed. "Let me stop you there, young lady. If you wish for death, I cannot grant it. If you wish for life, I cannot grant it either. A protected exodus through the woods? Well, I could . . . but it would cost you."

Her mind reeled. At the limitations he had confessed, but also at what they implied. He said he couldn't grant life, which meant the missing men were dead. *Chares* was dead. Her throat tightened as she fought back the wave of emotion. Everyone had suspected but now their fears were confirmed.

"No," Aglaia replied firmly. "These woods are our home. Generations of us have lived and died here, learned every tree. It's an extension of our homes. We know how it changes with the seasons, where to hunt and which berries to pick. We know the stories of the trees. These woods are a part of us as much as we are a part of it."

The Barterer raised his hands to appease her. "Apologies. If you don't wish to leave, what *do* you wish for?"

Now or never. Something had to give.

"I wish for the ability to fight the monster."

Silence met her words, making her heartbeat seem so much louder. The Barterer considered her seriously for the first time. He rubbed a hand over his chin, through the stubble on his cheeks. Then he frowned and scratched his head. Aglaia waited, her teeth worrying at her lips. It couldn't be good if the Barterer himself had to think about it.

"The monster stalking the woods, do you even know what it is?"

She shook her head. She suspected but she didn't know.

The man sighed, exasperated, as though dealing with a child. "It's called a gorgon. A woman cursed to wander and has lost her humanity over time, taking on the form we know from legends. Serpents for hair, and a single look at her eyes will turn anyone to stone."

At the revelation, Aglaia's hope vanished. She knew the gorgon tales.

"They lure their victims with sweet songs," Aglaia muttered to herself. She lifted her eyes to the Barterer, "Is it true the only way to fight them is blindfolded?" How did one fight a creature one couldn't look at?

"I highly discourage it, what with the claws and all." He waved dismissively and paced back and forth. "I suppose something could be done to grant your wish. It's powerful magic though. The consequences would be far greater than you might imagine. Not to mention the continent's magical balance."

Abruptly, he stopped, facing her once more. His eyes had recovered their brightness.

"I can grant your wish," the Barterer declared. "You will have the ability to fight the gorgon. Next time you pick up a weapon, your body will instinctively know how to wield it. When you meet the gorgon, her gaze won't affect you. There is only one way to defeat such a creature."

Aglaia swallowed. "I know what I need to do.".

"Good." He nodded, satisfied. "Then tell me, my brave young lady, shall I grant your wish?"

"What consequences will there be?"

His smirk returned as he circled her once more.

"As clever as she is brave. Not all remember to ask before they rush headlong into their desire." He waited a moment before continuing, which only made Aglaia more nervous. "For the ability to fight the gorgon, you will have to wander this earth as she has for as long as she has. You will have to leave your home and your family and travel from place to place without ever being able to settle somewhere."

"Will I become a gorgon too?" she asked, not having forgotten the Barterer's earlier words.

"Perhaps. Perhaps not. Not all who wander lose their humanity in the journey. Only your own actions will determine the outcome."

Aglaia thought about it. If she didn't do this, how long before anyone else thought to ask the Barterer? The whole village might have been turned to stone by then. What was to say the price hadn't gone up for the same wish by then? Something had to give. Aglaia could be the one to make the sacrifice. Though the thought of being without a home scared her, she straightened her spine and looked the man in his colorless eyes.

"Barterer, please grant me my wish."

* * *

THE HOUSE CREAKED SOFTLY. Aglaia listened from her bed, eyes focused on the window. It had been a long day. The Barterer's magic wasted no time, urging her out of the house at sunrise and struggling against her as she returned at the end of the day. But it was only for a few hours—hours that had gone by in the blink of an eye.

Everyone had gone to bed a while ago. Ikralis's snores were easy to make out, as their rooms shared a wall. More faint were her father's snores on the other side of the house. Lavrentios was a quiet and light sleeper. Passing in front of his door would be tricky: the floorboard squeaked loudly.

If they truly slept, that is. All day they had watched her. Her brothers had trailed her through the village streets in the morning and her mother had watched her as she did her chores in the afternoon. Her father had watched her push her dinner around her plate without appetite. They knew something was up. How could they not, distracted as she had been?

It would be her brothers she'd miss the most. She had spent countless hours stalking them through the woods as they tried to run from her because, at ten years old, Chares, Ikralis and Lavrentios wanted nothing to do with her. They had argued and laughed, played and done chores. She had comforted Lavrentios when he had nightmares. She had tended to Chares's cuts and scrapes. She had covered for Ikralis whenever he snuck out. Together they had attempted to form a united front against Mother, who would have none of it.

Eighteen years was a lot of time spent together.

After another minute, Aglaia rose and dressed quietly. She laced her boots, drew on her cloak, and shouldered her pack. She had filled it with some of her things, preparing for a long journey: clean clothes, an extra pair of shoes, and her coin purse, but also sentimental items such as the owl figurine Lavrentios had carved for her, a recipe book from her mother, and her favorite beaded necklace, which she knew Chares had won for her at the traveling fair no matter how much he denied it.

On her dresser lay a folded piece of paper: a letter for her family, telling them about her wish and insisting they did not come after her. She couldn't bear to tell it to their face, witnessing their reactions and giving them the chance to try to convince her to stay. They couldn't change her decision, and even if they convinced her, the magic wouldn't let her. So the letter would have to be enough.

After one last look around, she left.

With each light step, the floor groaned and protested. The stairs were much worse. Luckily, no one woke. In the kitchen, she tore a fresh bread loaf in half, unlocked the door, and stepped outside. The night was colder than the one before. She thought longingly of her bed. But, no, she had to keep going.

"Time to go," she muttered to herself.

First, Aglaia went to the woodshed, where she retrieved two splitting axes. They were sharp and light. They were also the only weapons she had ever held in her life. Lifting them now made her body want to move in a way she never had; her mind plotted out movements with swift precision to cut through invisible foes. Her steps felt suddenly lighter, steadier, as if she normally stumbled along. She hefted the weapons resolutely.

"You can do this."

And she could! No one else would get hurt because Aglaia could do what needed to be done.

Without a backward glance, Aglaia ventured out, moving through the deserted streets until the houses were replaced by trees. The branches blocked most moonlight, shrouding everything in near-darkness. The forest spread for miles and miles; the gorgon could hide anywhere. How to find the creature?

Somewhere deep within her, she felt a sharp tug. Her feet stumbled over the uneven ground and her hands bushed against rough bark to catch herself. She scanned the dark terrain. Perhaps she should have taken a lantern but she hadn't wanted to carry around a beacon for the gorgon to follow.

Rodents rustled in the undergrowth. In the distance, an owl hooted and a buck grunted somewhere to her right. Away from the road and the village, the forest teemed with life despite the late hour and, perhaps more surprisingly, the monster that roamed among them.

She kept up a steady pace. Her breath came out in white puffs of air as she locked her jaw to minimize the chattering of her teeth. Anything resembling manmade paths disappeared as she traveled deeper into the woods, leaving only the occasional deer trail to guide her.

Something crunched under her boot, the sound incredibly loud in the silent forest. When had it become so quiet? Aglaia squatted down for a closer look and recognized a small stone bird, its wings spread wide as if midflight. A sparrow, perhaps? One wing had broken off when Aglaia had stepped on it. Picking it up, she noticed the details in the feathers that felt quite real, in stark contrast to its blank, lifeless eyes. The work was incredible, far too perfect to have been manmade. The gorgon must have caught it in mid-air; it could have easily shattered as it fell from the sky.

Putting it down, Aglaia cast a look around. Stones, some large, some small, all shaped too perfectly into something to be natural occurrences. She rose, gripping the axes tightly as they tugged at her, eager for a fight. Aglaia wasn't sure what she had expected from the Barterer's wish, but this wasn't it.

Aglaia moved on. Knowing she was in the right place, she advanced cautiously. Her eyes surveyed what they could in the dark. She had entered the gorgon's territory: broken rocks littered the ground, a stone squirrel sat on a branch, an entire pile of rubble lay half-hidden under a bush. And there. . . . Aglaia gasped. There stood a man, slightly bent backward, his arms up in front of him and his mouth and eyes wide. He wore the thick boots of a lumberjack, an axe sheath hanging empty on his belt. Taking a closer look, she thought she recognized the slight aquiline nose and large ears. Gray and frozen as he was, she couldn't be sure.

The gorgon couldn't be far. All around her, the forest felt deserted.

No more rustling, no more hooting, no more grunting. An invisible line had been crossed. No one with any sense would travel onward.

Except for Aglaia. Her gut feeling continued to pull her forward, and she continued to follow it.

After the first human statue, she found more. Some vaguely familiar, others disturbingly so, and others still not at all. She gasped as she recognized Dimos; he had disappeared at the beginning of spring. He had been here for months. Aglaia and her mother had baked his parents a mutton pie and sat with them as they cried.

As she spun slowly and inventoried the numerous statues, there was no doubt about it: they had been arranged as if they were congregating somewhere. Subjects on their way to a beast's court. Only this creature had no throne, just a lair in the middle of the woods. The arrogant audacity of it made Algaia want to scream, igniting something hot and dangerous in her.

The statues led the way onward until she reached a cave. Aglaia couldn't remember any kind of rock formations like this near the village. Or perhaps she'd always known, just like the animals did, not to venture this way. The Barterer's magic must have dulled her self-preservation instinct.

At the cave mouth stood two more statues. Guards . . . or a final warning. Upon closer inspection, Aglaia decided they were meant as the latter. The first was a little boy, who had crouched down and hidden, doubtlessly hoping to go unnoticed. The other . . .

"No!"

The second statue was none other than Chares. She recognized his face even in stone. The long nose. The slightly hollow cheeks. He stood a foot taller than her, preparing to face his foe, his arms behind him as he prepared to swing his axe down. His head was tilted upwards, which Algaia took as a bad sign; how tall was this gorgon?

If the gorgon hadn't known Aglaia was coming, her horrified cry would have alerted it now.

It was hard to care. Tears rolled down her cheeks. To look at him was painful. Nothing of her lively brother remained, just a lifeless statue. Knowing what had happened and seeing it wasn't the same. This hurt. This hurt tremendously more than just knowing. And it fueled her rage further, to where she wanted to smash every statue to bits.

Before she could do anything, a high-pitched screech echoed through the cave. Startled, Aglaia twisted to face the cavemouth but dropped her axes. She hurriedly picked them up, cursing herself. She should have taken the day to practice with them. From inside came the sound of bare feet on rock. They rushed towards her. She backed away and ducked behind a tree.

Careful not to make any noise, Aglaia peered around and watched the cave.

Glowing yellow eyes appeared in the dark. They shone like a lantern's flame as they swept the surroundings and found Aglaia. The creature's pace slowed as it stepped into the moonlight at the cave entrance. It assessed Aglaia, who did the same to it.

The gorgon's body was that of a human woman, though no one could ever mistake it for one. Its curvaceous form was clad in the remnants of a once beautiful dress with a high slit up its leg. Where hands should have been, Aglaia saw only claw-like fingers with skin that had turned black like a festering wound, in stark contrast to the pale-as-moonlight skin of its legs and face.

The creature's face had once been beautiful, Aglaia could tell, before the predatory eyes had overtaken its features. Sharp teeth poked out from between its lips. On the creature's head, she realized what she had thought to be long hair was instead a collection of serpent tails growing straight out of its skull.

This mixture of woman and beast left her horrified.

The yellow eyes drew her attention back to its face. Eyes that no bard had ever been able to describe; who could look at them?

But Aglaia could. Unconsciously, she had leaned further around the tree to stare at the creature directly.

Her grip on the bark slipped and she stumbled forward, trying to catch her balance. The gorgon had already spotted her, fixing her with its unnatural gaze, only to come to the same realization as Aglaia: she couldn't be petrified.

The gorgon shrieked. In a rather human act of rage, she smashed her fist into the nearest surface —Chares's shoulder. A crack, and the arm fell to the ground. Aglaia's eyes followed it then moved back to the gorgon. Turning her brother to stone was one thing, but carelessly breaking it to bits?

Her hands gripped the wooden axe handles. Further down for a longer reach, her fingers around, her thumb on top. Not too tight as to cramp up, not too loose as to drop them. Perfect for a powerful swing. But Aglaia held off making the first move, afraid the gorgon might lure her into its cave where it would have the advantage. The instinct guiding her weapons also told her the gorgon was an ambush predator.

Instead, Aglaia slid backward, pushing into the shrubbery and forcing the gorgon to follow if it wanted to keep her within sight. And it would follow, she knew; she had come into its territory, and she couldn't be turned to stone. It was an insult.

The gorgon was quiet but, in the silent forest, Aglaia heard it. With careful steps of her own, she slipped behind a tree and waited.

The only way to protect the village from the gorgon was to kill it. The only way to kill a gorgon was to cut off its head. She couldn't imagine doing it yet, but she would. Her people depended on her.

The gorgon advanced with caution. Aglaia's breaths were even and low. The bushes rustled at the gorgon's passage. A slight tapping sound joined the footsteps, like claws on wood.

Aglaia leapt out, both axeheads aimed at the gorgon. The creature screeched and stumbled backward at her appearance, but Aglaia pressed the attack, pushing forward as she swung one axe in an under-handed attack. The second followed in a horizontal swipe from the other side.

The yellow eyes tracked her movements. A serpent tail caught the axe handle at the shoulder, the sharp edge only a breath from pale skin. The sudden halt and loss of velocity rattled Aglaia and her wide eyes met the gorgon's. This creature relied on its ability to petrify, so it shouldn't have the ability to fend off her attacks. Yet it did. How much experience could it have battling humans? There wasn't a hint of fear in those animalistic eyes; only cold determination, and perhaps a hint of wicked satisfaction. Aglaia suppressed a shudder.

With unexpected strength, the tail forced the weapon back. Aglaia staggered, her foot halting against a protruding root. Then she pushed off with renewed determination to rush the gorgon once more.

The darkness sharpened as she focused on the silhouette moving to meet her. She planted her feet firmly and ducked under the gorgon's attack. Aglaia threw herself to the left, then swung her right axe at the gorgon's waist. Jerking it back, she only had a second to note the thick, clear blood dripping sluggishly from the creature's wound before the gorgon made another swipe with its clawed hand .

Aglaia aimed for an exposed shoulder but only cut through a few snake tails as the gorgon spun. It shrieked and clawed at her face, only to be deflected by Aglaia's axes. One nail raked across her arm. The pain burned sharply then dulled as her mind dismissed the information for now. Aglaia danced back and rounded a tree. She swung an axe, catching another serpent tail. She brought the second axe down after it, slicing through skin and flesh.

Too slow on the drawback, the creature's claws sliced through Algaia's cloak and shirt through to the delicate skin of her wrist. A snake tail flew out, grabbing her, putting pressure on the wound while simultaneously accentuating the pain. The bite of it dazed her for a second. Her senses sharpened just in time to dodge another attack coming for her eyes. The gorgon merely scratched her cheek as she lurched back.

Aglaia cut herself free and was quick to go on the offensive again. She swung, throwing her weight behind the attack. She wanted this to end. She *needed* this to end.

A final swipe and it could all be over.

"Aglaia!"

The sound of her name ripped through the night, breaking her concentration. Thrown off-balance, she floundered to stay on her feet. She couldn't have heard it right; the gorgon played a trick on her somehow.

"Aglaia!"

Her name sounded again, but the voice was different. She hadn't imagined anything at all. She locked eyes with the gorgon and, while the eyes were anything but human, she *knew* they thought the same thing; someone else had ventured into the woods. Aglaia spun and sprinted away, deeper into the forest toward the sound. Her cloak billowed around her, the clasp pressed on her throat.

The gorgon screamed and pursued her, its light footsteps close behind. Sharp claws hooked into her cloak, pulling hard enough to break the clasp. It fell from her shoulders, fluttering behind her. Her pursuer became tangled in it, which drifted to Algaia's ears as a soft thud followed by an enraged cry. Aglaia didn't look back. Her feet flew over the forest floor. Around her, everything became a blur.

Until she came to a crashing stop, colliding with a hard body and knocking them both to the ground.

"Aglaia!"

"Ikralis," she breathed, pushing herself up. Disbelief and dread swept through her in equal measures. She pulled on her brother's hand, urging him to his feet. "You have to go! You and Lavrentios both! It's not safe." Because both her brothers had come after her, the lovable idiots.

"I know it's not safe. Why do you think we're here?" His eyes slid down to the axes she had dropped again. "Are those ours?"

"They were." In the distance, she heard the gorgon's swift steps. "It's not like you need them. You obviously came fully prepared." She eyed the butcher knife he had tied to his belt. It wouldn't do him much good if he couldn't look at the gorgon, but he wouldn't be entirely defenseless either. "We have to go. It's coming."

Aglaia pushed him ahead, following him to make sure he kept moving. They found Lavrentios not too long after that. Before he could hug her, she pushed him ahead. There was no time for this with the gorgon gained on them. Before long, it would catch up. She might be impervious to her petrifying powers, her brothers were not.

"What were you thinking?" Ikralis demanded. "I know you're upset but you can't take off alone. You have no idea what's out there. Do you want to end up dead?"

"It's a gorgon," she deadpanned. There was a time to be the protective brother. This wasn't it. "It turns its victims to stone with a single look—whatever you do, don't look at it! Chares's statue stands guard at her lair."

Her brothers exchanged a look. "How do you know this?"

The gorgon was close, hidden but only a few steps away. It stalked them, waiting to ambush them. Aglaia stopped and the two men copied her. She scanned the dark forest, hoping for a glimpse of those glowing yellow eyes.

"Close your eyes. Whatever you do, do *not* open them for anything."

"What? Aglaia," Lavrentios started.

"On the full moon," she said, needing to explain. She desperately needed them to understand and trust her. Her instincts picked up the slightest noise: Ikralis's rapid breathing, the gorgon pushing against a bush. "I went to the crossroads and made a wish. The Barterer granted it. I can fight the gorgon."

There.

Aglaia spun, adjusting her stance. The more she practiced it, the more it came naturally.

"Aglaia," Lavrentios started again.

"Eyes. Closed!" she commanded

As the gorgon sprung from the bushes, Aglaia caught the attack with her axes, cutting the pale skin. She could only hope her brothers listened to her. The claws came at her again and again. She wielded her weapons in a flurry of motion. It shrieked and huffed, forcing her backward with every attack. Aglaia allowed it, leading it away from her brothers.

Twigs caught in her hair and brambles in her skirt. Somehow, through it all, she kept up her defense. Until they were far enough, then Aglaia blocked her feet and ducked under an attack, preparing her retaliation. She swiped at the gorgon's ankles, then at its stomach, cutting cloth and skin and drawing thick, pale blood. But while it frustrated the gorgon, the creature kept delivering its own attacks.

The speed at which they exchanged blows made it impossible to avoid all hits. Its claws caught her left cheek, the wound weeping blood and soaking her collar. Her axe sliced through the creature's upper shoulder. A blow landed hard on her elbow, causing her entire arm to throb painfully. She kicked out her leg, the momentum swinging her axe around. The gorgon pushed Aglaia backward, knocking her head against a tree.

Both opponents were bleeding and covered in scratches. They were equal in strength, neither gaining on the other.

"Aglaia," Lavrentios called, his voice distant.

How far had they gone? More importantly, why would her brother call out? Their mother always insisted she hadn't raised a single idiot but, at that moment, Algaia wondered.

The gorgon perked up at the sound. She thought something mischievous gleamed in those beastly eyes. With another hard shove at Aglaia that left her unbalanced and tumbling, the gorgon took off.

Easy prey.

"No!" Aglaia yelled. She swore and followed the gorgon again. "Be careful! It's coming for you!"

She hoped they heard her warning . . . that they could do what, exactly? Close their eyes to not see those wicked claws coming? Defend themselves against the monster but freeze under its yellow eyes?

Aglaia pushed herself harder.

Their fight had left a path of devastation through the brush. She followed it now, hoping to catch the creature before it caught her brothers. Ahead, something pale caught her attention. Her sides burned as she sped towards it even as branches whipped at her face. The gorgon had moved so fast.

Beyond the sound of her heavy breathing and her thundering heart, Aglaia's ears picked up a new noise, sweet and clear. A song of some kind. A lullaby, perhaps? It clicked a second later; the gorgon sang. A song so innocent and pure it could lure its victims to their death.

Ikralis and Lavrentios stood together, their eyes shut, as the gorgon glided closer and closer. Aglaia wondered what the song sounded like to them. Did it whisper of days spent in the sun for all eternity if only they opened their eyes? Did it plead with them to open their eyes and take in the beauty of the world? Anything to convince them to open their eyes.

It hardly mattered.

Aglaia threw her shoulder against the gorgon's back with her entire weight. The song stopped abruptly, replaced by a cry. It turned to face her, claws raised to attack, but Aglaia didn't give it the opportunity. Her new instincts had kept her on her feet ready to carry through.

The first axe caught the moonlight as Aglaia brought it down on the gorgon's right forearm, cutting deeper into flesh and muscle than her blows before. She brought the second down a fraction later, embedding itinto the creature's abdomen. Blood flowed. The pain-filled shriek it released almost broke Aglaia's heart.

The pity only lasted a second. Her instincts guided her, shifting her grip on the handles as she pulled them free and the axes worked together to decapitate the gorgon in one powerful, final blow.

The monster's head fell to the ground with a thud, its body following a moment later. She watched as the glowing yellow eyes extinguished, the way a firefly's glow might fade: slowly, until all was black.

When the light was entirely gone, Aglaia exhaled and dropped the axes. She had done it. She had killed the gorgon.

She'd thought she'd feel happier.

Her brothers came rushing to her side but paused at the sight before them. Their sister, covered in blood and standing over a beheaded corpse. Aglaia wasn't sure what to say to them. Instead, she turned and walked to where she thought the cavemouth had been, though her arms and legs felt boneless, trembling under the strain to keep her upright.

Following the path of destruction made it easy enough. Her brothers followed.

"Let's hurry home. Hopefully, Mama won't have noticed we slipped out." Ikralis cringed at the possibility.

"I'm sure you'll be fine," she muttered.

The cave soon appeared through the trees and, still standing guard at the entrance was Chares, forever frozen. She paused in front of him, taking in the missing arm, but also the details of the stonework. His frown was half-hidden under that awful lock of hair he refused to cut. The folds in his coat and the top that hung partway open, one hand reaching into his pants pocket. She wondered what he had in there. Had he been reaching for a weapon or something entirely mundane? They would never know.

"Chares," Lavrentios breathed.

Aglaia left them there in search of her pack. She couldn't remember where she had dropped it. Her cloak had been lost in the woods, which was bad as it was the only one she had. She'd have to get a new one, though how could she afford one? Until now, she hadn't thought much about leaving home beyond the actual leaving. Would she be forced to turn to a life of crime? How could she hope to search for honest work if she couldn't remain in one place? And where was her pack?

"Should we take him home?" one of her brothers asked.

"Not yet," replied the other. "Let's get Papa out here; he might know what to do. I'm not sure Mama could handle seeing Chares like this."

"Good point."

"Aglaia, could you find this place again in the morning?"

Her brothers watched her expectantly. With tears welling up, she shook her head. "I won't be here tomorrow. You will have to find him on your own."

In seconds, her brothers were at her side. Lavrentios gripped her shoulder, shaking her. He leaned down so their faces were level and he could look her in the eye. "What do you mean? Why won't you?"

Before Aglaia could answer them, a new voice cut through the darkness, startling them all.

"Her wish came with a consequence."

The Barterer stood behind her brothers, leaning against a pine much as he had the night before. His arms were crossed over his chest, his bright eyes taking in the three siblings with interest. Ikralis took a step towards him, placing himself between the newcomer and his brother and sister. Lavrentios stopped him from going further.

"What consequence?"

Aglaia's voice came out small and shaky. "For the ability to kill the gorgon I must wander in her stead for as long as it had."

The Barterer nodded. He reached for something at his feet: it was her pack. "I came to see if you might like a traveling companion. The world can be a lonely place for wanderers."

"What?" Lavrentios exclaimed. "No, Aglaia, no. You can't go! It will break Mama's heart."

"It will! Especially after Chares," Ikralis insisted." You can't do that to her. You can't do that to *us*."

The rest of their protests fell on deaf ears. Aglaia's focus remained on the Barterer, on the longing she heard in *his* words.

"Lavrentios, Ikralis," she interrupted, "it's all right. I've made my peace. This was the price to pay for safety. Besides, it doesn't have to be forever, right?"

She glanced at the Barterer, who nodded. Relief flooded her. A weight she hadn't known was there until it lifted had disappeared. There would be another day.

Ikralis was the first to nod, as she knew he would. It was a stiff nod but a nod all the same. Aglaia offered him a weak smile before wrapping her arms around him. She held onto him tightly and felt him do the same.

"Stupid little thing," he muttered into her hair. "Brave, but stupid."

As he let her go, she turned to Lavrentios. "The wish has been granted. Nothing can change that now. Don't make me leave while you're mad at me."

He opened his mouth to answer but closed it with a huff at the sharp glare Ikralis shot him. Finally, reluctantly, he opened his arms. She held onto him for longer, breathing in the scent of home. Her wish had been granted, now they must all live with the consequences.

When she finally let Lavrentios go, she moved to stand with the Barterer. He studied her for a minute. Although he didn't move, Aglaia felt the magic as it went to work on her sore muscles and the numerous cuts. Her aches faded away and crusts of dried blood flaked from her skin. Then warmth enveloped her as a new cloak materialized over her shoulders and around her body.

"That's better; all cleaned up," he declared. The Barterer shouldered her pack and added, "We will get you a proper pair of war axes, and we'll train you. A gorgon is far from the scariest thing out there, but I think you'll find your new skills quite transferable."

Without looking at her brothers, the Barterer set off into the woods. Ikralis and Lavrentios watched her wordlessly. She wanted to hug them again, to go home with them. But the longer she stood there, the stronger the tug in her gut became; the urge to follow the Barterer and discover the world beyond her village and the woods.

The urge to move.

Finally, Aglaia raised her hand and waved at Ikralis and Lavrentios one last time. Then she turned and followed the Barterer, knowing she would be back one day.

AUTHOR SOCIAL MEDIA

Alex Harvey
Twitter: DracoNako
Instagram: DracoNako or Cosmina_Miki
Website: Authoralexharvey.com

Alex K Masse
Twitter: @itsfairything
Tiktok: @itsfairything
Website: https://alexkmasse.ca/
E-mail: alexmasse2000@gmail.com

Ally Kelly
Facebook: https://www.facebook.com/AKFantasyWriter
Twitter: https://twitter.com/AKFantasyWriter
Instagram: http://instagram.com/AKFantasyWriter
Tiktok: https://www.tiktok.com/@akfantasywriter
Website: http://akfantasywriter.com
E-mail: ally@akfantasywriter.com

D.A. Gatlin
Twitter: http://twitter.com/daniel_gatlin
Instagram: http://instagram.com/dagatlin_author
Website: https://danielgatlin.com/
E-mail: dagatlin.author@gmail.com

Emma Schouten
Instagram: http://instagram.com/emskiewings
Website: https://emmaschoutenwrites.tumblr.com/

Erin Slegaitis-Smith
Twitter: http://twitter.com/eslegaitissmith
Instagram: http://instagram.com/eslegaitissmith
Tiktok: http://www.tiktok.com/@eslegaitissmith
E-mail: essauthor@gmail.com

Freya Bell
Twitter: http://twitter.com/FreyaEH
Instagram: http://instagram.com/darkneptune_19
Titktok: http://tiktok.com/@freyabellauthor
Website: www.freyabellcreates.com

Irene Bowie-Johnson
Twitter: http://twitter.com/irenebowiejohn1
Website: irenebowiejohnson.com
E-mail: irenebowiej@gmail.com

Jess Monnier
Website: http://jessmonnier.com
Email jessmonnier.author@gmail.com

Kieran Lamoureux
Instagram: http://instagram.com/kjlamoureux.writes
Website: kieranlamoureux.com
E-mail: kieranlamoureux@gmail.com

Nicole L. Soper Gorden

Facebook: https://www.facebook.com/NicoleLSoperGorden
Twitter: http://twitter.com/NLSoperGorden
Instagram: http://instagram.com/NicoleLSoperGorden
Website: http://www.nicolelsopergorden.com

WORLDSMYTHS SOCIAL MEDIA

Website:

http://worldsmyths.com

Facebook:

http://facebook.com/Worldsmyths

Instagram:

http://instagram.com/WorldsmythsWriters

Twitter:

http://twitter.com/Worldsmyths

E-Mail:

publishing@worldsmyths.com

WORLDSMYTHS NEWSLETTER

Did you enjoy this anthology? Follow us at our newsletter here http://worldsmyths.com for up-to-date information.

You'll find community updates, future submission calls, featured authors, informative blog posts, tips for writers, and the occasional short story.

STEPHANIE CULLEN EDITING SERVICES

This book was edited by the amazing Stephanie Cullen. If you'd like to book her yourself, please visit her website at https://stephaniecullenediting.com/.

CALL FOR 2023 SUBMISSIONS

Interested in submitting to our next anthology? Our love themed anthology, *Sugar and Spice*, is open for submissions June 2022 until August 30th, 2022. Visit http://worldsmyths.com for more info!

www.ingramcontent.com/pod-product-compliance
Lightning Source LLC
Chambersburg PA
CBHW071437200726
48294CB00002B/675